Gilded Wagons

By

F E Wharmby

First Published in 2013
By Gingernut Books Ltd

Cataloguing in Publication Data is available from the British Library

ISBN 978-1-907939-34-1

Ed2

Cover Art © T Gent

Printed and bound in Great Britain

Dedication:

I dedicate this book to my lovely daughter, Janet, who was promoted to glory at the age of 41.

To my good friend, Angela Rigley, and also Michelle Gent who has helped me with her editing and guidance.

Over the years many people have been kind and passed on their knowledge which has made this book into what it is.

All profits from the sale of this book will be given to The Salvation Army

Table of contents:

Chapter 1

The Gypsy, Tawno Ardry sat on the steps of his bow-top caravan, spooning his evening meal of rabbit stew into his mouth. As he ate, eyes narrowed, he examined the faces of those seated near him. His coat was grease stained so he ignored any fresh splashes of gravy.

"Horse thieves hang," muttered a member of the group with contempt, then he spat into the flames of the communal fire.

Tawno scowled and sat up straight, letting his tin plate fall to the ground with a clatter. Horses were Tawno's love; his life, and trading in horses, although always a precarious trade; was how he made his living.

"What's that? Who said that? Stand up and say what you bloody mean!" Under the brim of his battered hat, his brown eyes darted to his brother, Culvato, then to each of their companions seated around the fire. Everyone there knew very well that the man who had spoken had meant Tawno, but one and all kept their heads lowered; they knew better than to quarrel with him. They had seen, more than once, how his expertise with a knife could scar a man for life. Tawno's eyes settled on his brother's wife, Ursula. She was

1

seated outside a bender tent feeding her new baby under a spotlessly clean shawl which she had modestly draped over herself and the baby. He saw her give him a disapproving stare. It was well known that Ursula hated dishonesty and that she believed good fortune and happiness came from a hard day's work and living life in a God-fearing way. His brother had told Tawno more than once that he and Ursula didn't like the way he made his livelihood. His thin lips turned down in a sneer. *That's why I've got a vardo and you tramp the byways pushing a barrow*, he thought.

Tawno was sullen and disagreeable, and towards most people, his demeanour was somewhat menacing. If he didn't like a conversation or disagreed with a point of view, he'd brush past the other person, who was probably still speaking, and walk away. People could pick him out in a crowd since he usually wore his favourite green knee-length coat with six pockets. One of the pockets was large enough to hide a small animal or bird out of sight of suspicious gamekeepers. Another pocket was always filled with corn kernels. His high black leather boots had been stolen from a drunken nobleman and Tawno was very proud of them. Synfye polished the boots daily. Moleskin breeches fitted his muscular thighs like a second skin. A red bandanna under his hat almost covered his dark curls, and a gold earring swung from one ear.

Someone threw a piece of wood onto the flames, and sparks flew up towards the stars. In the shadows on the far side of the fire, a Gypsy youth had been playing a lively melody on a squeezebox and had been accompanied by a woman humming in time to the music. Tawno's cursing and sharp voice had drawn attention to the group around the fire, and the Gypsies had now fallen silent. The plaintive cry of an infant and the whicker of a picketed horse sounded loud in the hush.

Rising to his feet, Tawno stood on the top step of his caravan and towered over everyone. The firelight which illuminated the swarthy faces of the group also emphasised the venomous glare Tawno directed at Ursula.

At that moment it seemed to Ursula that he was standing within the very flames of the campfire. The back of her hands tingled, warning her of dire events in the future.

"One day, fire will bring you sorrow," she predicted in a whisper.

"Romni!" Tawno had only to bark the word to make Synfye Ardry, carrying her baby daughter Mikaila, hurry towards the firelight and follow her husband into the caravan.

Ursula looked down at her baby and sighed. She had already borne two boys, but her husband had not yet been told that her state of health meant she couldn't bear any more children.

Culvato Ardry placidly puffed on his pipe; he looked askance at his brother. The Ardry brothers had shown very little emotion when they had met in the encampment two days earlier, even though their paths seldom crossed. They were as unalike in nature as they were different in looks. Culvato, a well-built man with skin darkened to a rich coffee colour by the weather, had a rounded face with kind eyes which twinkled merrily, especially when he was surrounded by his children.

After placing baby Mikailia in her elaborately carved cradle, Synfye checked that their two-year-old son, Seth, was still asleep on the goose down mattress under the bed at the end of the caravan.

Smiling at her husband, Synfye helped him to remove his coat and pulled off his muddied boots - as every well-brought-up Gypsy woman should.

She was washing Tawno's hands and face when he barked

3

the instruction: "We leave here in the morning!"

Synfye showed no surprise and calmly patted Tawno dry with a towel. She carried on with her tasks in silence. She and the children were his, to take or leave whether she wanted to go with him or not. A flannel nightshirt, sewn by her, and a tasselled nightcap were laid out on the bed. She then combed her husband's curls and moustache, ending his grooming with a hug. He shrugged it off and held out his arms so as to be undressed. She pulled his shirt free from his trousers, and unfastened the laces before pulling the shirt up and over his head. The shirt was replaced with the nightshirt before she removed his trousers. When her hand slipped between his thighs, he pushed her away with a curse. What had been said earlier had hit home, and he was in no mood for love-making.

***

Tawno noticed a fine strawberry roan mare contentedly cropping the grass in a field when out walking that morning. Gleeful at his stroke of good fortune, Tawno had looked up and down the country lane. No one had been about. Breaking and slashing branches with his knife, he'd widened a gap in the hedge then whistled to attract the mare's attention. He'd encouraged it nearer by offering a handful of sweet grass. Speaking quietly, Tawno had allowed the mare to smell and then taste a handful of corn kernels. Holding its head halter, he'd persuaded the mare to squeeze through the enlarged gap into the lane. Tawno had cursed under his breath upon noticing that thorns had scratched the mare's neck and a trickle of blood was staining its glossy coat, but the wound wasn't deep. He took a cord from his pocket, tied it to the halter and sprang onto the bare back of the mare. Fortunately for him, the lane was still deserted. Kicking the mare to a trot and leaning back with outstretched legs, he'd ridden her towards the Gypsy encampment.

Some Gypsies had seen how Tawno had ridden into the camp at a fast trot, and they'd watched with disapproval as he tied the strawberry roan mare to the back of his caravan. They were inclined to think that the horse had been stolen; the well-cared for condition of its coat was a giveaway, as was the way Tawno had quickly thrown a large blanket over its back, and thrown shifty glances at people nearby.

They all turned away; it was none of their business how he made his living - though it would not be in their best interest if parish officials came searching the campsite.

In the year 1790, parish officials needed little inducement to hang Gypsies who stole from landowners. If a gamekeeper caught a Gypsy in possession of a rabbit, a hare, or even a hedgehog, it was enough reason to call for a law enforcer and have the culprit and his entire family thrown into gaol. A horse thief took an enormous risk.

During that afternoon, a few Gypsy children joined Tawno and Synfye when they went to collect wild mint - Egyptian's herb - which grew in and around a gently flowing stream nearby. They watched with interest as Tawno made a fire, and, using an old tin can, boiled the mint roots until the liquid was thick and reduced by half. The result was a brown dye. He collected a bunch of green twigs and tied them together with blades of grass. Tawno crushed the ends of the twigs with a stone to make brushes. He avoided touching the dye with his hands as the dark stain would take months to fade away. With Synfye's help, he covered the mare's coat with the dye until the strawberry roan mare was unrecognisable. A small star was all that was left of the white blaze and three white socks. By the time darkness fell, the mare looked as though it belonged with Tawno's other dirty horses, tethered near his caravan.

"I've collected all the best horses from these parts now, only rubbish left." Tawno spoke quickly. He didn't bother to explain to Synfye that the local magistrate, Squire Pomffite, would be searching the lanes in the vicinity for his fine strawberry roan mare, nor that he wanted to get well away before the other Gypsies in the encampment were questioned about the theft.

"Shouldn't you tell Culvato and Ursula you are leaving the camp and where you're travelling to?"

"No need," Tawno said and gave a shrug. "Culvato will be going back to Nottingham Town. He thinks he'll get rich by selling wooden skewers to butchers, whittling clothes pegs and mending pots and pans. He'll never own a vardo doing that." He gave a mocking grin.

"I can see Culvato pushing his barrow when he has a grey beard growing to his knees. Him and that goody-goody wife of his will tramp the byways of England forever with that barrow." With a chuckle, Tawno dismissed his brother from his mind, then stretched and flexed his muscles.

Synfye picked up his trousers and began folding them. "The boys out there, will they know where to find us?" she asked.

"They will if they want to carry on working for me,' Tawno said and gave a smirk. "Not young Rick, though. He'll probably nasher, come Tuesday."

As he spoke, he bent his head to let Synfye put his nightcap on. He showed no sign of grief at the forthcoming demise of five-year-old Rick. The urchin had become involved with some older boys when stealing for Tawno and they had put the blame for a theft and murder on his young shoulders. Fortunately for Tawno, Rick was scared by the situation in which he had found himself, and hadn't divulged to the authorities the name of the man who had employed him to steal. Synfye gave a shiver. She had begun to get to know the child and liked him, but there was nothing she or anyone else could do to prevent his fate now. There would be another to take his place, lonely ragged children appeared regularly. Another factory apprentice runaway or some town child would very quickly replace little Rick.

Like gaunt shadows, children followed the Gypsies from camp to camp. Lurking near caravans or bender tents, they waited to pounce and devour any food thrown out by the Gypsies before snarling dogs could snatch the scraps. Many men, like Tawno used the children as beggars and thieves. The children's reward was a crust of bread, a bone, or the remains of a meal when the family had finished eating.

***

Campfires smouldered beneath large, flat stones, and dogs still slumbered under the starlit sky as Tawno and Synfye prepared to leave the camp in silence. The pans that usually hung outside, together with anything else that clanged or clattered had been wrapped with cloths and placed inside the caravan. A string of four horses and a donkey followed behind as the caravan moved slowly away from the encampment and along tree-lined lanes. A couple of lurchers kept pace, avoiding the wheels of the vehicle and the hooves of the horses and donkey.

Two dirty boys, their pale faces turned up to the moon lay under a hedge near Tawno's caravan trying to keep warm by sleeping close to each other. As they made ready to leave, the family's noise awakened Ben. With a sharp elbow he nudged the other boy.

"What's you a doing?"

"They're going. If you wants to keep getting a meal a day, you had best wake and follow them," Ben whispered.

"What about the others?"

Ben eyed some other ragged children sleeping nearby and put a finger to his lips. "More for us if them others don't come. You're good at thieving. We make a good team. Well?"

The other boy scrambled to his feet and rubbed the sleep from his eyes.

"He ain't a bad cove, gave me an extra crust the other day."

Ben hitched up his filthy trousers and wiped the back of his hand across his running nose. "He always gives us a fair price, or some food for what we filch from the Gorjios, but I wouldn't like to cross him."

The boys crouched under the hedge and waited until the caravan was clear of the camp before setting off. Ben was six years old. He had run away from a cruel master, and was now keeping himself alive by stealing for Tawno. It would be a good thing if the other boy was Ben's companion, and in truth both boys needed reliable company. Two boys working together would be less likely to be caught stealing. The more they stole, the better they would eat. Half-walking and half-running, the two urchins dressed in rags and bare-footed, kept a discreet distance from the caravan as it travelled along.

***

The sun shone on Tawno as he leaned back against the door of his living wagon. His body rocked with the motion of the caravan as its wheels dipped in and out of the muddy ruts on the road. Holding the reins loosely, he allowed it to move at its own pace. "I make for Peterborough Town," he said.

Open mouthed, Synfye stared at her husband. A couple of years before he had promised they would never return to

Peterborough Town. Her body stiffened as she recalled the whipping she had received in the market place. In the town's courthouse, she had been convicted of begging. She only missed a three-month sentence in the house of correction because she was eight months pregnant with Seth. He was now a sturdy two-year-old, a quiet, dark-haired boy with brown eyes. Pressing her lips tightly together, Synfye held her baby daughter close. She knew from past experiences that if she tried to change Tawno's mind, or quarrelled with him, he would become even more determined to have his way. She would have to abide by his decision and be very careful to keep out of trouble.

Reaching the outskirts of Peterborough Town, Tawno drove the caravan along lanes shaded by overhanging trees. He camped on a patch of grass behind a bush and near a fast-flowing stream. It took only minutes for him to drive a wooden peg into the ground and picket the donkey so that it could safely graze on the grass. Then he roped all the horses together and leapt onto the back of the lead horse.

"Be back before nightfall, I'll wait for you here! Don't get caught monging this time, Romni!"

Synfye stood with her head held high. Her hands were clenched, her nails cutting into her skin, and she bit back a sharp reply as she watched Tawno ride away along the lane, closely followed by both lurchers.

"You make it very hard for me to love you, Rom. You think more of your grais than you do of your children and me," she said.

Leaving the baby in her cradle, she went to the back of the caravan and removed a deep rush basket from the outside cupboard. It was where Tawno sometimes kept his game birds for fighting, but at the moment the cupboard was used by Synfye to store her saleable wares. Any spare time she had

9

when travelling was spent making willow clothes pegs, lace, and dried grass arrangements, in the hope of selling them at cottages. After filling the basket with some of her handiwork, she closed the door of the living wagon and checked to see that the donkey was still safely tethered. Throwing a woollen shawl around her shoulders, she tied baby Mikailia within its russet-coloured folds, and with an arm supporting the babe, Synfye held her comfortably on her hip. Seth clung to her long skirt as she walked in the direction Tawno had taken.

Synfye ignored the two urchins slinking along behind. Each night since leaving the Gypsy encampment, she had thrown food to the boys, but had not bothered to see if they or the dogs ate it.

The urchins had sat partly hidden by a tree, eating a turnip Ben had stolen from a field, and watched Tawno rope the horses and ride away. They stayed where they were until Synfye and Seth reached the bend in the lane.

Waiting until the woman was out of sight; Ben scrambled to his feet and motioned his companion to join him.

"Come on, stay near me. They'll not notice us following. When we get to town we'll go to the market and chore a purse or two. Mr Ardry will be pleased if we do well." Ben grinned, but the smile didn't light up his hazel eyes, which looked empty.

Soon Synfye and the children reached a row of low, thatched dwellings. Her eyes roved over every back door and window in search of her most fruitful source of income; the gullible servant girl.

Dogs snarled, showing yellow teeth and straining their tethers. At one cottage, when strangers approached the gate, patrolling geese hissed and ran towards them with outstretched necks; Synfye walked past that cottage quickly.

Keeping a safe distance from any dogs, Synfye approached

each door. Many of them stayed tightly closed, but some were opened by women who, either from superstition or pity bought something from her.

"Would the child like some milk?"

This question, from an elderly woman, took Synfye by surprise. It was a rare thing indeed to have a Gauji woman offer sustenance to a traveller without waiting to be asked.

"The boy is thirsty. You have a lucky face, lady. Fortune will be good to you for your kindness." Synfye smiled gratefully and took the cup. Seth drank quickly, wiped his mouth on his hand, and then hid behind his mother's skirt to peep at the woman.

"I was once a traveller myself," the woman confided as she moved a stool and seated herself in the sunshine by the door. "It took me a long while to settle in a house, for I was born on the straw."

This meant the woman had been born of Gypsy parents who had lived in a bender tent.

"I could never settle in one place. My man has a vardo and we travel all over the country," Synfye said, with a proud toss of her head which set her gold earrings dancing.

"A house on wheels can come to grief, the same as a house set down. It's the people living inside that make a home fit to live in." The woman gave Synfye a strange look as she spoke. With an involuntary shiver, Synfye pulled her shawl closer and clutched baby Mikailia a little tighter. A cloud obscured the sun and the woman's words sounded like a prophecy. As she walked towards the garden gate, Synfye was struck by a sudden fear and she shivered again. As her hand reached out to open the gate, she heard the woman call out:

"Put this in your basket, Chai! You may be pleased to have it by the end of the day."

The woman held out a freshly baked cake loaf. Synfye's

11

face glowed with pleasure at receiving such a welcome and unexpected gift. She took the loaf, felt its warmth and savoured the smell of the fruit and spices before placing it in her basket.

"Thank you. Thank you." Gratitude made her voice sound gruff. She gave the woman another smiling nod, caught Seth by his hand and led him out of the garden, closing the gate securely behind her.

***

Peterborough market was composed of two parts; one a general market laid out in front of the church, with stalls set in rows for trading; the other a beast market. Tawno found the beast market crowded and noisy both with animals and people. Shouldering a mild-looking farmer to one side, he tied his horses to a hitching rail and put his stained clay pipe between his lips. With eyes narrowed, he assessed the other traders nearby and decided it was best to stay where he was; it seemed the best place to be to attract customers.

Tawno had just sold his second horse when he caught sight of Ben and the other urchin working on the far side of the market square. He watched them with keen interest as both boys slipped stealthily in between richly clothed townsmen and the farmers who carried heavy purses hanging from their belt. *Chore didikais, chore tradderly*, (steal rough travellers, steal carefully,) he thought. He nodded and half smiled, satisfied both boys were busy on his behalf. He would be ready and waiting for them that night when they brought their loot to the caravan.

The church clock showed half past four by the time Tawno had sold the last of his horses. Enjoying the feel of money in his pocket and smirking with self-satisfaction, he

12

strode into the taproom of an alehouse. His eyes smarted and he grimaced as the smoke from the log fire, mingling with that of the customers' long clay pipes met him. Blinking and rubbing his eyes, he pushed through the crowded room and found a seat at a table. It took a moment or two for him to catch the attention of the tavern wench; he ordered her to bring him some ale, and to be quick about it. She returned with a tankard and a jug of the tavern's best brew. Tawno threw a coin on the table and eyed the woman's breasts while she filled his tankard. In her hurry to please, she let the ale spill over the table.

Tawno half rose to his feet, scowling and cursing at the woman's carelessness, but a heavy hand on his shoulder made him spin on his heel with fists raised, ready to fight.

"Tawno, it is you! I thought I saw you earlier in the market place, but by the time I reached you…" The Gypsy facing him gave an eloquent shrug of his broad shoulders. His dark hair was covered by the customary scarlet bandanna and stained felt hat. Tawno watched sullenly as the man pushed a pewter tankard forward and winked at the serving wench who filled it for him from the ale jug.

Ignoring the spillage dripping from the table, Tawno stared at the other Gypsy in silence. Brandy-Joe Lincolin gulped down most of the ale without pause. Brandy-Joe grinned at Tawno. He was young, about twenty, with dark, penetrating eyes that made Tawno feel uncomfortable. Tawno tried to hide his unease by taking a drink.

"Did you know the Lincolin family are camped in the vesh by the river? They still talk of how you and those Gaujo choramengros working for you robbed them," said Brandy-Joe.

They both lifted their tankards to drink, staring at each other in silence. Neither man dropped his eyes. Brandy-Joe spoke again.

"Did you hear about the old sherrekano who rode that piebald grai you sold him? It was a bad buy. He broke his back when it threw him. He can't travel no more; too painful. He has to lay flat. Can't move nowt but his head."

His eyes staring wildly, Tawno leapt to his feet, his shaking forefinger thrusting at the younger Gypsy's nose.

"You tell that thieving Lincoln family of yours that I deal straight wi' them that deal straight wi' me. There was nowt wrong with that grai he bought from me. It was the fool of a rider, not the grai that caused the accident." Grabbing Brandy-Joe's necktie, Tawno pulled him close and ground his heel into the man's foot before pushing him away with such force he fell across the table. With a foul curse and smouldering eyes, Brandy-Joe sprang back to his feet, a curved knife in his hand. Too late: his enemy was gone.

Elbowing his way through the crowds to reach the door, Brandy-Joe yelled after Tawno: "Just you watch out. I ain't atrashed, Tawno Ardry. Now they've found you at long last, the Lincoln family will get their revenge. They never bister and let insults pass." Softly, he added, "And neither do I."

Chapter 2

Culvato Ardry had chosen an admirable wife for his life on the road; Ursula could walk all day without tiring. She was able to cook delicious meals from the fruits of the land and she knew the greater part of middle England as well as she knew the inside of her own pocket. She believed with all sincerity that ghosts walked at night and that cuckoos were the souls of evil Gypsies, but she had a vein of shrewd common-sense; woe betide the shopkeeper who tried to cheat her or best her at bargaining.

The stench of Nottingham Town was borne on the wind. It first reached Culvato and Ursula as they travelled over the wooden bridge spanning the river Leen. Ursula wrinkled her nose and wondered if she could persuade Culvato to journey to the east coast during the summer, to enjoy the bracing air.

Happy with their love for each other, she held the tail of her Gypsy husband's coat as he pushed the two-wheeled barrow towards the centre of town. The barrow contained all they owned, including vital pieces of an oiled canvas tilt for constructing a bender tent in a lane or field in which they wanted to spend the night.

Halting part way up a steep road, Culvato drew his wife

and young son Hugo close. Loud shouting and the sound of marching boots came from the direction of the top of the street. They looked towards the market place with some ' trepidation when they heard repeated shouts.

"Hold it there. Hold steady boys. Keep the ropes to the side!"

A crowd of townsfolk came towards the Gypsies at speed. A squad of armed soldiers wearing red coats, white breeches and plumes in their hats flanked them.

Market days in Nottingham were always full of the noise of traffic and people calling out their wares for sale, but the hullabaloo sounded unusually unpleasant.

The baby was strapped to Ursula's chest and, for added protection she pulled her woollen shawl over her head, draping it over the infant. Hugo held his mother's hand tightly.

Ursula noticed Culvato's healthy complexion had paled, and he looked around frantically for somewhere to go, somewhere to keep his family from harm. The only real place of safety they could see was an opening between two buildings a few yards further along the road.

Speaking Romani, Culvato said: "Stand well back in here. With any luck no one will notice us." Following Ursula, he pushed his barrow into a long narrow alley, which curved around the back of some cottages until it re-joined the road. As the crowd drew nearer, the Gypsies moved further inside the alley and pressed themselves against the wall.

About twenty men holding strong ropes struggled to keep a foothold on the cobbles as they manoeuvred an enormous iron and wooden knitting machine down the steep road. The contraption was covered with numerous levers and wheels and a number of bobbins with wind-tangled threads hanging from them. It was mounted on a low cart that threatened to collapse under its weight.

Another group of men, a few yards behind were striving to control a similar load. Other men and boys were milling around, shouting advice and the barking dogs darting around people's legs added to the pandemonium.

Ursula was a slim young woman with a happy nature, but at that moment, in place of her usual smile she wore a worried frown. Only four-foot-five, she needed to stand on tiptoe to see over the loaded barrow and into the road. She gasped when she saw the arrival of the mayor, dressed in his rich and colourful robes and his gold chain of office. It was the closest she had ever been to an important person. The mayor strode up the street towards the men. Close behind him followed the town dignitaries puffed up with self-importance and dressed in velvets and fur. It was seldom such exalted people walked the mucky streets of Nottingham to mingle among the populace. Usually they rode in carriages or were carried in sedan chairs, to avoid sullying their shoes and grand clothes.

"Who might they be, Rom?" Ursula whispered, pointing towards the first group of straining men.

"Stockingers. The machine is for making stockings. The men pulling it are probably something to do with the Luddites. We'll keep well away from them. Now hold your tongue, I don't want us to be caught up in their troubles." Culvato's voice was sharp with worry.

He pushed Ursula out of sight with his arm, but not before she saw the mayor stop in the centre of the road. The imposing man stood facing the crowd with legs apart and both hands raised high. The Gypsies were not to know that the machine belonged to the mayor. The people stopped, but the first machine continued down the hill towards the mayor and his party. No majestic command could stop its progress. Aplomb and dignity gone; the robed personages fled in all directions to avoid the knitting frame. The few men still holding the ropes were not strong enough, and it was only when others sprang to help them that they were able to save the machine from being wrecked. They hauled on the ropes, yelled orders and brought the contraption to a standstill just as it reached the door of a house at the bottom of the hill.

There was no need for Culvato and Ursula to speak. They were in one mind as they hurried along the alleyway, Ursula carrying the baby and leading Hugo, Culvato pulling the barrow behind them. By the time they reached the end of the alley and stopped to draw breath, it was all quiet. Peering out, they saw that most of the crowd in the road had dispersed. The Gypsies had no need to worry, for no one had noticed them. They exchanged amused glances when they saw someone lift the mayor's hat from a filth-filled gutter, slime dripping from its once curled feathers. It looked no better after a vigorous shaking. The mayor would need to purchase a new hat.

Culvato and Ursula were still chuckling as they took an indirect route to the centre of town. They entered the Nottingham market place from a street on the north side. As they expected, the market was busy. On the far side of the market, a number of people were standing next to a row of empty wooden stalls, furiously complaining to each other about the high price of corn and dairy products. The way they were dressed marked them out as farmers.

With his wife following, Culvato pushed the barrow as far as the Exchange Building. They stopped close to a stall stocked with vegetables; well away from the angry people and empty stalls.

"If we stay over here we won't get into bother with any of the Gaujo problems."

Ursula nodded. She knew that Culvato was always careful not to involve himself in the problems of townsfolk; it would give the parish constables an excuse to question them and class him as a vagrant, and after that, she and the children would be quickly incarcerated in a parish workhouse.

***

Ursula bought a large round cheese and some apples from a fresh-faced country girl, before taking a moss-lined rush basket from the barrow. She put the basket in a shady spot near the wall of the Exchange Building. With tender care, she placed her baby boy in the basket and covered him with a shawl. Hugo crouched by his brother and watched as Ursula took a caged linnet from the barrow. She attached the wooden cage securely to the top of a five-foot pole; it was the trademark of the Gypsy fortune-teller.

Ursula, leaned the pole against the wall and glanced at the passing people with an enquiring expression. She was well known for her predictions. Her professional spiel and patter convinced all who listened that she could really predict future events. Her mother and grandmother had taught Ursula their secrets, and they had taught her well.

Having business of his own to attend to in the town, Culvato walked away, pushing the barrow, leaving Ursula with both children.

A man and woman arrived and stood near Ursula, nudging and encouraging each other to have their future told. The woman was the first to step forward and hold out her hand. She gave a self-conscious titter when Ursula traced the lines on the woman's work-worn hand with a gentle finger and murmured in a low voice, so only she could hear.

"You have had a journey, and this journey has brought you to the start of a time of great happiness." She took a crystal ball made of fine quartz from a specially made pocket in her skirt and held it out towards the man, beckoning him closer. "Come. Let me tell you of the happiness that will be yours, good sir," she said. After his spouse had spoken crossly, and pulled him forward to face Ursula, he agreed, his ears reddening with embarrassment.

"You are to place a baby in a cradle very soon," Ursula chanted. She had already noticed the woman's thickened waistline under her half-opened cloak. Ursula stared deep into the crystal, and by degrees the crystal's cloudiness began to clear. She saw a breathtaking image take form. "You are to have wealth. Great wealth," she said, in awe.

A cluster of beautiful objects showed themselves in the depths of the crystal ball; gold chains tumbled over a pile of bright coins, multicoloured stones twinkled and flashed their incandescent fire between the gold.

"Do you see more, Gypsy? Do you see happiness?" The anxious tone and a touch on her arm brought Ursula's attention away from the picture. Dazed and disorientated for a moment, Ursula blinked and wiped her eyes with a finger.

"I see happiness and a long life for you both. My crystal sphere always tells me true."

As the couple disappeared among the crowds, Ursula stared at the crystal ball and blinked. The picture had cleared. The glass had returned to its usual cloudy depths. It was one of Ursula's most treasured possessions for it had belonged to her grandmother and mother. If Ursula ever had a daughter, she would teach her the fortune-telling procedures, passing on her knowledge. But she knew it was not to be. Her mother, who had been the midwife for the clan, had told her that Lionel would be Ursula's last baby.

Raised voices made Ursula hesitate as she replaced the ball in her pocket. Peering around the corner of the Exchange Building, she saw two gentlemen coming towards her. The older man was stout, and had his white wig tied with a black ribbon at the nape of his neck. His face was painted and brightly rouged on the cheeks and chin. There was a black patch in the shape of a coach and horses stuck on the side of his mouth, which was ugly with anger. Something flashed from between the folds of the older man's white cravat. *I bet that's a doodi-bar he has fastened there, and that knob on his cane is gold,* she thought, Ursula's interest was caught, and she leaned out farther. The men were too busy talking to notice her. The younger man had a weak, narrow face, and wore his fair hair tied with a blue ribbon which matched the colour of his coat. Although his clothes were fashionable, they looked shabby, and his shoes were dusty.

By the look of that young one, he'll have to face a deal of trouble before he's much older, she thought.

Ursula became aware of a tingling sensation on the back of her hands. Whenever that happened in the past, some event always changed the direction of her life. She began listening more carefully to the men's conversation.

"My wedding to the widow Rials is tomorrow, Jonas Bigsby. Even if I wanted to marry into your family, and I don't, the upkeep of my town house couldn't be met by your sister's paltry dowry. Money accompanies the widow and it will be enough to pay for the latest gas lighting, as well as many other things I have planned for my town house."

Dangling a perfumed handkerchief from his fingers and holding a gold snuff box in his hand, the older man scrutinised the far side of the market place as though bored with the conversation. With a flick of his wrist he tossed back his lace cuff, took a pinch of snuff, and then brushed a minute speck of dust from his coat sleeve with his handkerchief.

Ursula heard the sulky voice of Jonas Bigsby: "You have wronged my sister, sir. Our agreement was that you and your friends should dance with her, not take her to your home, rape her and get her in the family way. You have ruined any chance of her having a decent husband."

"Everyone at the assembly was drinking heavily on that night if you remember, Bigsby. Including your sister, who quickly found a taste for champagne; and when she was merry, she readily agreed to accompany my friends and me to my home. Miss Charlotte Bigsby was extremely willing to please us all, each and every one of us if my memory serves me right. You were her escort to Lady Bracaster's soirée. You alone were accountable for your young sister's behaviour and safety. Her ruination is of your own doing."

Wetting a finger, the other smoothed his eyebrow and gave Jonas a sharp glance. Then, as he spoke again, he prodded Jonas in the chest with the knob of his cane, relentlessly pointing out the facts.

"You gave permission for her to dance with every gentleman in our party, and you must take full responsibility for the consequences. Remember also that she was bedded by all of us that night. Any one of us could be the father."

Jonas hid his shifty expression by staring at the cobblestones. Should he speak to the widow Rials? Would she believe his story? He shook his head; probably not. Blackmail had crossed his mind weeks ago, but he had dismissed the idea, thinking that the man would probably ridicule him; it was true, how could he prove who was the father? Because he was having the conversation in the street, Jonas felt at a disadvantage, and he raised his voice.

"Lord Corredence I only agreed to let her dance with everyone so as to pay my gambling debts! How was I to know you would take the silly girl's virtue?"

"If I remember, you were only too pleased to cancel your gambling debts in such a way. You are not the first to engage this ploy, sir. Others much older and wiser than you have tried the same trick. Don't come whimpering and whining to me now with your predicament. How do I know you haven't used the same ploy on my other friends to try and gain a titled husband for your sister and a father for her coming bastard?"

It was clear from Lord Corredence's expression and from the way he used his gold snuffbox that he would give no help to the young woman, or give her expected baby any assistance whatsoever.

Ursula saw Jonas give a loose cobblestone a vicious kick. His former gambling friend turned and sauntered away, with heels clicking, to where his carriage waited.

It was at that moment that Culvato rejoined his family. Ursula put out a hand and gestured to him not to approach when she saw Jonas walking towards her. Culvato turned away and stood near the entrance to the Exchange Building, watching Ursula.

Ursula stepped forward and held the crystal ball out towards Jonas Bigsby. "Let me tell your fortune, sir? I may see love and a happy life in the future for you," she said.

"What's that you say; a happy life? I think not, Gypsy," Jonas said, walking past.

On reaching a nearby market stall, Jonas spun around on his heel and swiftly retraced his steps. He stood in front of Ursula, studying her face, feature by feature. He saw a guileless, open face of olive complexion. Honesty and intelligence shone in her eyes. She stood with a tilt to her head, as haughty as a marchioness. Then his attention dropped to her chest and the amber-coloured glass beads she wore. She blushed and was about to say something scathing, but she bit back the words as Jonas flashed an insincere smile at her and crooked his finger.

"Follow me at a distance, woman!" he barked.

Ursula glanced towards Culvato. No sensible Gypsy woman, whatever her age, would move far from the protection of her men folk. If there was any suggestion of the man attacking her, his brains would be spilled or his throat slashed. Ursula left the linnet and pole for Culvato to pick up on his way past with the barrow, lifted baby Lionel from the basket and took hold of Hugo's hand. Keeping a few steps behind Jonas, she glanced over her shoulder. Her husband, pushing the barrow, now laden with the basket and linnet cage was keeping pace with her.

They didn't have to go very far. They followed the worried man around the corner, across the street and into a small, deserted courtyard. Although Jonas gave a start of surprised to see that Culvato had joined them, he made no comment when he faced the Gypsies.

Jonas tilted his nose in the air and said, in a haughty manner: "My name is Bigsby. We will soon have a babe in our home, new born and unwanted by its mother. It will need a home. You appear to be a caring woman. Will you take the child and raise it with your family?"

Without realising what he was doing, he clenched and unclenched his hands. Ursula was quick to notice his agitation and, as always, she hoped there might be some profit in helping the gaujo. She looked at Culvato and stood back waiting for him to speak.

He rubbed the stubble on his chin, a note of doubt crept into his voice.

"We have many children of our own to feed and clothe, and another baby will be here very soon."

Ursula, carrying Lionel in her arms, shifted him to rest on one hip and stuck out her stomach in support of her husband's claim - although there was no possibility that she was pregnant.

"You will be well paid. I'll give you enough money to take the babe far away from here. You can do with it whatever you want; we don't want to see the child again."

Culvato glanced at Ursula, and Jonas saw her shrug her shoulders with an air of indifference. Culvato held out his hand, palm up, and Jonas, giving a sigh of relief, knew a deal had been made.

Ursula trusted her husband; he would do what was best for their family. She heard Jonas telling Culvato his address before she left and returned to the market place with the children. Culvato would make the necessary arrangements. Ursula was fond of all tiknies and she would find room in her heart to love the unwanted baby. Maybe it would be a girl. A surge of expectancy ran through her, and she began to plan how she could make the child look pretty in lace and ribbons.

Suddenly weary, she sat on the steps below a high stone fountain and made baby Lionel comfortable on her knee. The sound of water tumbling over the stone basin soothed her, and her eyes half closed. A friendly smile at a passing matron encouraged the woman to stop and have her fortune told. Taking out her crystal ball once again, Ursula gazed deep into it.

"Your life could be long, and I see great riches coming to you and your family."

"How rich? Will we have children?" the matron asked, in great excitement.

Ursula nodded. "You will have everything money can buy," she chanted.

Accepting a coin from the woman and replacing the crystal ball in her pocket, Ursula got to her feet and glanced at the sky. Summer storm clouds were threatening rain. The market was emptying of customers. Stallholders were packing away their unsold goods and beggars were sorting through the rubbish in the hope of finding food or something to exchange for drink. At a stall selling fruit at a reduced price, Ursula, knowing his fondness for them, bought an orange for Culvato. Another stall displayed sweetmeats and candied peel. She bought a sugar twist for little Hugo. As she gave the sweet-bit to him, down came the rain. Quickly securing her shawl over baby Lionel and taking hold of Hugo's hand, she hurried away to meet her husband.

Culvato had waited for them on the edge of town. Ursula smiled as he scooped up Hugo and put him under the oiled canvas which covered the barrow, making the little boy squeal with delight. Then the couple hastened to find shelter from the heavy rain.

The weary family found a low barn in the middle of a field, one door hanging half off its hinges; to them it was heaven sent. They entered it cautiously. The old barn welcomed them with warmth, a strong, familiar smell of horse and crushed, fusty straw. To their relief, it was unoccupied by man or beast.

As her husband shook the water from his hat, Ursula threw an old sack over a heap of straw in a corner away from the draught of the door and made Hugo lie down on it to rest.

Ursula made herself comfortable on an old wooden box and placed the baby to her breast. Leaning his shoulder against the doorframe, Culvato looked out at the sodden field.

"Did you earn much?" he asked.

Ursula finished feeding Lionel and laced up her bodice. In answer, she held out some coins with a broad smile.

"Not much there." Culvato started to peel his orange as he spoke; the spray and citrus aroma made his mouth water. "Some of our clan are camped on Mapperley Common. If we spend the night here, we will join the others tomorrow. We'll need to stay somewhere near Nottingham until the Bigsby gauji has her baby." He put a segment of orange in his mouth and chewed it with enjoyment before adding: "I'm pleased to be away from the town. I dare bet there'll be trouble tonight if what I've heard about the Luddites is true. Some men were saying that they were taking those machines to block the doors of a master hosier's house, but if we keep well away from the town, the Luddites won't bother us."

"I wonder if the Mayor's hat has dried. It will never look the same again." As Ursula broke into spontaneous laughter, Culvato grinned and nodded at her.

"Shame we had no feathers to sell him," he chuckled.

Looking beyond the field, listening to the rhythm of the rain beating a tattoo on the earth-covered roof, Culvato noticed a rider's head and shoulders bobbing up and down above the hedge as he travelled along the lane. The rider turned into the field, and Culvato realised the man was riding towards the barn.

"Quick! Get everything together, Romni, someone is coming," Culvato said, in an urgent whisper. He tossed his orange peel into a clump of grass, and then turned the barrow so that it faced the door, ready for a quick departure.

With a bad-tempered grumble at his mount, and cursing the mud underfoot, the rider dismounted, led his steaming horse inside the barn and tied it to a ring set into the wall. Ursula and Culvato stood side-by-side, partially hidden by the barrow. The man used a handful of straw to rub the horse down, and started a tuneless whistling between his teeth. He was so intent on the job in hand that he didn't notice Culvato and Ursula until he had thrown an old blanket over the horse. Startled, he faced them with a curse. Realizing the family were Gypsies, he grabbed hold of the nearest weapon, a twin-pronged hayfork.

"Gurt off me land! Thieving vagabonds! Dirty peddlers! Causing me trouble, gurt out before I use me whip about your shoulders!" he yelled, jabbing the hayfork towards Culvato and Ursula.

Culvato lifted Hugo from his resting place and, without

awakening the child, laid him inside the barrow. Ursula placed Lionel by his brother's side and covered them with blankets, and Culvato quickly pulled the oiled canvas tilt over them.

With his lips compressed and his back stiff with anger, Culvato pushed the barrow out of the barn. Throwing her shawl around herself and covering her head, Ursula gave the man a dark look before following her husband. The rain had turned the field into a sticky quagmire, and Culvato had difficulty pushing the heavy barrow over the sodden earth. The lane was firmer underfoot, but water lay in the deep ruts.

As soon as they were out of earshot, Culvato said: "We'll go to the other side of Connie Wood, near the old ruined house, and make camp. I'd chosen it earlier. 'Twas only the rain made me stop at the barn."

Ursula didn't reply, but flashed him a trusting smile; Culvato knew all the campsites in the county where Gypsies could stay safely, and where there was clean running water.

They plodded on for several miles without speaking, and eventually the rain stopped. Culvato gave a grunt when he recognised where they were. He took a candle lamp out of the barrow, lit it, and handed it to Ursula.

"Not far now. We will still have enough daylight to see what we are doing as we build the tent, but when we go through this wood, we'll need this to light our way," he said.

"I haven't been here before. Where are we?" Ursula said.

"Used to be a country manor. The owner went mad. I've heard tell that he did all kinds of strange things. When he died, it's said that the family searched all over the house for his wealth, but they never found a penny piece. Pulled the place apart and made it a ruin. The house hasn't been lived in for years. Follow close behind, and hold the lamp up high."

Turning off the lane, she had to help Culvato, he was having difficulty in manoeuvring the barrow along a narrow mossy path flanked by high bushes and trees whose branches laced together overhead. Ursula held the lamp high, but it gave scant light through its thin horn window. It took some effort, but together, they steered the barrow through a gap in the bushes and into a field; placing it near a hawthorn hedge for protection from the wind. Culvato let out a mild curse when he staggered backwards and almost fell over a clump of thistles.

"By the state of these weeds, this field hasn't been used for crop or beast since the family moved away from the big house," Culvato said, stamping the thistles down.

"I'll see to the tiknies if you go and cut some willow." Ursula said when she saw Culvato take his long, curved knife from his belt; he honed it daily to razor-sharpness.

Ursula rolled the oiled tilt off the barrow and shook the water from it. The baby whimpered as Ursula lifted him from the barrow and spots of rain splashed him. She laid him on a quilt, protected from the wet grass by sacks. Hugo continued to sleep soundly. He gave a soft moan as he was gently placed next to his brother.

Culvato returned carrying an armful of long slender willow boughs and the couple pushed them into the ground until they formed a part-circle. A tilt, a rug and some blankets were spread on the ground inside before they lifted and pulled the largest of their oiled tilts over the upright willow boughs. They both fetched large stones from a broken wall at the far side of the field and put them around the bottom of the tent. It would help to stop the entry of vermin and other unwanted visitors, and it would prevent the wind from blowing it all away.

Culvato pointed to the bottom of the slope where the stream was swollen to the point of overflowing.

"I had to wade in the stream to cut the willow. The water is murky and won't be any good for drinking. We'd be wise to move on in the morning."

In the cosy warmth of the tent, the family fell asleep to the gentle lullaby of gurgling water and birds roosting in the trees.

Ursula awoke first the following morning. Stepping out of the bender tent, she lifted her face to the sky and took deep breaths of sweet-scented air. She walked across the meadow to the broken wall. Sitting on a moss-covered stone, she shook out her hair and combed perfumed oil into her long, dark tresses before braiding and pinning it neatly into place with combs.

Early morning was the time of day Ursula enjoyed most. The birds were giving their first chirp of the morning. Orbs of dew covered the grass. Spider webs were as yet unbroken. The echoing bark of a dog fox made her peer towards the trees, but its camouflage was too good, and a white mist, clinging like smoke on the ground, prevented her from seeing it.

During years of storms, the stones, which had formed a boundary wall, had shifted and were buried among the high weeds and grass. The wall was of little use. Recently, a stone had fallen across a deep, rusted metal box, eighteen inches square, and had gouged a bright groove in the rusty lid. The mark attracted Ursula's attention. She pulled the box free from the tumbling rubble. It was locked. Her mouth set with determination, she hammered at it with a hand-sized stone and soon broke apart the rotting leather clasp. Her eyes widened with astonishment as she looked at numerous gold coins, chains, and an assortment of jewellery set with precious gems. A pair of gold earrings took Ursula's fancy, and she held them high to admire them.

"It's mendis. It's mendis; we're rich. I saw the future in the glass, for us," Ursula said.

"What's you got there, monushi?"

Ursula hadn't noticed Culvato leave the tent and come across the field to join her. When she heard his voice she turned, her face aglow. She held the earrings out towards him.

"We are barvali! Look here. Lovva and sonakai. Look at these Kan-fornies. I saw it all in my crystal ball, yesterday, but I never dreamt it was for us. It's all quality stuff, Culvato, and now it's mendis!"

Culvato gave a glance around the field to check they were unobserved before crouching down to poke at the contents of the box with a finger. He lifted a gold chain, and an emerald shifted and shone in the dawn's light. Lines crinkled around his brown eyes as he smiled at Ursula.

"I dare bet it's the madman's family treasure. Tales were told about how the family pulled panels off the walls and lifted all the floorboards as they tried to find his wealth. The madman must have hidden it out here without telling anyone. We'd best leave this place as soon as we can. No one saw us arrive last night. I'll make sure no one can tell we've camped here. Get Hugo awake and I'll pack away the tent." Culvato closed the lid of the box and stood up.

"Have you got a bag or something to keep everything secure? I can't use the box now it's broken," Ursula said, springing to her feet.

"Yes. I've an old leather gonner with strings. You must tie it under your skirt. It'll be safer with you." Culvato handed the heavy box to his wife. With a wide grin, he added, "We are rich, girl. At long last we're barvali-fellows."

Culvato slipped an arm around his wife's slim waist. Ursula nearly lost her grip on the box when he pulled her close and kissed her. With a sigh of ecstasy, she slipped her arm around his neck. The kiss would have quickly turned to passion, but Culvato moved away.

"We haven't time, my Romni. Later, later we will celebrate

and plan what we will do." Another hug and a quick kiss brought a becoming blush to his wife's face.

They hurried back to the tent, the box carried by Ursula. Culvato rummaged through the contents of the cart and found the leather bag.

"When we make camp tonight, we'll count everything," he said.

"What shall I do with the empty mokto?" Ursula asked, holding out the box towards Culvato.

"Give it to me. I'll throw it into the water. With the stream running so fast, no one will find it until we're far away." Dropping the box on the ground, he stamped on it until it was misshapen. "If they do, I'd doubt if anyone would know what it used to hold."

Ursula watched him go to the stream, and heard the splash as the box hit the water. It didn't take the couple long to dismantle the tent and pack their belongings into the barrow. Culvato helped Ursula to fold and lift the tilts, which were heavy with the previous day's rain.

He hid the willow boughs among the trees and replaced the turf that he had lifted the previous night so that they could make a fire; it looked as though it had never been disturbed. When the family left the field, a casual observer wouldn't have known anyone had spent the night there.

They set off along the lane, showered with moisture dripping from the trees, and thought of wonderful ways to spend their newfound wealth. Dreams, half-formed and unspoken, could, if they wished, become a reality. Ursula followed her husband and held baby Lionel close to her heart. She wondered if they might travel to the coast and show Hugo the sea and sand. To paddle had always been one of Ursula's ambitions. She remembered how her father had once told her tales about a place called Scarborough, with green water and white foam that stretched out towards the sky for a million miles.

By mid-morning, Culvato was striding well ahead of his family, along a towpath beside the River Trent. Ursula was beginning to feel tired, both from her early rising and at the excitement of their find.

"Culvato! Shall we rest here?" she called.

Turning with a hand on the handle of his barrow, he scanned the area; no one was in sight. He ruffled Hugo's dark curls before pushing the barrow behind a fallen tree which lay beside the path. He made it secure by kicking two large stones against the wheels.

Where they had stopped, fine gravel shelved down to the river. The warm sunshine was accompanied by buzzing insects, water slopping over stones, and other soothing and peaceful countryside sounds. Culvato lay down on the grass, closed his eyes and began to talk about his ideas for his family's future. The first thing they agreed upon would be to have something better than the barrow. Ursula, taking a knife from the sheath on her belt, cut into a bread loaf and the cheese she had bought the previous day in the market. She handed pieces to Culvato and Hugo, and then lifted baby Lionel to her breast.

The pleasing silence was broken when Culvato said: "Once we have the new baby, we're going to Eastwood."

Ursula nodded. She smiled at the contented face of her baby as he fed, and thought how like his father he looked.

Hugo was eager to explore, and he pulled at Culvato's arm.

"Dadrus, can I go and look at the fishes in the river?"

Culvato gave his son an empty enamel mug and he watched the child approach the water's edge.

Ursula rose to her feet, so as to keep a more effective watch on Hugo.

"It means we'll have to travel through Nottingham Town again," she said.

"I heard my brother and his family will be travelling this way after they've been to Peterborough. He'll get a good price for that young strawberry roan grai," Culvato said, placing an arm around Hugo and examining the mug of water for make-believe fish. Hugo leaned against his father and yawned. Seeing that the child's eyelids were drooping, Culvato scooped him up and put him in the barrow. Within minutes, Hugo was fast asleep.

"You could buy a moila. Tawno would certainly wonder where you had the money from to buy such a luxury as a donkey." Ursula gave a giggle at the thought of her surly brother-in-law's likely puzzlement at the sight of them with a donkey.

"You could tell him that all the butchers in Nottingham wanted to buy your wooden skewers and baskets. My brother might believe you and travel this way again next year." Culvato joined in her merry laughter, before adding, "A pony would be better to pull a vardo."

Ursula almost choked.

"Vardo? A real bow-top caravan with vazo windows and a stove?" she asked, almost unable to believe that such a wonderful thing could possibly become theirs.

"I once saw a beautiful Reading Caravan. Wouldn't mind having one like that. Don't know if we'll have a stove, but I think glass windows might be put in." Culvato laughed aloud at the expression on Ursula's face, and was then suddenly serious. "I've always wanted to make a chavvies' merry-go-round. I thought one with farm animals - a horse, cock, pig and cow, all turning in a circle. Painted in bright colours and with leather saddles and reins. It would attract children. You could take the money for the ride while Tawno and I made it spin." Culvato's eyes gazed into the distance as he voiced his dream.

"Oh, Culvato, you could have your name written in gold on each animal." Putting her arm round her husband, Ursula drew him close.

"I'm so happy you picked me to be your woman," she whispered. Her tongue tickled as it touched the outside of his ear. She giggled when his arm snaked round her waist and found a ticklish spot. After a quick glance around, Culvato unlaced Ursula's blouse and tantalised her breasts with his tongue until the nipples were hard. Ursula knew wonderful ways to arouse and please Culvato, and slowly they made love.

They were sated with lovemaking, and had begun to doze in each other's arms, when two swans flew down and splashed into the river. Culvato sat up and nudged Ursula.

"Best get on our way. We'll stay a while at the travellers' camp, the one at Arnold. Mr Bigsby is to let me know when the baby is born. While we're in Nottingham, I'll exchange some of the gold sovereigns into smaller coins, and maybe I'll sell some of the jewellery. A long time ago my dadrus and my Kaka Piramus told me about a wheelwright who builds Romani vardos. The man has a workshop at the Eastwood Village. We'll ask him if he will make our new home. Think of what colour you would like it to be and I'll paint it. Then you can sit behind the grai and drive our very own smart vardo all around the country."

Culvato laughed when Ursula squealed in delight and kissed him passionately. Neither of them was in a hurry to move and they lay for another hour in each other's arms, kissing and being kissed, whispering and dreaming of their future plans. It wasn't until the children awoke and disturbed them that they set off in the direction of Nottingham.

Chapter 3

Culvato leaned on the wall of the Nottingham Exchange Building, smoking his clay pipe and watching the people going about their business in the marketplace. As usual at this time of day, he waited for Jonas Bigsby to walk past.

It was Saturday. The country folk always arrived early to sell their wares and it was past midday. Discerning housewives had already bought the best of the live poultry, homemade preserves and the home-grown produce from the stallholders.

On Culvato's left were people selling penned geese, turkeys, ducks and pigeons. He noticed a number of quarrelsome pigs in the care of small boys, who tried to control the animals with sharp sticks. The noise of cackling, quacking, gobbling and squealing was intermingled with the cries of street traders and stallholders, each of whom was trying to outshout his or her neighbour. Culvato grinned widely when a couple of chickens broke loose from their coop and make their escape. In the commotion, a basket of eggs was swept from the stall. Two women, attempting to catch the eggs, banged their heads together and the inevitable happened. Rubbing their heads, the women looked ruefully at the mess on their long skirts before walking away in opposite directions.

This was the first time Culvato had been kept waiting. Usually at midday, Jonas Bigsby would acknowledge Culvato's presence by raising his hand. The Gypsy would then understand that the baby had not yet been born. After waiting for more than an hour with no sign of the man, Culvato decided to go to his house.

When he'd first been told the address of the Bigsby family, Culvato had accompanied Ursula as she worked her way, dukkerering, along the street. A servant girl had been happy to have her fortune told and to gossip about her neighbour. She had warned Ursula not to go to the Bigsby house.

'They only have one servant and she won't open the door to anyone in case it's a tradesman wanting to collect his debts,' she had said.

Culvato pushed his barrow through the back garden gate and put it out of sight behind a shed. No one was about, and the shed door was ajar. A wooden pail, covered in cobwebs, stood near the door. The usual clutter of garden implements were lying around, neglected and rusting.

Rain began to spit in the wind. Taking a piece of sacking from the barrow, he threw it around his shoulders and seated himself on the upturned pail. From where he sat he could see the kitchen window and the scullery door. He settled down to wait for a member of the household to appear—or anyone else who could give him some information about the birth.

* * *

Charlotte Bigsby kept her eyes lowered. This was the first time since her disgrace that her mother had allowed her in the drawing room for tea. She sat on the window seat. The thin curtains that hung each side of her did little to keep out the draught from the casement window.

37

The chilly temperature of the September afternoon matched the dismal atmosphere inside the drawing room. Jonas stood with an arm resting on the mantelpiece, swinging his quizzing glass by its ribbon and looking at her. The weak glow from the fire hardly warmed them at all.

'We do not seem to be enjoying your sixteenth birthday as I would have hoped, Charlotte,' he said.

Their mother shivered exaggeratedly, and pulled her shawl closer around her shoulders. Jonas glanced at her with barely hidden irritation. He rolled his eyes towards the ceiling and then turned his attention back to Charlotte. He lifted his quizzing glass to stare through it at his sister.

'You have been silent since you entered the room, Charlotte,' he said. 'You aren't eating your birthday cake, and you haven't even thanked me for the present I bought to improve your mind.'

At her brother's mocking words, Charlotte let her glance pass over the framed embroidered text she had placed beside her on the windowsill. It said, "Fallen women must learn to rise in the sight of men and God." As he spoke she looked at him with loathing. Her blue eyes were huge in her gaunt face, and her beautiful golden hair was lank and tied back with an old ribbon.

During her pregnancy, she had tried to recall the night of the ball and constantly wondered why her mother believed the lie she had been told by Jonas. She knew she had behaved that evening as protocol dictated. Following her brother's recommendation, she had been charming and danced with each of his friends. She clearly remembered dancing with a Mr Soult, who stuttered and was most courteous. She had behaved with decorum when she had been introduced to Lord Corredence, although she had taken a dislike to him. It had been he who had offered her champagne when she was thirsty.

After that, everything became unclear. Why she should bring to mind a long carriage ride, she couldn't say, for Nurse Grant had told her Jonas had brought her home in a hansom cab.

On a cold day in February, Charlotte had been working in the kitchen when she had noticed Mr Soult approaching the house, bearing a bunch of flowers. Nothing could have persuaded her to receive the young man. She had thought him to have been a member of the party on the night of her rape. Jonas hadn't bothered to mention that Mr Soult had not been involved, and had known nothing about the dreadful incident.

'I... I'm not very hungry, Jonas,' Charlotte whispered. She dropped her gaze to a tiny piece of the birthday cake on her plate. Her mother had ordered her to bake the cake that morning and, with the help of Nurse Grant, it had turned out tolerably well.

'That, Jonas, is all the thanks you get for presenting the ungrateful wretch with a gift and for allowing her to celebrate her birthday in the drawing room. Had it been left to me, well...' Charlotte heard her mother's peevish voice echoing as though from a distance. She let her mind wander as her mother voiced her accusations, for she had heard the words many times in the recent months.

'As usual you show bad manners, Charlotte. I don't know where you get them from; not from my side of the family, that I do know.' Shrugging, she lifted her cup, grimacing when she found it empty. 'If you'd come downstairs on the day when that nice Mr Soult called to see you, instead of sulking in your bedchamber, I dare say you would be safely married by now. But you had to have the vapours, and missed your chance to find a husband before the child is born. The man is still clearly besotted but he won't wait forever.'

The teacup rattled in its saucer as she held it out towards Jonas. There was nowhere to put it. The beautiful inlaid table which used to stand by her chair had been sold months ago, together with most of the other furniture and carpets. Both Charlotte and her mother knew that any money raised had gone to pay the gambling debts incurred by Jonas. He would swagger around the town wearing the latest fashions. "Top show" was everything to Jonas Bigsby.

The paintings and gilded mirrors were all gone, leaving light patches on the walls. Charlotte and her mother had been told the furnishings would be brought back after they had been cleaned, but they dared not ask Jonas why they were not yet returned, in case he flew into one of his terrifying rages. The only things of value left in the house were the essential pieces of furniture and a lantern clock which had been made by Edward East and bought by her great grandfather.

The rent was in arrears and tradesmen constantly knocked at the door asking for bills to be paid, so they suspected Jonas was still gambling and attending race meetings, but they had to appear to be affluent for, after the baby was born, Charlotte would have to marry a man of substance. Otherwise, she and her mother would have no other option but to go and live in the workhouse.

Charlotte shivered and pulled her loose robe together to cover her nightgown. Both garments were neatly darned and patched. They were the only clothes that fitted her. Having been up since dawn, she rubbed the index and middle fingers of her hand over her forehead in a weary gesture.

As it struck the hour, they all looked at the lantern clock standing on the mantelpiece. Jonas placed his mother's cup and saucer next to the clock and put his quizzing glass to his eye. He examined the clock in detail. It was a beautiful thing: sixteen inches high with tulips engraved on the brass dial and a double dolphin fret across the gilded top.

Her mother arose from her seat, holding both hands out

imploringly.

'Jonas, please, not my clock. Please leave me that. It's all I have left of my family things.' She pressed her knuckles against her teeth while her eyes filled with tears.

His face a stony mask, Jonas spun round on his heel to face her. 'You told me earlier that tradesmen are continually knocking at the door. Yet when I see a way to pay your debts, you have the vapours. I really don't know why I bother to return to this house. I should stay in comfort with my friends.'

Charlotte looked at him with an expression of revulsion and he pointed to the door. 'Get back to the scullery where you belong. You aren't fit to be seen in your condition.'

She eased herself from her seat and moved towards the door without a word. She heard Jonas say to their mother, 'Each time I see my sister I could swear she's larger. I've never seen a woman so big. She's like a balloon on stilts.'

She was too weary to care.

Her mother lowered her voice. 'Nurse Grant says it may be twins. Charlotte should rest or she will not have the strength to give birth.'

Jonas gave a barking laugh.

'Rest? Rubbish, she's as strong as old iron. What she needs is hard work. You have nothing worth polishing now, so set her on scrubbing. That should slim her down.'

Turning back towards the fireplace, he reached for the clock as Charlotte let out a piercing scream.

With a sharp cry, her mother quickly rose to her feet.

'Charlotte's ready to take to her bed, Jonas,' she said.

'If that's so, Mama, get her to a room on the top floor. I have letters to write and I need quiet so I can collect my thoughts.' Jonas kicked the logs in the fire grate, causing a rush of sparks to fly up the chimney, as his mother took Charlotte from the room.

41

Reaching the bottom of the staircase, she bent double with pain, forced to cling onto the banisters to pull herself upstairs. With an arm around her, her nurse encouraged the frightened girl to take each step upwards. Her mother followed them but when they were about to enter Charlotte's bedchamber she pointed along the landing to another, uncarpeted staircase.

'Not that room, use one of the rooms on the upper floor.' She reddened and bit her lip when the nurse flashed a look at her mistress. Nurse Grant had attended her when she had given birth to Charlotte, when she'd had every possible attention at her laying in, paid for by her adoring husband.

The nurse supported Charlotte as they climbed the second wooden staircase which led to a fusty attic once used by servants, and abandoned long ago. The only furniture in the room was a small chest of drawers, a rickety chair and a low bed near one wall. The wooden slats of the bed were partly covered by a straw-filled palliasse.

A mouse scurried across the bed and under the chest of drawers. Nurse Grant shuddered. 'Stay where you are, mouse, until we've finished here,' she muttered.

'Here now, Miss Charlotte. Let me spread your robe over the bed so you can lie down. Then I'll fetch the things I have made ready for you.'

Standing with her fingers in her mouth like a child, tense and terrified, Charlotte glanced towards her mother. She was chilled by her expression. Silently, she began to say the Lord's Prayer, but kept forgetting the words and was forced to start again. Her lips moved as she allowed Nurse Grant to remove her robe. She put both hands on her stomach, and watched the nurse without interest as the woman shook the straw-filled palliasse in a vain attempt to make it comfortable.

The nurse gasped and quickly caught hold of Charlotte when she suddenly bent double and let out another piercing scream. 'Come, Miss Charlotte, get on the bed. You will feel better soon.' As she helped her lie down, her mother stood by the door, her face a pale, cold mask. 'Will you stay with her, mistress? I need to fetch hot water, blankets and the cradle.'

Mrs Bigsby pointed to the chest of drawers. 'Use one of those. The babe will not be with us long enough to lie in a cradle.'

Nurse Grant's face turned ashen, as if she thought the treatment at such a time was downright cruel. Her hurrying footsteps echoed on the uncarpeted floor as she fetched what was needed from the kitchen and bedchamber. Each time she entered the attic room, Charlotte was writhing in pain. The nurse had no help whatsoever from her mistress who stayed near the door with her arms folded and did nothing to ease her daughter's suffering.

A blanket, folded and placed in one of the small top drawers, was ready to receive the baby. Nurse Grant gave a relieved sigh at the arrival of a perfect baby girl and, holding the baby by the feet, she gave her a sharp smack. A sound of satisfaction escaped her as the baby gave a cry.

Wrapping her up, she gently placed her in the drawer then quickly turned her attention back to Charlotte when the girl gave a low moan and began to bear down again. Another baby slid into the world and gave a healthy cry. She had more hair than her sister. Wrapping up the second baby, the nurse placed her in the drawer and covered them both with another blanket.

'You'll both have to wait to be cleaned until I've finished making your mother comfortable,' she murmured.

Charlotte closed her eyes. Nurse Grant gently wiped the sweat and tears from her face, but a moan and a sudden arching of the girl's body produced another baby, smaller but perfect, lying between her legs.

Mrs Bigsby's eyes were as round as the nurse's as the third

baby girl was placed with her sisters.

Nurse Grant was busy with Charlotte as her mother moved closer and, with a quick movement, slipped an amethyst necklet under one of the babies. Then, with some difficulty, she picked up the drawer and carried it out of the room. Jonas was waiting for her in the corridor. He hurried towards her.

'There are three. All girls. Is the man outside waiting for them?' Mrs Bigsby didn't wait for an answer as she held the drawer out towards him. 'Here. Take them quickly, before Charlotte asks for them. And if she does want to see them, we will tell her they are dead.'

Jonas snatched the drawer. Holding the stair banister rail for support, she watched him hurrying downstairs, and gave a tearful sniff.

Hearing Charlotte give a long sobbing moan, she took a deep breath before re-entering the bedchamber.

A look of dread filled Charlotte's half open eyes. 'My babies?' she whispered.

Mrs Bigsby looked away.

'There were more than one. What happened? Why don't you answer?' her distraught daughter cried. Somehow she found the strength to lift herself up, and looked first at Nurse Grant and then at her mother.

'There, there, hush, hush,' said Nurse Grant, stroking a strand of damp hair from the girl's face. 'You had three little girls.'

'Three? Where are they? Can I see them?'

'Gone. They were monsters. Jonas has taken them away,' her mother said briskly. 'We now have to make you strong again. If anyone asks, we can say you have been very ill, but you are now recovered. No one whom we are acquainted with will ever know about your disgrace, and now you can marry that nice Mr Soult. I will ask him to take tea in a few days. Have a sleep, and later we'll help you down to your bedchamber.'

She ignored Nurse Grant and quickly turned to leave the room before the woman could ask awkward questions, but as she reached the door, the nurse spoke to her in a cold voice. 'Miss Charlotte needs someone to stay with her for a while, mistress.'

'You stay. I will not be needing you.' She closed the door softly behind her.

The sight of Jonas removing her grandchildren with such obvious revulsion had shaken her to the core. She had believed him when he had lied about his sister's behaviour at the ball but now, with Charlotte's constant denial about her so-called wanton behaviour, she was beginning to have doubts. *It's time for us to look to the future, and if my plans for Charlotte come to pass, it will be without Jonas*, she thought.

Chapter 4

Synfye Ardry felt wretched. She trudged along and pulled her shawl further over her head. She held baby Mikailia so tight in her arms, the baby began to whimper. There was no sight of Tawno and she felt alone and vulnerable. She couldn't enjoy the atmosphere of Peterborough market because she had to continually to look about her, hoping not to be recognised. The last time she had been there, the parish constable himself had escorted her to the parish boundary, with a stern warning that she would probably be hanged if she returned. Her back still bore the scars of her clash with Peterborough officialdom.

Remembering that time, Synfye's body shrank into itself. The thought of being stripped to the waist, tied to the back of a cart, to endure another bloody whipping terrified her.

Skirting around the edge of the market place, she managed to sell a few pieces of narrow lace from her basket. More often, upon approaching people with an outstretched hand and a whining voice, she was ignored, though some swore or even spat at her. At a stall selling hot peas, a woman threw a pail of cold, greasy water that drenched Synfye's skirt and soaked Seth's dark curls. Raising her fist and shaking with anger, she cursed the woman at the stall. That was a mistake she couldn't afford. She could see through the shifting crowd that a person in uniform was approaching. With a last dark look at the stallholder, she pulled her shawl further over her head and drew back. She glanced around to see if she had invited trouble, but no one was taking any notice of her and grabbing Seth by the hand, she hurried away.

More than once, Synfye had to pull Seth into a doorway for safety from the wagons and carriages which careered past at dangerous speed, perilously close to the buildings. On market days the streets stunk of the household liquid messes thrown from windows and doors; it mixed with stallholders' litter and ran along the street's shallow gullies. Synfye wrinkled her nose in disgust at the body of a dead dog, bloated and fly-ridden.

Looking down, she felt pity for the child trotting by her side. She smiled and placed a hand on his head. "Not long to go now. We'll soon be tramping through sweet meadow land, my chavvi."

Throughout the town there were rogues and vagabonds. They passed many who were crouched by walls or sitting on stone steps, holding out their hands. Shifty-eyed peddlers seemed to be on every street, hawking their wares. Above the sounds of hoarse voices and rumbling wheels, Synfye heard a furious commotion, distant at first, but coming closer. Shouts and yells headed in her direction, and warned her of trouble. Catching hold of Seth, she dragged him into the shelter of a doorway and trembling, she pushed him behind her skirts.

"Keep still, my chavvi. Stay out of sight and be a mouse."

Peering cautiously around the corner, Synfye saw the smallest of Tawno's two runaway urchins haring along the street. For an instant she let him see her. None of his pursuers saw the boy toss his three stolen purses into the doorway. More importantly, they didn't see Synfye cover them with her feet and long skirts. A dozen or more people ran past the

47

doorway crying out: "Stop thief! Stop that boy!" But none of them noticed Synfye.

Were the urchin to be caught with stolen property, he would meet the same fate as little Rick and be hanged. If by some miracle the boy was found to be clean, and no one could swear to have seen him stealing, he might be fortunate and be taken to the parish workhouse to be fed. Tradespeople found most of their new apprentices at the workhouse and the boy at five years old was the right age to be chosen for years of misery. But even a future of drudgery was better than death by hanging.

When the hue and cry had passed and the street was back to normality, Synfye crouched down as though attending to her child. With her skirts pooling around her feet, she gave a quick glance over her shoulder to see if anyone was paying any attention to her, but for the moment no one was nearby. She picked up the three purses and felt their weight. The coins were thick, and their size and weight suggested that they were gold. With an exultant smile, she lifted her skirt and placed the purses into a deep pocket sewn inside her petticoat. She seldom needed to use the pocket as she rarely had money of her own; Tawno always appropriated any coins she earned by dukkering or selling her scraps of lace.

Knowing that she could now buy her way out of trouble, Synfye tucked the purses away and confidently led Seth back towards the market place.

The aroma of hot apple and cinnamon made her mouth water. She saw a pie-man walking towards her, balancing a tray on his head and calling: "Pies for sale!" in time to the ringing of a hand bell. She grinned when a horse lifted its head to steal a tasty morsel - but the pie-man was too quick, and moved the tray from temptation. She spent one of her newly acquired coins on a couple of pies, and was pleased to find they were still warm. With Seth following closely behind, she made her way to a grassy spot beside a stream and sat down to eat, hidden from the view of the jostling crowds by bushes. The pies were delicious. While Seth finished his, Synfye prepared to feed baby Mikailia, pulling her shawl over them both for modesty. Seth became interested in exploring the bank of the stream, though his recent fright in the doorway ensured he kept his mother in sight. Remembering the purses, she felt for them through the fabric of her skirt and tried to count the coins. *No need for me to beg or sell any more from the basket today*, she thought. She had only sold some scraps of lace at a farthing each, and the remaining contents of the basket could be sold tomorrow. It also still contained the cake loaf.

Smiling, she put the baby over her shoulder. She patted her back, and enjoyed feeling the baby curls against her cheek. She called to Seth.

"Let us go home to your dadrus now. Maybe he will want to buy you something nice when he sees what we have to give him."

Synfye was sure that Tawno would be pleased with her, and that he might even give her a kind word or a kiss or two. Swinging the basket by its handle, she sauntered along, daydreaming and allowing Seth to examine the hedgerows. The child darted around, looking for berries and birds nests.

Nearing the place where they had left the caravan, Synfye was jolted from her reverie. A cry; a dreadful cry ending in a long, sobbing moan and her first thought was to run for the safety of home and her husband.

***

Dropping the basket, she picked up Seth, and clutching both

her children tightly, she raced around the bend in the lane. She could smell smoke and scorching before she saw what was causing it, and her heart pounded. She found Tawno on his knees in front of a smouldering pile of ash and twisted metal. Letting Seth slip to the ground and holding Mikailia tightly to her chest, she fought her swimming senses and tried not to faint as she listened to her husband.

"Chikli-Beng outbreeds! Taking the home from children! A curse I put on all ill-doers who'd do such a waffedipen thing to a poor family. You're nothing but a set of grai thieves. Sons of draggle-tailed whores!" Tawno spat his curses with venom and hatred at the people who had destroyed his home.

Synfye's eyes stung from the smoke which still rose from the smouldering mess, as Tawno lifted out pieces of charred wood and leather, scattering the ash in the breeze. He cursed wildly upon discovering the broken hand-carved shafts of the caravan. Picking them up, he dashed them to the ground in anger. The blankets were singed and in holes. The goose down mattress and pillows had been slashed and lay useless, their feathers floating across the field in the breeze. The sight of the smashed crockery and the pans bent out of shape added to Synfye's misery. Even the carved cradle, lovingly created by Tawno's father, was burnt beyond repair.

The flap of wings and the harsh caw of crows turned Synfye's attention to the grim sight of their donkey which lay stiff legged, its eyes staring and its throat cut. A crow balanced unsteadily on the donkey's head. Synfye gave a long drawn out wail that lifted a flock of sparrows from the trees. With a sob, her hand covering her mouth, Synfye sank to the ground, tears flowing. She watched Tawno move around the debris to pick up items from the ashes; a tin mug, a plate, charred pieces of the canvas tilt, bloodstained leather taken from the bridle of the donkey. He collected everything usable and put it together in a pile.

A whimper made Tawno lift his head and stare at one of the dogs cowering in the long grass. The second lurcher stood beside it as though on guard. Tawno snapped his fingers and they moved cautiously towards him. The dogs were nervous, and one limped and held up his front paw to be examined by its master. With a click of his fingers, Tawno directed them to return to the long grass and lie down.

Tawno spent some time trying to bend the smoke-blackened kettle into a semblance of its old shape, and then shook the ash from the two longest pieces of the broken shafts and dropped them on the ground beside Synfye.

"Need to tie these together. Rip one of your skirts into strips to use as rope."

Synfye did as Tawno asked, but she turned away so that he didn't see the weighty purses hidden inside her petticoat pocket. As she handed the torn fabric to Tawno, she whispered, "Why? Do you know who did this?"

"No." Seething with anger, Tawno walked to a nearby alder tree and broke off two branches. He'd no intention of telling Synfye about the meeting with Brandy-Joe Lincoln in the tavern, or of his suspicions, until he had more proof.

Tawno set to work, placing the pieces of wood to make an A-frame for Synfye to pull along. With quick strokes of his knife, he shaped three branches to fit over the shafts. He had found a few nails and a hammer, which, though some of the handle had burnt away, was still useable.

"I'll fix that piece of tilt over the frame so you can pull it; it should carry all you'll need. The tikni can go on top if you get tired of carrying her." As he spoke, he bound the donkey's leather bridle around the wood. It took only a moment to hammer the nails in place, after which he shaved the end of the frame with his knife to make a rough handle.

51

Tawno checked again to see if there was anything else he could salvage. He grunted when he found the blade of a knife and the remains of a wooden spoon. With a flick of his wrist, he flung the spoon into the still smouldering embers.

"I can make this knife usable," he said, holding it out towards Synfye. "A piece of beech wood should do the trick."

She gave a watery smile and nodded, too upset to speak. All Synfye could think of was that her beautiful home and all her personal possessions were gone, forever.

Tawno set off towards the trees to find the beech wood he needed to mend his knife, but he stopped when his belly growled, and called to Synfye: "You got anything to eat?"

Synfye hurried to fetch her basket from where she had dropped it and took out the cake loaf which the gorjified woman had given her. Breaking it, she took a large piece to Tawno. As she did so, she remembered what the woman at the cottage had said.

"A house on wheels can come to grief the same as a house set down."

It was as though she knew, she thought.

A movement caught Synfye's eye. Ben, the runaway urchin, was crouched under the hedge. She looked to see if the other boy was with him, but he was alone. With a sigh, she broke the remainder of the cake loaf and threw some towards the boy. It fell on the ground, but Ben, smiling gratefully, scurried on all fours to pick it up.

The light was fading and Synfye glanced nervously at the cloudy sky. No one would wish to be caught without shelter if it rained during the night, but now she had no other choice; sleeping under a hedgerow was far more desirable than a bed in a workhouse. If luck favoured her she might be able to spend the night in comfort, under a haystack or in a barn.

Tawno crouched down and ate his piece of bread whilst

he pondered who had done that awful thing to him and why. Hours had passed since he had visited the alehouse and had had his meal there interrupted by his fight with Brandy-Joe Lincoln. Tawno suddenly leapt to his feet. *He was meant to keep me there while his family came and found my vardo*, he thought. *They've met me here in the past, and knew that I'd probably have made my camp near these woods.*

As he had walked home along the lane, he had noticed a group of horsemen riding hard across the fields. Although they were too far away for Tawno to see them clearly, he thought that he had recognised one of the horses. It was the grai he had sold to the chief of the Lincoln tribe. His eyes narrowed with temper. *It's that Brandy-Joe and his family who are to blame for this destruction. This all came about because of a bloody skittish horse. If that's the way of things, they will soon find that I can be twice as evil*, he thought. *They'll find it don't do to cross Tawno Ardry.*

He knew that Brandy-Joe was sometimes employed in fairgrounds as a fire-eater, and often used by the Gypsies as a farrier. It should be easy enough to track him down. Tawno spat on the ground. *I'll get my revenge. Something someday will help me raise my hand against that mochadi Lincoln family*, he thought.

Chapter 5

Poor orphan Ben scurried back under the hedgerow to eat his bread cake. He chewed slowly, rolling the tasty bread around in his mouth to make it last longer. He had seen the chase through Peterborough Town, and the arrest of his companion. Ben knew that the boy had had stolen property in his possession, and he didn't expect to see him again. He shuddered; it could so easily have been him fleeing for freedom. Already he missed the company of his ragged companion - though he was pleased he no longer had to share the food.

He finished eating, searched for crumbs, and then remained crouched, elbows on knees and the fingers of both hands interlaced behind his head. Ben didn't look his six years. An absence of love, care and inadequate food had made him small for his age. His dirt-ingrained skin, his ragged clothing and his stillness allowed him to merge into his surroundings. He had learned how to keep quiet and perfectly still when he had been employed as an apprentice in a cotton mill. It had sometimes saved him from an unjust beating.

Only his hazel eyes moved as he watched Tawno sorting through the burnt items and constructing the carrying frame. It was a common sight: poor Gypsy women using a pulling frame to carry their small children and possessions.

Ben had a heavy purse in his pocket, taken from a woman in the town. When he had stolen it, his first impulse had been to keep the money and run away, but he had quickly dismissed the idea. If he attempted to spend any of the money, someone would be sure to demand how he had come by it and guess that he was a thief. No, best to give it to Tawno as usual, in exchange for the man's slight protection as they tramped the byways together.

"You! Come here!"

Ben's brief dream of a new life as an honest citizen was shattered by Tawno's shadow falling across him. Trembling, he looked into Tawno's narrowed eyes and scowling face. He rose to his feet and, cowering as though expecting a blow, moved closer to the hulking figure.

"Give." As he spoke, Tawno reached out, grabbed Ben's hair and shook him violently.

With a squeal, Ben hurriedly held out the purse and the two handkerchiefs.

"And the rest."

He was shaken again, and with a pitiful whimper Ben took the small enamelled silver snuffbox he'd hidden inside his shirt and held it out. Tawno snatched the snuffbox and half threw and half pushed the child away, leaving him sprawled on the ground.

"You stay with her and the brats! Don't you run off! If you do, I'll find you and kill you!"

The man loomed over the boy; Ben stared with fear-filled eyes at a shining knife, its sharp blade held ready to cut his throat. Tawno made another threatening gesture with the knife before striding towards Synfye and the children. Scrambling back to the safety of the hedgerow, Ben heard Tawno issue his commands.

"Make your way back to Nottingham. Me brother Culvato and his wife will still be camped over that way. I'll find you when I'm ready."

Synfye nodded. Not only was it was dangerous to ask her husband questions when he was so angry, it would be suicidal to argue with him at the moment. Tawno thrust the purse and the handkerchiefs into his coat pocket. After examining the snuffbox, he slipped it into a small pocket in his waistcoat. Synfye, keeping her head down and her back to him, fastened Mikaila and their few remaining possessions securely to the frame. The purses inside her petticoat knocked against her thighs and she was rigid with terror that he might discover them.

Giving Synfye a sly glance, Tawno picked up his hat. Placing it over his red bandanna at a jaunty angle, he took hold of the walking stick that he had fashioned from a stout ash branch and whistled the lurcher dogs, which obediently moved towards him with their tongues hanging out. Striding smartly along the lane, he set off in the direction of Stamford, accompanied by the dogs, without another word or look at the stricken woman and Ben.

Synfye's face was expressionless as she beckoned to Ben, who was still sheltering under the hedgerow.

"Get yourself on your feet, boy. We've a long way to travel," she called, harshly.

Synfye saw the boy glance in the direction that Tawno had taken. Indecision written on his face, he took a tentative step forward as though to follow his master, but Tawno was out of sight. Ben's shoulders slumped and he took a deep breath and gave a sigh before moving slowly towards her.

Synfye lifted the handle of the wooden frame and began to pull.

Two grooves in the dusty ground marked their progress. Seth, trotting along beside his mother, kept a thumb in his mouth and clutched his mother's skirt. The day had been long and the unusual situation had bewildered the child. Ben, also bemused by the recent events, followed a few paces behind, carrying the kettle.

Because Seth was tired, their progress was slow. Doors were closed sharply when Synfye and the children approached any of the cottages along their route. Only one compassionate woman threw some stale bread on the doorstep, but even she pointed silently down the lane before slamming the door closed.

When they arrived at an inn, Synfye left the children sitting under a tree, with strict instructions not to move while she went inside. She soon discovered however, that the only occupant was the landlord, so she had no opportunity to read palms or beg. Disappointed that she was not able to earn a penny or two but thankful she had kept the purses a secret from Tawno, she purchased a gill of whisky.

As darkness fell, Synfye led the children into a coppice. They found a fallen tree which lay near the path in such a way that the branches and dried leaves formed a little nest. Synfye busied herself making Mikailia and Seth comfortable, and it was not until she started to make a fire that she realised Ben was missing.

"Drat the didikai! He's run off already," she muttered.

Synfye dropped a handful of broken twigs on top of some burning moss and knelt down. She blew on the twigs to encourage them to catch fire until, hearing a leaf rustle, she lifted her head to find Ben watching her.

"Thought you could use a shushi," Ben said, holding out a dead rabbit. Uncertain of her reaction he stood half turned, as if to flee.

Taking the rabbit, Synfye nodded.

"Roasting will be the best way to deal with this beauty," she said, feeling the animal's plump flesh. "Washed down with some whisky in hot water, it will make us a fine supper."

"I'll skin it, Rauni. I've a sharp knife."

Tying its back legs together with the stem of a creeping vine and suspending the rabbit on a low branch of a tree, Ben skinned and prepared the meat for cooking. He cleaned his knife by plunging it into the soil as Synfye impaled the rabbit on an iron contraption, ready to roast over the smoke and flames of the fire.

"I found a stream through there. Shall I fetch some water now, Rauni?" Ben asked. He was apprehensive and stood well away from the busy woman. It was the first time he had been part of a real family, and he wasn't sure if he would be accepted.

With a smile, Synfye gestured towards the kettle. As Ben bent to pick it up, she noticed a sling tucked inside the waistband of his trousers.

The urchins who followed the Gypsy wagons were quick to learn how to make and become skilled in the use of slings. And woe betide any Gypsy tormentor who left the camp and walked in the woods alone to pee; the urchins would take a silent and a painful revenge.

For the first time, Synfye examined Ben. His skin was almost as dark as her complexion, but his unkempt hair was many shades lighter and his eyes were hazel.

The rabbit eaten and her children asleep, Synfye asked Ben where he was from.

Ben said, in a voice like wind sighing through leaves. "I can remember living in a big house and then I think we went to live in a prison. The door was locked and we slept together on straw. From the day I was taken to the poorhouse, I never saw my papa or my mamma again. They told me they were both dead." Ben tried to stifle a sob, but in the light of the fire,

Gilded Wagons

Synfye saw a tear rolling down the boy's face, leaving a track in the dirt. With an angry gesture, he brushed it away. "When I was five, four others and me left the workhouse and went to work in the Basford Cotton Mill near Nottingham. The men who took us there said we'd have roast beef and currant tarts every day, and ride in coaches driven by the mill bosses. It was all lies. They said that to stop us running off."

Synfye made no comment. They both sat enjoying the warmth of the fire and listening to the sounds of animals and birds moving in the shadows.

"The smell was first thing I noticed. The food was awful. For supper we had thin porridge and rye bread, hard as stone on the outside and sticky glue on the inside." Ben shuddered. "Never saw the sky for a long time. Worked for nothing, and I never dared to ask if I could go and have a pee. I stayed till spring came. After that I ran away. I was lucky I found you and Mr Tawno." Ben paused, hugging his knees and sniffing back tears. "I think the worst thing at the mill was the whips and leather straps whistling over us all day. Everyone got hurt. If you were cut on your head, you were taken to see the doctor and to have hot tar poured over your head. After a few days, the doctor would put his fingers under the tar cap and off it would come, all in one go. Took most of the hair off with it." Putting both hands on his lank curls, Ben scowled. "Not me, though. I ran away. Cut healed all by itself. I wasn't having that happen to me."

The blood drained from her face as Synfye listened to the boy. She shivered and pulled her shawl closer around her shoulders, then held it under her chin. It was only one of the gruesome tales she had heard about the cruel treatment of apprentices. If children died at the hands of their sadistic taskmasters, there were plenty more waiting to take their place.

Ben had never talked to a sympathetic adult before.

Overcome, he lay face down on the grass, and slept.

***

On reaching the outskirts of Melton Mowbray, Synfye and the children fell in with two other families of Gypsies who were journeying to Nottingham. Because Tawno had not yet joined her, Synfye felt that they would be more secure in the company of other people. In each parish she passed through, there was the danger that she could be labelled a vagrant, have the children taken from her and put in a workhouse. Ben would then be made to work for another master.

On a fine, sunny morning, the boys joined the other Gypsy children who were enjoying splashing in the river. Ben hid his surprise when he found that Seth couldn't swim, and encouraged the child to venture into deeper water. After a great deal of coughing and sputtering by them both, Seth had learned to swim a few strokes, and Ben could swim across the river and back. Both boys were bright and happy as they walked with Synfye into the town. Ben certainly looked cleaner, and it gave him an air of confidence.

Synfye had only the little to sell which was still in her basket, and once in the town her plan was to part company with the other Gypsy women, and beg or, if the opportunity arose, pick a pocket or steal food from a stallholder. She would have to be in dire straits to spend the money in the purses. After giving the matter a great deal of thought, her intention was to save as much as she could, find Tawno, and have a new living wagon built.

Nothing prepared Synfye for the shock to come. She saw Tawno, with his wrists chained together. A crowd of yelling townsfolk, keeping pace with a horse-drawn cart carrying the cursing man, ran alongside whilst pelting the Gypsy with rubbish taken from the gutters. The crowd shouted their appreciation each time the filth found its target.

"Tawno! Tawno! It's me, my Rom. What's happened?" Synfye called, in the Romani tongue. At first she didn't think he'd heard through the noise of the mob. But her heart gave a leap when Tawno's eyes swept over the faces of the crowd and he saw Synfye waving and calling his name. She saw him smile ruefully as she lifted Mikailia up for him to see.

"Go to Eastwood! It's on the other side of Nottingham! Find my brother, Culvato! He'll take care of you!" Tawno yelled.

Half blinded with tears, Synfye watched the cart rumble down the street and turn a corner. Clutching the arm of a passing woman, she sobbed out: "What has happened here? Do you know why that man was taken? What will they do to him?"

"'Dirty Gypsy! Whip them all, I say. Get rid of all vagrants and vagabonds and leave the streets clean for decent people." The woman, eying Synfye up and down, spat and hurried on. The spectacle of a man being whipped was too good to miss.

Synfye's eyes were wide with horror. How could her proud Rom be so humiliated?

Drawing Synfye to one side, Ben tried to shield both her and Seth from the passing crowd. In that mood the townsfolk were quite capable of turning on any other Gypsy person they saw and doing them harm.

"You go back to the camp, Rauni. I'll see if I can do anything to help your rom," he said.

Ben's face was as white as Synfye's. Parish officials would certainly arrest him if they caught him helping the Gypsy man, but he had to try.

Chained to the back of the cart, Tawno was prepared for whipping. With his shirt hanging in tatters around his waist, he yelled defiance at the mob. Blood flowed from a blow across his mouth. A threat from one of the constables silenced him. He spotted Ben pushing and squirming his way to the front of the crowd. Fixing his gaze on the boy, he clenched his teeth. The whip was raised and the crowd roared approval.

Tears filled Ben's eyes. Surrounded by the shifting crowd, he thought himself unnoticed. He flinched when a hand gripped his shoulder.

"Friend of yours, young un?" The man loomed over Ben, a sly smile breaking through dirty stubble. It was Brandy-Joe Lincolin. There was a smear of blood on the handle of the knife in the man's belt, which was level with Ben's eyes.

"No. Never met him," Ben answered. Keeping his head lowered, he looked anxiously for an escape. This man was a sharp, if ever Ben saw one.

"We could use a friend of Tawno Ardry. Has a good name among us in the town." The man's fingers dug deep into Ben's bony shoulder. "We want to know all about Tawno. Why he's here and where he's going. My friend here could maybe use you in our gang, young shaver. Pay you well and feed you regular."

"No, mister! I must go. See my master. He will beat me if I'm missing for long."

The fingers loosened. In a flash, Ben twisted and pulled away. The next instant he was off in the crowds. Sobbing, crying, running, alone, snotty-nosed and full of fear, Ben didn't know it, but he needed Synfye.

Luck led Ben along the right streets and lanes to the Gypsy encampment. Synfye was there, sitting under a tree with Seth by her side and the baby asleep at her feet. She held out her arms towards Ben when he stumbled into the camp.

"Did anyone help him, Ben?"

The boy's body shuddered as he sobbed and shook his head.

"You did your best, boy," Synfye said.

Chapter 6

Jonas felt no pangs of remorse as he listened to Nurse Grant's footsteps, but when Charlotte screamed as she struggled to give birth, he glanced at the ceiling. It suddenly occurred to him that he had missed his appointment with Culvato. *I wonder if the Gypsy had the sense to come here when I didn't meet him at the market place,* he thought. Jonas peered through the window, but the view was of the street. Carrying an oil lamp, he hurried through the ground floor rooms. Standing on the scullery doorstep, he looked into the garden.

The Gypsy saw the light shining through the kitchen window and then heard Jonas open the door. He walked cautiously across the yard.

"Is that you, Gypsy?" Jonas called.

Culvato moved into the light so that Jonas could see him.

"Where is your woman?" Jonas wasted no time in polite greetings.

Pulling off his hat and screwing it up in both hands, Culvato bowed humbly to Jonas.

"She is camped just outside the town, master. I'll fetch her if your lady needs help with the birthing." Ursula had the knowledge of how to bring a baby safely into the world and she always kept a variety of herbal medicines ready for use. "It'll only take me half an hour to fetch my woman."

"No. Wait here. I don't want anyone to see you. I'll bring the child out to you."

Jonas slammed the door and Culvato returned to the shed. He resigned himself to a further wait and continued whittling pieces of willow to make clothes pegs.

The scullery door banged hard against the wall as it was flung open, and the light from the oil lamp glistened on the wet leaves in the garden. Jonas Bigsby stood in the doorway, peering across the yard, holding the drawer in his arms.

As soon as he heard the door latch rattle, Culvato leapt to his feet and hurried forward, putting a finger to his hat. As Jonas moved towards him, Culvato's expression changed from eager expectancy to narrow-eyed caution; he could hear the mewing cry of more than one baby. He stepped back when Jonas attempted to thrust the drawer into his arms.

"Here, fellow. The purse I promised is on the blanket. Take the box from me." Jonas' haughty tone almost, but not quite, hid his anxiety.

Instead of taking hold of the drawer, Culvato gently drew back the top blanket.

"What's this, mister? You said a babe. You've brought three!"

Jonas gave a half laugh, but Culvato stared him out and he flushed with embarrassment.

"I know. Silly bitch had three bastards. No one can say how many will be born until they arrive, can they? They're all healthy. Not a mark on them. It's a damn shame we can't keep them, but my sister is to be married. Her betrothed doesn't want a ready-made family of girls."

What appeared to be the Gypsy's reluctance to take the drawer was in fact his pondering that the girls, once grown, might become a valuable asset - assuming his half formed plans for a fair developed into reality.

"If you want me to take all three babies, I'll need three times as much as we'd agreed on. That's only fair. And my woman will have three times as much trouble to raise them. " Culvato's mouth was set hard and his dark eyes glittered in the light that shone from the house. He saw no reason why Jonas shouldn't pay him more to take the other two babies. He could also foresee all kinds of difficulties when he arrived home and showed the babies to Ursula.

"I don't keep much cash in the house, only enough to pay the bills. But I'll get you more. Wait here, fellow."

Culvato grabbed hold of the drawer as Jonas pushed it at him again. One room after another lit up as Jonas went in search of valuables. With a rueful sigh, Culvato pulled back the oiled tilt covering the barrow, and, with care, put the drawer and the babies inside. When Jonas returned, he had replaced the tilt and was tying it in place.

The young man held another leather purse, and also carried the lantern clock by its handle.

"This is all the money I have in the house," he said, giving the purse to Culvato. "I've also brought you this. It's very valuable and should make you a considerable amount if you sell it." Jonas held the clock out towards the Gypsy who looked at him without speaking.

"You'd better have this as well." Jonas gave a sardonic laugh. "I've had it for years. It was my father's. It's supposed to be my lucky ring. Done nothing to help me make a fortune, but it might just work for you."

Culvato wedged the clock in the corner of the barrow next to the drawer. The extra money jingled as the purse joined the other one in his pocket. He examined the ring, and was dubious about its value until the facets on the stone caught the lamplight. *Ursula would like to have that,* he thought. Without speaking, he slipped it onto his finger. It took only a moment to push the barrow through the garden gate. Jonas stood with his arms folded and his face expressionless, watching without a hint of emotion.

"I never want to see you or those three bastards again. If you ever return and try to speak to me or any member of my family, not only will I deny ever knowing you, but I'll also have you horse-whipped, then hanged."

The contemptuous glance the Gypsy threw at Jonas made the young man take a step back.

"You won't hear from me, mister; but one day, not so far distant, you'll wish you were as rich as I am."

Jonas shuddered at hearing Culvato's prophesy. Hurrying back into the house, he slammed the scullery door and shot home the bolts as though to keep out evil.

Culvato took much longer to reach Mapperley Common than he had expected. Trying to give the babies a comfortable ride, he did his best to avoid the deepest ruts in the road. His clumsy efforts to lull the babies to sleep by rocking the barrow were in vain. He looked constantly over his shoulder, if anyone heard them crying, they would assume he had stolen them. Without a good explanation of how or why he had possession of the babies (and he knew Jonas would not corroborate his story) it would mean prison and then he would be swiftly hanging from the gallows.

***

All three babies were yelling when Culvato approached the bender tent. Ursula had been keeping a watch out for him, and, hearing him calling her name, she threw her shawl over her shoulders and hurried outside. She held a lamp high to guide

Culvato across the common. When he had not returned home by the late afternoon, she had guessed the baby had arrived. As the hours passed, the excitement had built up inside her. As Culvato brought the barrow to a halt, she hung the lamp on the side of it and held out her hands.

"Have you got it? What is it? Is it a boy or girl?" She took the baby from Culvato with a tender smile curving her lips.

"The poor mite is hungry," she said, covering the baby with her shawl.

Her smile widened when Culvato held out another blanket-wrapped baby.

"Twins. She bore twins," she said.

With great care, Culvato placed the second baby in her arms.

Ursula tenderly kissed each baby in her arms. She was delighted to have them both, but then she realised what a great responsibly an extra baby would be.

"No. She didn't have twins."

Her mouth dropped open. She squealed when she saw Culvato lift another baby from the barrow. Pulling the blanket aside, Culvato held baby number three so that Ursula could see her. That infant was slightly larger than her sisters, and she waved her fists angrily as she cried.

"Culvato. I can't look after three! I can feed one now that Lionel is ready to take soft food. With some help I could perhaps manage two, but…" Each tiny red face was screwed up, and demanding attention. Ursula shook her head. "They are so small. It will be very difficult to raise all three." She hid a smile at the sight of her husband awkwardly holding the third baby at arms length. "We'd best get them inside before they die of cold," she said.

With a worried frown, Culvato followed her inside the tent. Tucking the blanket around the tiny body, he placed her on the pegged rug near Ursula's feet.

"They're all girls, triplet girls," she said, unlacing her bodice. "You always said that you wanted a big family. I hope five children are enough for you."

When Culvato saw Ursula was preparing to feed the babies, he hastily backed out of the tent.

"I'll fetch you the mokto they were put in," he said.

With a sigh, Ursula tried to feed two of the babies. After a few false starts they fastened their tiny mouths on Ursula's nipples and began to suckle.

"This is what he gave me to carry them in." Culvato's voice was cold with disapproval as he placed the drawer on the floor. The drawer tipped, the blanket inside moved and he saw the amethyst and gold necklace which had been placed there by Mrs Bigsby. He let it swing from his fingers so that Ursula could see it.

"That's nice," she said, and turned her attention back to the baby she was nursing.

"I shall never understand the ways of Gaujo people. Romani folk wouldn't even make a dog kennel out of a worm-eaten mokto like this. Do you like this?" Culvato said, holding the lantern clock near the lamp so that Ursula could see it.

"Is that all he gave you?" Her voice was sharp.

"Money. Not as much as he should, but I don't think he had any more. Before it was dark I looked through the windows. They didn't notice me. They'd nothing much in the way of furniture. I saw no sign of servants working in the kitchen and no dogs were in the yard to eat scraps." Culvato began examining the clock. He breathed on it and rubbed it with a finger. "This is old and I think it might be valuable. We might try and sell it. If not we'll give it to one of the girls when they're grown," he said.

Ursula moved. The babies immediately began crying.

"These two know what to do now. I don't know about that

one, though. She is smaller than these two. Take these, Culvato, and put them in the box. Pass the other one to me and I'll try her again. If she won't feed we'll lose her," Ursula said. "When I've finished with this one, I'll try to give them all some milk and water."

The babies looked tiny in Culvato's big hands. With great concentration, he placed the baby girls, one by one, on the blanket inside the drawer, and handed the third triplet to his wife. He let out his breath in a long 'phew', and wiped his face with the back of his hand. Gypsy men never handled infants; that kind of thing was left to the women.

"I wish your dai was still with us. She would have helped you with them," he said.

Ursula bit her lip. She still grieved for her mother and she knew Culvato missed both his parents, although he rarely mentioned them.

When the smallest baby began rhythmic sucking, Ursula smiled triumphantly.

"What do you think about this?" said Culvato.

"Where did you get it?"

"Bigsby gave it to me. Said it was his lucky ring. By the looks of him, I think he needs more than a ring to change his fortune."

Ursula held out her hand so that he could try the ring on her finger. She frowned when it slipped off.

"It's a man's ring. Much too heavy for me," she said.

"I'll put it with the clock. Maybe we'll sell them together, but we'll keep the necklace for when the girls are older," he said.

When the babies were fed and all the children were asleep, Ursula and Culvato agreed that the triplets would be reared as though they were their own children, but, so there would be no risk of prevarication, they would be kept out of sight until the family had left Nottingham.

The following day was stormy. Culvato and Ursula decided, for the sake of the babies, to stay on the Mapperley Common a few more days before setting off for Eastwood. While Ursula stayed inside the tent and took care of the babies, Culvato helped as much as he could with his sons. On the instruction of Ursula, he took Hugo with him to fetch fresh cow's milk from a nearby farm, and hoped other Gypsies would not see him doing women's work.

Culvato explained to Hugo that he was a big boy now and that he must take care of his brother and little sisters. It would help the child take pride in being the older brother.

The sun peeped through the clouds on the day the long walk to Eastwood began. Culvato packed the barrow with their belongings and the drawer was wedged securely on the top. The triplets and Lionel were placed in a nest of straw and tucked into crocheted blankets.

It took a few days before the family arrived at Hill Top, a small hamlet on the Turnpike Road. Having secured the barrow by pushing a stone against the wheels, the couple rested on a patch of grass near a hedge. They didn't notice Hugo climb through a gate which led to a meadow. Seeing a donkey foal lying on the grass, the child ran to place his arms around its neck.

Ursula suddenly missed him. She shouted Hugo's name when she spotted him and saw the danger his was in. A female donkey was heading in a very purposeful manner towards the child.

Alerted by Ursula's cry of alarm, Culvato leapt to his feet.

"Lord preserve us!" With a bound he vaulted over the gate and raced across the field. He scooped Hugo into his arms as the jenny thundered towards them. With nostrils flared and teeth showing, the donkey chased Culvato and Hugo. They just managed to scramble over the gate. Annoyed, the animal vented her anger by braying long and loud.

Culvato let Hugo slip to the ground and bent over to catch his breath. Ursula enveloped Hugo in her arms. She was pale and shaking with fright.

"Why ever did you go inside the field, you imp? I've told you before about wandering out of my sight. You might have been killed if that dai donkey had caught you," Ursula said.

"I thought it was Kaka Tawno's moila," Hugo sobbed.

Culvato drew the child to him and held him tight.

"Not all donkeys are gentle like Uncle Tawno's Betty, my son," he said.

"Hey, you there! Gypsies! What are you doing to my donkeys?" The call came from a man who was waving a twisted hazel walking stick.

Culvato pushed Hugo towards Ursula before turning to face the man.

"We were looking at them. Fine beasts," he said, with a knowing nod.

"They go to market tomorrow," the man said. He leaned on his walking stick and stared distrustfully at Culvato.

Putting his arm on the top of the gate and studying the donkeys, Culvato rubbed his nose with a finger.

"The jenny seems a strong animal."

He felt the gate move as the man rested his weight against it.

"She's one of my best."

"What we're looking for is a strong mule or a well-boned horse, already broken in for ride or drive."

The man glanced behind him and saw Ursula and Hugo standing next to the barrow. He gave a grunt and nod in their direction.

"You don't need much of a beast to pull that," he said.

"Mr Watson over at Eastwood is going to build us a caravan, but if you don't want to trade..." Culvato, pulling the brim of his hat down to his eyebrows, moved slowly towards Ursula.

"No. No, I meant no offence, just my little joke. I'm known for my humour around here."

Culvato glanced first at the hand placed on his sleeve, then into the man's eyes.

"No offence taken. I'll come to see you when we're nearer to wanting an animal."

"I'll look out for you at Eastwood," the man called as the family moved away.

The couple saw the Eastwood Mill in the distance. After a half an hour's walk, they could hear the mill's huge sails turning in the wind.

Unexpectedly, a horse, frightened by the turning sails, bolted past them pulling an empty wagon. It missed the family by inches, and its owner panted along behind, quite unable to catch it.

Culvato walked along the streets of Eastwood with a confident stride. There was a good campsite on the far side of the village with a natural spring; in the summertime his clan occasionally used it, but at that time of year most Gipsies preferred to camp closer to a large town.

Hearing music, Culvato joined a small crowd gathered on the road outside the Parish Church of St Mary's. He exchanged delighted glances with Ursula on seeing an old man in the centre of the crowd. Piramus Ardry, playing a catchy tune on a homemade whistle, danced a jig as he entertained the onlookers with his music. To one side, but never out of his sight, stood a wooden peepshow with leather straps. The Gypsy wore a long coat which once had been black but was now green with age. His gaudy red and orange neckerchief peeped out from beneath his grizzled beard. Half a dozen pheasant feathers were stuck into the band of his top hat, which he wore at a jaunty angle. They bobbed up and down as he moved.

"It's Kaka Piramus. Kaka Piramus!" As Culvato called out his uncle's name, the thought occurred to him that the old man looked very like his dear, departed father.

Finding a shady place under a tree, the family made themselves comfortable within calling distance of the old man. With her shawl covering the infant, Ursula fed one of the whimpering babies, and watched as Hugo inched his way to the front of the crowd. Culvato gave a worried frown when he noticed Ursula slumping wearily back against the wheel of the barrow, closing her eyes. Slipping his arm around her, he gave her a hug.

"We'll reach our campsite soon, and then you can rest for a few days," he said.

"Well met, Culvato. The drom has curved and grown long since our last meeting." With his black eyes twinkling and a thousand lines creasing his face, the old man leaned on his staff and held his hand out to his favourite nephew.

Culvato jumped to his feet and took the old man's hand in a warm clasp before giving the old man a hug. The last time they had met was at the funeral of Culvato's parents.

"May an old didikai join your campfire this night, Culvato?" Uncle Piramus nodded and smiled at Culvato.

"Oh yes. You most of all are welcome, Kaka. We are on our way to see Samuel Watson, the wainwright who lives at New Eastwood. I'm going to ask him to build us a vardo."

"A home on wheels, a vardo of your own?" Uncle Piramus lifted his eyebrows in surprise and then smiled sweetly at Ursula.

Uncle Piramus swept his hat from his head and used it to give an elaborate flourish as he bowed low.

"I see you have another tikni. How many is that now, merry rauni?"

"Five, Uncle Piramus." Ursula giggled when the old man's hand tightened on his staff and he pretended to stagger.

"I hope your man plans to build a large vardo to house such a growing family." Laughing so hard his gold earring swung and glinted in the sunlight; uncle Piramus winked at Ursula and gave Culvato a nudge with his elbow.

"I've a lot of ideas whirling around in my head. I'm hoping the wainwright can build the kind of vardo I am wanting. If he says he can, we'll make our camp on the old site in the beech wood until it's finished."

Culvato's parents had reared their family in a bow-top caravan built by Samuel Watson. In keeping with Gypsy tradition, the beautiful vehicle, containing all of their possessions, was burnt after their funeral.

The wainwright's premises, only a short walk down to the bottom of the hill, were close to the old badger woods at New Eastwood.

It took only a few minutes for the old man to pack away his peepshow. Carrying it like a knapsack on his back, uncle Piramus used his staff to steady his steps. They travelled slowly down the hill, exchanging gossip and news of family and friends. Hugo was excited at meeting his great-uncle. He questioned the old man about badgers and danced from one adult to the other, asking when he could be taken to see the nocturnal animals, until his father quietened him with a frowning look. Then, the child walked quietly, holding his mother's hand.

Chapter 7

At first glance, you would think the lane in New Eastwood ended at the entrance to Mr Watson's timber yard. The ruts in the road curved to the right and halted in a wide yard in front of a wooden workshop. It was moss green and silver grey from years of exposure to the weather. A pair of high doors were held open by logs, and the sound of hammering from somewhere at the back of the building reverberated, suggesting someone was hard at work.

Culvato spotted a seat in the sunshine beside a stack of planked timber where Ursula could be sheltered from the wind. She crossed the yard and sat down and Culvato pushed the barrow into a patch of shade near her so that she could easily hear if the babies needed attention.

"Have a rest, Romni. We'll be a while telling the man what kind of vardo we want built," he said.

Culvato felt a pang of guilt when she gave a nod, and then closed her eyes.

Undoing the straps and shrugging the wooden peep-show from his shoulders, Piramus leaned it against the timber and put a hand on Hugo's head.

"Don't you go near that deep sawing pit over there, chavvi.

If you falls into it you'll be buried in sawdust and you won't be able to climb out," the old man warned.

"Stay near your mother," Culvato said, sharply.

He was, like most Gypsy fathers, kind and loving; but he expected to be obeyed without argument by his children.

Mr Watson's young grandson had been playing with a whip and top. Upon seeing the Gypsies enter the yard, he ran into the workshop to tell his grandpapa of their arrival. The din ceased. The elderly wainwright put down his hammer and looked across the well-swept workshop. He saw Culvato and Piramus coming towards him and immediately he recognised the elder Gypsy. Moving forward, Mr Watson held out his hand.

"It's some years since you came to see me, Mr Ardry."

"I was last here with my brother," Piramus said, shaking hands with Mr Watson.

"Eh! I remember. Nice little wagon we made for him. A bow-top, if I remember rightly."

"This is his son. He has need of a vardo and he has other plans he wants to talk over with you."

With a nod of greeting to Culvato, the wainwright led the way to the back of his workshop with its pleasant scent of newly sawn wood.

Both Gypsies looked around with interest at the assortment of tools placed in racks on the wall over the carpenter's benches. Different sized felloe patterns hung in rows on hooks from the ceiling. A foot-operated lathe, various tools, cradles, and wheels of assorted sizes were stacked in a tidy fashion around the workshop walls, which still left plenty of working space.

"What size and style vardo was you thinking of?" Mr Watson asked, picking up a lump of chalk and a large piece of slate. He listened carefully as Culvato described the living wagon he wanted built. The wainwright, asking questions, drew rough sketches on the slate.

"A bow-top like you made for my father. About twelve foot long and with a front and back porch made of pine?" Culvato relaxed when he saw Mr Watson nodding approval. "Slip half doors, canvas roof over wooden hoops, and a pan box under the floor," he added.

When he saw how his ideas were taking shape in the sketch on the slate, Culvato glanced at Piramus, who grinned. Culvato pointed to the sketch.

"Oh, I nearly forgot. We want a stove, and windows in the door."

Mr Watson paused and glanced outside, noticing that Ursula was speaking to his grandson and Hugo, and making the children laugh. Pushing his dusty hat to the back of his head, Mr Watson turned his attention back to Culvato.

"It'll be heavy. It will weigh a ton or more. You'll need a strong horse, maybe two to pull it in comfort. Best have a spreader fitted. Anything else?"

"Iron-rimmed wheels?"

"Hmm… Cost will be high. I suppose you'll want it painting and carving front and back?"

Culvato nodded. "Cash. Some when you make a start, the rest when it's finished," He said.

"Furniture?"

"Yes. I'll have to be guided by you about what we need. We've five small children, so..."

Mr Watson wiped the chalk from his fingers onto his sacking apron and smiled.

"I'd say the caravan sounds about the right size for comfort."

"Dadrus, I've made a new friend," Hugo called.

The two boys were standing in the doorway, shoulder-to-shoulder; already the best of pals.

"Ah, Richard. He's my youngest grandson," said Mr Watson. He was proud of the lad, who was already showing an interest in his grandfather's work.

"Richard, go tell your dad we have a new job to do and to leave what he's doing. Tell him to go over to Brook-hill Leas and bring John Bailey here. Your dad's working at the far end of the yard. Hurry up, lad." As the boy disappeared, Mr Watson turned to the Gypsies again. "Bailey is the best blacksmith in these 'ere parts. He'll make your springs and hoops for the wheels. Can turn his hand to making anything in metal."

Culvato had been eying a tree stump which lay beside a sturdy wheelbarrow and, moving nearer, he tapped the stump with his foot.

"I'll come back and look at that piece of wood later. I've a mind to do a bit of carving while the living wagon's being built."

Mr Watson took off his hat and wiped his forehead with a piece of rag.

"It's time I got rid of a few of those old tree stumps. If they're any use I'll give them to you, Mr Ardry."

Mr Watson led the way to the far end of the yard, and the men examined some partially covered stacks of planked timber.

"I've got nice seasoned pieces of ash and ten year elm here, and I've some beech I could use for furniture. Maybe you'd rather have pine. That would look nice stained and not be so heavy." Mr Watson grunted as he pulled out a thick plank from the stack. "We must watch the weight for the sake of the horses," he said.

The next hour or so passed quickly as the three men discussed the merits of various pieces of timber pulled from the stack. They broke off from what they were doing when Mr Bailey arrived. The blacksmith was a burly man with a dark curly beard. In his haste to get to the wood yard, he had forgotten to remove his leather apron. Mr Watson showed him the sketch he had drawn, and explained what metalwork would be required for the caravan.

"It looks a straightforward job. I can do that easy enough. When are you making a start?" Mr Bailey asked.

Everyone looked at Mr Watson. He pushed back his hat again, stared at the sky and scratched his head with his thumb.

"Got that sedan chair to finish for Lady Emma; she's in London Town, and not likely to be back for a month or two. The wagon over there, that's finished and only needs taking to the farm. I've a coffin almost ready if one's needed, but no one has complained of sickness for a while. I reckon we can start work tomorrow on your job, Mr Ardry. But I'll need to have my best two handle saw reset before I start. That will cost a bit."

"Dear things to set." John Bailey grinned.

"Would this be enough?" With a twinkle in his eye, Culvato held out a gold sovereign.

"I'll finish the sedan chair later. I've plenty of timber to start on your job," Mr Watson put the coin straight into his waistcoat pocket. Because the Ardry family had been honest when he had dealt with them before, he didn't bother to check if any of the gold had been shaved off.

The men watched as Hugo attempted to copy Richard. The boy had been turning cartwheels and now stood on his head, next to a pile of wheel spokes in the shade of the barn.

"A pair of acrobats, those two," Piramus laughed.

When Hugo managed to balance on his head successfully, everyone clapped and called 'bravo'. Culvato looked thoughtful. Watching Hugo, his earlier half-formed idea began to take shape. *If the triplets and the two boys can be trained to be acrobats, we could have more than just a children's ride. I'll speak to Ursula about it later*, he thought. He turned back to the workmen, and asked,

"I heard there's a glass works close by, somewhere near a coal pit?"

Mr Bailey took a clay pipe out of his pocket and used it as a pointer, as he said,

"You're right, Mr Ardry. Mr Nicholson and Mr Pauncefote own the glasshouse. It's not far, over at Awsworth. They turn out some right fancy patterns. They'll make your windows in any shape you ask for."

Mr Watson began to draw on his slate again and gave Culvato a rough idea of the expected size of the caravan windows.

***

To keep the boys out of mischief while the men were talking, Ursula had put them to work, collecting bags of sawdust and wood shavings. Each baby wore a light cotton nappy, and to keep it clean and fresh, Ursula placed a bag of the sweet-scented sawdust underneath them. Refreshed after her rest, she was eager to find the new campsite. Hugo ran towards his mother and called goodbye to Mr Watson's grandson.

"Come along, Hugo," she said, taking his hand. "It looks as though Mr Watson will be building us our very own vardo to live in." Her eyes were shining, and although she tried to hide it, her excitement was clear from the tone of her voice. *I wonder what Tawno and Synfye will have to say when they know about it,* she thought.

***

The babies were fed and sleeping peacefully as Culvato pushed the barrow along the winding lane. Ursula smiled and placed a hand lightly on his arm. She lifted her eyes to the sky and spoke quietly.

"This moment is a piece of happiness I wish to remember

forever."

As they walked along the lane, she saw blackberries growing in profusion. *I'll be able to pick those and make cordial ready for the winter coughs and colds,* she thought. Wild dog-rose hips grew fat and golden, supported by other bushes, and she took notice of their location so that she could return and pick them. The sweet syrup would nourish the babies.

Piramus was a few paces behind the young couple, and Hugo skipped along beside the old man.

"Richard has a grandpapa."

"Yes, I know."

"Have I got a grandpapa?"

"No. He's mullered."

"Did you burn his vardo?"

"Yes."

The answer satisfied the child and he ran off to explore the hedgerows. When he tired of investigating the remnants of an old bird's nest, he rejoined the old man.

"Have you been here before, Kaka Piramus?" asked Hugo when they had walked on for a while.

With a sigh of relief at the change of question, the old man smiled.

"The last time I camped at Eastwood we saw lots and lots of badgers. Probably there's still a sett somewhere in the woods. They make their home in the same place for years. If I find they still live in the woods, I'll take you to see them. Would you like that?"

Hugo's eyes were round with hope. He had only seen a badger once; usually he was fast asleep when the shy nocturnal creatures cleaned out their home and hunted for food. He ran forward to tell his parents what Piramus had promised him.

"Hugo would like that, wouldn't you, chavvi?" Culvato said, smiling at Ursula.

"Will you show me the badgers tonight, Kaka Piramus, please? Now I'm a big boy I can stay up late," he pleaded.

The old man's eyes twinkled as he looked at the child. Hugo was so like Culvato at the same age. Already, the child knew many Gypsy skills, including making snares for catching hedgehogs and rabbits. Ursula approved of children being kept busy; that way they were less likely to get into mischief.

"When the moon is full and your mother says you can, I'll take you out with me."

The family halted at a high spot where the bushes were sparse. Aware of the beauty around him, Culvato pointed into the valley. The trees were still in full leaf and shone bronze and golden in the sunlight and in the distance, hills melted into the sky. The pleasant warmth of the early autumn sun was on his back.

"We'll make our camp in the field by the beech woods. Maybe we will stay until spring if the brook still runs clear and the water is sweet," he said.

They found a level piece of ground suitable to erect their tents on. Culvato placed the barrow under a tree and cast a critical eye over the place. The grass was springy underfoot and alder and willow trees grew nearby. Thorn bushes were growing just in the right place to protect the back of the bender tents from intruders, and the bushes were thick enough to make a windbreak. The brook, flanked by willow trees, ran along the bottom of the clearing before disappearing into the beech wood. Culvato saw minnows darting about in the clear water.

"Should be able to catch plenty of shushies around here, and I've seen signs of kannengros, so we won't starve," Ursula called to Culvato.

Piramus had disappeared. The old man seldom left his precious peepshow with anyone, but it was leaning against a tree.

"Stay here Romni, Hugo and I are going to cut branches for the tent,' Culvato said.

Pleased to be considered big enough to help his father, the little boy straightened his shoulders. "Now you are so busy with the small tiknies I shall need a great deal of help from my big chavvi." Without Hugo noticing, Culvato winked at Ursula before striding towards a clump of tall willow trees.

Left alone, Ursula laid a blanket on the ground. She cuddled and kissed each downy head before laying the babies side by side on the blanket. As she did so she examined each infant. Her sons had very dark skin tone compared to that of the triplets.

Ursula was unpacking the barrow when Hugo scampered across the clearing. He showed her his cap, which was filled with the beech and hazel nuts he had collected in the wood.

"They're lovely! We'll roast them in the fire and eat them for supper," she said.

Culvato joined them. He had cut a large amount of willow. The branches were long and pliable. Dropping them in a heap near the barrow, he examined the ground near the thorn bushes. It was flat, and the tent would be in a high enough position to be safe from the brook if it flooded later in the year. Culvato bent the willow branches around his knee until they were bowed, then he pushed them into the ground in such a way they formed a much higher and longer curved structure than usual. Hugo helped his father by picking up as many large stones as he could find, ready to be placed around the base of the bender tent.

"It will take Mr Watson a good many months to build the vardo. We'll probably be living here through the winter, and with all the tiknies and two men, I thought you would need extra room. I'll build another tent, next to this, for Uncle

Piramus to sleep in. We can all use that one in the daytime," Culvato said.

Ursula squeezed his arm and nuzzled close. Because of her husband's thoughtfulness, she intended to make the evening meal a little special by cooking honey balls, Culvato's favourite.

The bender tent would be semi-permanent quarters. Ursula already had some bright coloured cushions. It would not take her very long to make pegged rugs, which would make the tent into a comfortable home. In fact, it would be more comfortable than many of the low, earth-roof cottages in the district.

Culvato was ready to throw the oiled tilt over the framework of his new tent, but he left what he was doing when Piramus returned.

"I've brought some milk for the tiknies and flour from the Eastwood Mill. Will you make us some of your tasty bread tomorrow, Ursula?" Holding up a small can of milk, Uncle Piramus laughed as Hugo skipped around him, trying to reach it.

Winking at Hugo and then at Ursula, Piramus dropped the sack of flour at her feet and gave her the milk can.

The two men pulled and lifted another canvas tilt over the structure of the second tent. When it was in place, they tied it to the willow branches, then put heavy stones around the base.

"The girl looks tired," said Piramus in a low voice.

Culvato shot a swift glance at his wife. Ursula was preparing to feed the babies again and he saw how her head drooped with weariness.

"We should never have had all three tiknies, she had enough to do with our two boys," he said.

"If I can spend the winter here, I'll help you both. Always liked your woman, she's quiet."

Culvato gave a broad grin.

"You ain't heard her when I return home late and merry

from the ale house," he chuckled.

While the young couple made the inside of their bender tent comfortable, Piramus cut a large square of turf and put it on some dampened soil under the hedge. The piece of turf would be replaced on the scorched earth when they moved on. It didn't take him long to gather a bundle of sticks from the edge of the wood. Gypsies were taught at an early age that the best way to raise the temperature of a fire was to lay the sticks in the formation of the spokes of a wheel. It allowed a draught to run along to the centre, and the heat was drawn upwards. Piramus fetched a couple of long bent iron rods from the barrow. He found a large stone and hammered the rods into the ground, and Ursula, smiling her thanks, hung the iron cauldron over the fire.

Earlier, Piramus had caught a couple of rabbits in a snare. Taking them from his poacher's pocket, he tied their back legs together and, suspending them on a branch of a tree, he carefully peeled the skin from them. When cured, the fur would be perfect for use as winter clothing for the babies. By the time Ursula had fetched water from the brook, the meat was ready to put in the cauldron with fresh herbs. She then added vegetables tied in pieces of muslin. The smell of rabbit stew; bread, and honey balls cooked in a traditional Gypsy fashion pleased Culvato and he gave Ursula an appreciative glance.

As they waited for their meal to cook, Ursula nursed one of the babies. She listened to Culvato telling Piramus about seeing the knitting frames rolling down the hill in Nottingham. He embellished the story by putting a feather into his hat and miming the antics of the Lord Mayor. By the time the couple had finished the tale, Piramus was begging them to stop, he was laughing too much.

Chapter 8

Autumn leaves fluttered from the trees and red berries clung to the bare hedges, and still the caravan stood on a low wooden bogey in the Wainwright's wood yard. The wheels, already made and painted, would be the last items to be fitted to the vehicle. Culvato had worked alongside the wainwright and blacksmith to build his dream home and at last the caravan was looking as he had envisaged. Ursula passed what spare time she had by sewing curtains made from an old velvet gown (a gift from a housewife) and she cut the remainder of the fabric to make matching patchwork cushions for their new home.

Mr Watson's workshop smelled acrid. The men covered their faces with a scarf as they stirred pots of yellow ochre and white lead paint. Working quickly so as to obtain a smooth finish, the men first painted the bare wood of the caravan with the white lead, then with the yellow ochre. When each coat was hardened, Culvato rubbed the surface with a pumice stone and water until the woodwork was silky to the touch, without brush marks. The majority of the woodwork was finished in a rich dark green paint, with a contrasting burgundy red on the eves and door. It needed the final hand painted decorations to make the vehicle unique.

Culvato had spent a long time examining the tree stumps Mr Watson had given to him. He found six he considered suitable to carve into a set of animals for his child-sized roundabout. Most of the stumps were chopped into a rough animal shape. He had spoken to Mr Watson, and they had chosen the timber to make the base.

Ursula's skin was gilded by the sun to a warm honey colour. She wore a long, dark blue skirt fitting tightly to her waist, and a wide yoke of white lace around her neck over a mulberry-coloured, long-sleeved blouse. Her braided hair gleamed as black as a raven's wing in the sunlight. Culvato balanced on a sturdy ladder, borrowed from Mr Watson while Ursula steadied it. Stretching out his arm to the limit, he painted gold scrolls on the framework of the caravan with confident strokes. He flashed a jubilant smile at his wife as he finished painting the last scroll.

"These few touches of gold set off the red and green paint handsomely," he said. "I've only to put a pattern around the door and then the painting will be finished."

A movement in the lane caught Culvato's attention. He drew in a sharp breath when he saw Synfye watching them from the entrance to the wood yard. Two boys stood beside her. Expecting to see Tawno driving his vardo, Culvato frowned and scanned the lane.

Synfye had grown thin in the past weeks. Her cheekbones were prominent beneath her weather-beaten, darker-than-copper skin.

Nodding towards the small group of travellers, Culvato said quietly: "We have company, Romni."

Leaping to the ground, with his hand on Ursula's shoulder he waited to greet his brother's wife. Hugo had also noticed the travellers. Leaving the pile of logs where he had been playing with Mr Watson's grandson, he joined his parents as

Synfye, Seth, and the urchin Ben came towards them. When she saw Synfye using the pulling frame, Ursula's eyes widened in astonishment. Then her eyes narrowed with mistrust, she anticipated trouble brewing.

The difference between the two women was marked. Ursula moved gracefully, with her black hair carefully oiled and braided; Synfye's dusty hair hung in a long, tousled mop.

"I see you are without your husband," Ursula said, after their brief, traditional Gypsy greeting.

"The last I saw of Tawno, he was being taken through Melton Mowbray to be whipped in the Market Place. I've not heard from him since. Me and the boys have travelled far to find you. No one of our clan knew where you were. I happened to meet someone who had spoken to Uncle Piramus," Synfye said, lifting her chin. She looked at Culvato. "My Tawno told me I could stay in safety with his brother until he joined us."

Strange that Tawno should send her to us, he thought. *What bother has the man got himself into now?*

Culvato tried to hide his consternation. If he refused to give his brother's wife and her children his protection, it would be considered a disgrace, and their clan would discredit him. With a bold swagger, Synfye crossed the wood yard, followed by Seth and Ben. As she seated herself on a log, Culvato saw the two women exchange wary glances, and he gave a deep sigh.

***

It had been arranged by the chief of the Ardry tribe, that when she was of age, Synfye would marry Culvato. Tawno however, had wanted the pretty and voluptuous Gypsy girl for himself. With gifts and wild promises, Tawno had enticed Synfye to run away with him. The anger of both sets of parents eventually cooled and the couple returned to the Ardry camp. After a few days, they were accepted as man and wife and members of the tribe.

Tawno had always shown a wild streak, and Culvato thought that Synfye, who then had a flirtatious way about her, would make Tawno an ideal wife. He wished them well and began courting Ursula. Although she was from another tribe, Ursula knew Culvato and his family. She fell in love with the quiet young man. After a brief courtship, they approached the Gypsy Chief and asked his permission to marry. He consented on condition that he performed the ceremony over his own campfire. Culvato and Ursula were happy to agree. That arrangement pleased both sets of parents and both clans joined in the celebrations. Men played their fiddles and squeezeboxes while young girls danced, and the old women looked on, wishing they were still as spry. The rest of the party sang Romani songs and spoke of other weddings. Everyone fell silent when the women of Ursula's family escorted her from her tent. Her mother walked in front of Ursula carrying a white handkerchief tied to a stick. This was to signify the bride's purity. Wrapped in a multicoloured silk shawl and wearing the traditional Gypsy dress, the girl seated herself cross-legged beside Culvato. Her hair was plaited with imitation pearls and she wore silver rings on her thumbs. They sat by the fire with dignity as the adults raised their glasses and wished the couple wealth and health. Then the wedding party enjoyed the food prepared by the women that afternoon. The Chief rose to his feet and lifted his hands. Everyone fell silent.

"Now there is marrying to do," said the Chief, taking out his knife.

The couple stood so close to the fire, that the flames felt hot on their faces.

"Your hand, Culvato," the Chief said.

Culvato held out his hand. He felt a stinging pain as the Chief scratched his wrist. A drop of blood oozed out.

"Your hand, Ursula," he said.

Ursula stretched out her wrist. As the blade scraped her amber flesh, she flinched but looked confidently to Culvato.

The Chief bound their wrists together and their blood mingled.

"Say these words after me, Culvato. 'I take this monushi for my romni, but swear to let her free as soon as love has left my heart'."

Culvato repeated the words firmly. He knew the love he felt for Ursula would always stay with him.

"You now, Ursula," he said with a nod of encouragement.

Culvato felt a cold shudder as he heard Ursula say the words, but his fear disappeared when he saw the love shining in her eyes.

The brief ceremony finished, the music and singing began again. Everyone swayed to the rhythm, but kept their faces turned towards the fire as Culvato and Ursula left the camp. They had to pretend to run off together, taking a grai to ride - as is the custom of the Romani - and so began their married life.

***

Ursula was not pleased to see Synfye without her husband. Tawno would have kept a check on the woman's arrogant behaviour. In a tone which suggested that she wished Synfye had not turned up unannounced, she said: "We are camped in the beech woods yonder. I'll show you the way." Ursula walked towards the lane with Hugo skipping ahead, until she realised Synfye hadn't moved.

Staring at his aunt and uncle, Seth stood silently beside his mother. Culvato studied the child's features. *How like his dadrus he looks. I hope he has a sweeter nature and can control his temper better than Tawno*, he thought.

"Is that new living wagon yours?" Synfye asked. She ignored Ursula and stared at the caravan with her mouth open.

Retracing her steps, Ursula placed both hands on her hips and ran a satisfied eye over the sleek lines of the vehicle.

"As well as this, Culvato is having another wagon made - a flat one to carry a tiknies' fair ride. Uncle Piramus says he will drive that wagon for us."

Ursula's face was flushed with pride. She could not help boasting a little to the woman who had always treated her with disdain. Since their marriage, Culvato's family always had to walk and push a barrow holding their possessions; Synfye had made it plain many times that by having her own caravan she was socially a notch or so higher than Ursula.

"But how? Where have you got the money from for such a fine thing?" Synfye was unable to hide her envy and resentment, and it showed in the tone of her voice.

"I've been lucky and saved my coinage," Culvato growled, looking with narrowed eyes at his brother's wife.

"With its small front wheels it will turn in a tight lock. The shutters slide over the windows - Mr Watson calls them louvre shutters." Standing on tiptoe, Ursula proudly demonstrated how the shutters worked on her dream home.

"Who's the boy?" Culvato said.

He was still holding the paintbrush, and his eyebrows drew together with a frown as he regarded the Gaujo chavvi choramengro.

"This is Ben." Synfye took hold of the boy by his skinny arm and pulled him forward. "Without his help it would have been snowing afore we got here and he kept us in food. He used to work for Tawno, but now he does as I say."

Staring at Ben's undersized figure, and still frowning, Culvato nodded as though considering what she said.

"I know very well what kind of work you have been made to do for my brother. I want no trouble with parish officials, so no thieving! If you stay in my camp, you will do as you're told. Understand? Leave when you want."

Ben's face lit up. He had been afraid that once Synfye was with her family he would be cast out and would need to return to begging. Pulling off his dirty cap he moved a step nearer to Culvato.

"I'll work, sir, I'm a willing boy. Turn me 'and to most things, I can. I'll try, though I've never done no tinkering before. And, if there is anything else I can do, I'll do it."

Culvato studied the boy, his head tipped on one side, without speaking.

Ben moved uneasily.

"I'm as strong as a grown man!"

With a grunt, Culvato jerked his head in the direction of the women. They had left the wood yard and were now standing in the lane, calling Seth and Hugo to join them.

"Best go with them, nothing for you to do here. My woman will feed you."

Ben set off after the two women, giving Seth a piggyback - although he was just as tired as the boy he was carrying.

Hugo ran from one person to the other, chattering cheerfully about the woods, the village and everything else small boys love. He told Ben and Seth that he knew where a badger's sett was, and that he would show them the best places to lay snares for hedgehogs. He had caught two large hedgehogs the day before, and after his mother had killed, cleaned and rolled them in thick mud, she had baked them in the ashes of the cooking fire. Hugo remembered breaking open the clay to release the roasted meat's delicious aroma and his mouth watered.

Ben trudged after the women, the thought of a meal and a safe night's sleep spurred him on. Oh, how he wished that he had been born a Gypsy.

***

For the most part, the two women walked in silence, but as they neared the camp, Synfye began telling Ursula about the burning of the caravan and the fate of Betty the donkey.

"Don't you know why?" Ursula asked.

"Tawno didn't say. Don't think he knew. Maybe someone who holds a grudge against him." Sniffing back tears, she walked with weary steps, pulling the carrying frame.

Piramus was sitting outside the largest bender tent smoking his pipe when the boys and the two women walked into the camp. His eyes widened, and he exhaled a cloud of smoke when he saw who it was accompanying Ursula. The old man nodded an unsmiling welcome to Synfye. He remembered the sharp words he had exchanged with her and Tawno at their last meeting.

Holding up the tent flap, Ursula followed her inside the bender tent. Piramus stood at the opening, and said: "They've all been asleep since you left, Ursula. Good as can be. Not one chirp. I see you brought Hugo home." When the child heard his name mentioned he put both arms around the old man's legs and stood smiling up at him. "Couldn't your dadrus find you work painting the new vardo?" With a gentle hand, the old man ruffled the dark curls of the boy.

"My cousin Seth has come to stay, Kaka Piramus," Hugo said. "Can he come out with us tonight? I can show him where the fox had her cubs."

"So I see. Maybe I'll take you and Seth into the woods later, but only if you're both as quiet as mice." Piramus gave Synfye a hard look. "Your man with you?"

"No. He got himself into some kind of bother when he was in Melton Mowbray. Said I was to stay with Culvato and he'd find me when he was ready." Seating herself on a low stool, Synfye stared at the four babies who lay fast asleep on a muslin pillow filled with wood shavings. She glanced towards Ursula, an inquiring expression on her face.

"Lionel and Hugo now have three sisters," said Ursula. One of the triplets opened her eyes. Her face began to pucker as though she was about to start whimpering. Ursula lifted her and placed the infant to her breast before she awakened the other sleeping babies.

"I can see why you need such a large living wagon. With a family of this size you'll need extra help. Good thing I came." Synfye gave a mocking laugh. "You always said you and Culvato wanted plenty of tiknies. I never thought they would have fair hair, though. They look like Gaujo tiknies."

Letting out a deep breath, Piramus pulled out his knife. He saw that Ursula's cheeks were flushed and that she was biting her lip.

"I'm going to cut some hazel and willow. We'll need another bender tent. I'll leave you two to catch up with your gossip." He let the tent flap drop back into place and strode along the familiar paths in the woods. He had sometimes missed being part of a family group and the past few weeks had been idyllic. Would things change now Synfye had arrived? All he knew was that two women in one bender tent was one too many for his comfort.

***

Still nursing the baby, Ursula glanced at Ben. He was sitting on the floor on the far side of the tent with his arms folded close to his body, rocking backwards and forwards. Her heart went out to him. Seldom had she seen a traveller look so lost and forlorn as that undersized child.

"Boys, there's food cooking over the fire, help yourselves. Bring some in here for your dai, Seth."

Ben stayed where he was, unsure whether Ursula meant him. He leapt to his feet though, when she said, "You as well, boy."

Ursula turned her attention back to Synfye. "Where's Mikailia?"

"She grew sickly and died just after we left Melton Mowbray." Synfye's voice was flat. She still grieved a little for the infant, but it was her secret that she had taken the baby into the woods, covered her with leaves and branches, and left her to die.

"Tell me about her. Was she a good tikni?"

Synfye was prepared for Ursula's question and had her answer ready. She wouldn't reveal to anyone that she had grown tired of the baby's constant demands, and hadn't bothered to treat her with herbal remedies when she became ill.

"No. She was heavy. Tawno made me the frame to carry her, but she didn't like it. She kicked and screamed as though I was killing her when I tied her on, but I couldn't carry her far. After a week or two I found she had spots everywhere. She kept coughing and being sick. I tried all kinds of herbs to make her better, but nothing I did worked. She became worse. One morning she died in my arms. I didn't say anything to the boys. I left them guarding the frame while I went in a wood and buried her under a bush. They didn't even ask what had happened to her."

"I'm so sorry." Ursula's heart was touched by the sadness she thought she saw in Synfye's face. "Poor little thing, she looked so rosy when I last saw her."

Synfye looked at the baby in Ursula's arms. She stared back with big eyes the colour of cornflowers. She knew that blue eyes and fair hair were not in the Ardry clan, and wondered who had colouring like that in Ursula's family.

"What have you called them?" Synfye said, placing a finger in the baby's hand. When the tiny fingers closed around hers she smiled, although she felt a pang when she remembered how Mikailia had done the same thing.

"We gave them flower names. Lilly, Rose, and the one you are holding is Heather."

Synfye gave Ursula a startled glance.

"Not your mother's name?"

Ursula shook her head. She was about to explain why and how they had come to have the triplets when they heard a commotion outside. They heard Culvato shouting.

"Get out of the way, boy! If I tip up the barrow, it will roll out."

Ursula and Synfye poked their heads outside the tent. Culvato and Piramus were manoeuvring a thick tree stump, minus most of its roots, across the clearing. Ben hovered nearby, ready to help the men.

"What on earth is that for?" Synfye called. She got no reply and she looked at Ursula. "Strange kind of thing to bring home. I'd have thought there were enough tree stumps around here without bringing more."

Ursula frowned at Synfye's patronising tone.

"Culvato will trim it into the shape he needs, ready for carving," said Ursula, letting the tent flap fall back. Synfye hid her disdainful expression by putting Heather down beside her sisters. She could not help but notice how fair their skin was against the dark skin of her hands. *Glad both mine were black uns*, she thought, stroking a finger over the downy head of Rose.

Straightening up, she asked, "Carving? Carving what?"

"I told you. Culvato is having a tiknies' fair ride built. He has already begun to carve a set of animals for it; horses, or maybe farm animals. He hasn't decided yet. Mr Watson is making the ride, as well as a wagon to carry it. Uncle Piramus will drive the wagon when we leave."

"So you'll all be giving up the ways of the Romani. Start working in fairs?"

"Our own fair, Culvato has plans." Ursula ignored Synfye's embittered expression. She placed the baby she had been holding with the others and began lacing her bodice together. *Questions. Questions. She always has to know every little detail about everything what's happening. Wish she hadn't found us.*

"Well, I think he's got windmills in his head. Tawno never had daft ideas like this, and he always has plenty of money."

Biting back the tart reply that sprang to mind, Ursula kept her head lowered as she tugged at her laces and tied them. She didn't look up until Synfye had left the tent to help Piramus. As usual, Ben would have to find his own resting place - most likely under a hedge.

The caravan was almost ready to leave Mr Watson's wood yard. He had finished fitting the golden-stained pine furniture. Seats with lockers flanked a table on the right with a cupboard above and below. The table could be removed and used outside if required; upside-down, inside the caravan, it could be used as a bed. At the rear of the caravan was a shelf which extended to make a double bed. A rose-coloured glass window was above it - the etched glass had been chalked to make the pattern prominent - and a few inches from the floor was another bed, which would be pushed out of sight when not in use. There was a small stove on the left hand side of the door. On the right was a glass-fronted cabinet. Ursula had kept some of her mother's glassware packed in the barrow.

She intended to display it with her own modest collection of china.

Ursula felt that she could leave the babies with Synfye when she walked to the wood yard each day to admire the beautiful vehicle. The morning dew felt colder to her bare feet and the wind had an icy chill. One day, as she left the wood yard, she saw fallen leaves caught in spider webs among the piles of cut timber. They rustled and danced in the wind. *I shall be pleased when we can use the vardo. Draughty, leaky tents will be something I'll be glad to be rid of,* she thought. Pulling her shawl closer, she stepped over a puddle. Spurred on by the thought of the warming drink waiting for her, she hurried home.

One stump of wood had been carved into the shape of a horse with a hollowed out back, and Culvato had made a leather saddle with metal stirrups to fit it. A wooden goose with big feet stood next to the horse, and both were waiting to be painted.

Culvato was in the longer bender tent, within speaking distance of Piramus, chiselling another stump of wood and marvelling at the dexterity of the old man's fingers. With a pile of wheat straw and pieces of leather scattered around him, Piramus perched on a low stool, making the harness for the new horse. John Bailey had supplied the Gypsy with some metal hames, and Piramus had already sewn them into place. The old man whistled through his teeth as he padded a leather neck collar as tightly as he could with the straw, and then began to sew the leather with neat, even stitches. Hugo and Seth were near the doorway, each whittling a small piece of wood.

"What about the chal? Will he travel with us?" Piramus concentrated on his stitching as he asked the question.

Stopping work, chisel in position and hammer raised, Culvato looked at the old man.

"Ben makes himself very useful around the village. I did hear the man who lives at Hill Top is looking for a boy to help him with his donkeys. Ben would be ideal for the job, otherwise by the time the snow comes he might want to leave us and find work in Nottingham."

Suddenly Culvato became aware of Seth's worried expression.

"Don't want Ben to leave, Kaka Culvato. I love Ben. He's my bestest friend in all the world." Seth's bottom lip quivered.

"He can travel with us and welcome, Seth, but remember he is a Gaujo, not a Romani chal like you and Hugo."

The cousins exchanged a smile. They had already discussed it. Ben would always stay with them. He had often told them that he hated to be indoors, and he was every bit as good as any Gypsy at setting snares and acquiring food for the pot. Maybe one day, when he was a man, Ben would marry a Romani woman and become a pikie, and then he would stay with their family for always.

***

The finished caravan was beautiful indeed. Culvato stood with Ursula in the wood yard, admiring it. The craftsmen had been paid and the wheels, always fitted after the final payment, were in place. Sunlight glinted on the golden scrolls and the fine golden edges of the wheel spokes.

"Are you happy with the furniture, missus?" Mr Watson had just come out of his workshop and saw that Ursula was peering through one of the windows set high in the doors. The pine furniture, with amber glass handles, was fitted in such a way that not an inch of storage space was wasted.

Ursula nodded. "Oh, yes. It's lovely; everything is just what I wanted," she said.

"The stove only arrived Tuesday. We had a bit of trouble to get it in place. Do you like the grape vines etched on the windows?" Culvato asked.

"Everything's just perfect. The best vardo ever built." Ursula put her face on his waistcoat and tittered as he blew on her neck.

With his arm around Ursula, Culvato watched as Mr Watson walked across the yard to his workshop and went inside. He gave a quick glance around to make sure they were alone.

"I had a metal safe box built under the floor near the bed, as well as a sliding panel in the wall next to the stove. You still carry our money with you, don't you, Romni?" Culvato asked in a low voice.

Ursula's eyes darted towards the lane and then to the workshop.

"It's always with me. I never leave it where anyone could find it. For a start, I don't trust your pral's romni. She was in our tent, prying among things she shouldn't only a few days ago. I saw her examining the lantern clock, but no name is on it to give her a clue from where we had it. When she saw me watching, her excuse was that she was looking for a clean blanket for the tiknies. I didn't believe her. I've not told her about the girls. It might be best for them if I don't." Ursula's mouth was tight and her dark eyes flashed as she remembered the guilty look on Synfye's face when she had been caught snooping.

"She's asked Mr Watson to build her a small vardo. Nothing as grand as this one, but I wondered where the money was coming from to pay for it. When you get a moment alone, Romni, check your moneybag."

Ursula was seldom alone. Gypsy women mostly stayed together, mainly to protect their virtue.

Culvato gave her a nudge when he saw Ben running down

the lane and coming across the yard towards them. Laughter lit Ben's face, giving him a healthy glow.

"Hugo and Seth have a surprise for you both when you get back! Uncle Piramus has taught them how to hollow out a turnip and carve a face in it."

Exchanging an amused glance with Culvato, Ursula put her arm around Ben's shoulders and gave him a squeeze.

"I thought you'd be fatter with my cooking to fill your belly, but you're still a skinny rakkelo," she laughed.

Turning worshipful eyes towards her, Ben said: "I can't remember when I've been so happy as what I've been with you and Mr Ardry. Please let me stay with you when you travel on."

"Bless the child." Ursula felt her eyes fill and she sniffed. "We've done little enough for you, Ben."

"Just carry on helping like you have, young un. We'll be well satisfied with you, chal." Culvato looked at Ursula, and added, "I'll see you at the camp later."

Culvato wanted to make the final arrangements with Mr Watson, and as he went to find him, Ursula and Ben left the wood yard and walked along the lane to the camp.

"This will be your last night in a bender tent, Mrs Ardry. Will Mrs Synfye sleep in your vardo?"

"Oh!" She looked at the boy. The nights were getting colder and she suddenly realised that Ben had nowhere warm to sleep; but if Synfye's bender tent became empty, Ben could use that. "I'll see if we can find you a corner, chal. Somewhere to sleep out of the weather, maybe with the horse. Until she has her own vardo, Mrs Synfye will use a tent as usual, same as Uncle Piramus."

Ursula fell silent as she thought about Synfye. How could she possibly pay for a caravan? Even a small one would be expensive. Tawno would never have trusted Synfye with his money. She remembered that Ben had told her that when he couldn't catch birds or small animals, they had begged and stolen food on their journey. Milk was cheap enough, and someone could always milk a cow without the farmer's knowledge if it became necessary. *Surely Synfye wouldn't have let her baby die if it could have been prevented. But hadn't Mikailia died from sickness, not want of nourishment?* The thoughts in her head went round and round.

With a worried frown she placed a hand on her bag of gold and jewels and tested its weight. It felt the same and she had checked the stitching well before she used it. *I'll be pleased when it is all locked away in the vardo where it will be safe*, she thought.

***

Later, when Culvato returned to the camp and the babies were sleeping, he invited Ursula to walk with him in the woods. There was a taste of winter in the wind, and the couple walked with hips touching and arms entwined as they sauntered along. A nest of dried leaves had drifted against a hedge and they sat down. Culvato's hand moved over the front of Ursula's bodice and he pulled the laces undone. Her breasts were firm and rounded and she flinched as he gave them a gentle squeeze. As he bent to kiss them, the smell of babies and the flowery perfume she wore prompted in him a longing, an urge to love her. As they fell back on the ground, she pulled him on top of her, her arms and legs wrapped around him. She was moist and ready for him. He pulled away.

"What?"

"That bloody bag. I can't do anything while that money bag is tied to you."

They were both laughing as she pulled the treasure bag from under her skirts.

"Come here. That better?"

Using the bag as a pillow, she held out her arms. He didn't need any persuasion. Gently he put a finger inside her until she moaned softly.

"Now," she gasped, and quickly hooked her legs around his waist. His mouth stifled her moans of ecstasy.

At last, satisfied, they lay side by side. As Ursula retied the laces on her bodice, Culvato counted the treasure. It all tallied. He took one sovereign and a few smaller coins and placed them in his pocket. They would clear his debt for the new wagon and the horse. There was still plenty of money left in the bag, and Culvato knew a trustworthy member of their clan who would exchange the jewellery into cash needed.

"How can Synfye pay for a new vardo? Not only that, she's buying a mule to pull it. I can't understand it, especially as they arrived here half starved," Ursula said, refastening the treasure bag securely under her skirts.

"It's no use us wondering, Romni. Somehow she has managed to get her hands on some money and she don't want us to know how. Anyway, ours is safe so let's make the most of being alone." Ursula didn't need any persuading and Culvato pulled her closer, nuzzled into her neck and whispered in her ear. One lovely thing led to another and it was quite dark by the time they arrived home.

The fire had been dampened down and was smouldering under a large stone. Some wood thrown on it in the morning would soon make it burst into life.

"I'll take the chavvies with me tomorrow morning," said Culvato, watching Ursula check that a water jug had been emptied. "They'll want to go with me to buy the new donkey and horse. Mr Martin has promised me a fair deal. With me doing such a good job of pleaching the hedges in his donkey field, he won't try and cheat me."

Chapter 9

The horse chosen by the Ardry family was a sturdy animal, brown with a white patch on its belly, a white blaze on its face and white feathered fetlocks which fell in skirts over each hoof. It was young enough to be trained in ways to suit Culvato. He led it along the roads and lanes without difficulty, accompanied by Hugo and Seth. Everyone but Ben watched as it was brought into Mr Watson's wood yard, he had offered to stay at the camp to look after the triplets and Lionel. Piramus gave a satisfied grunt as he lifted the neck collar he had made over the horse's head. It was a snug fit, and it sat comfortably on its shoulders. His experience told him that the collar wouldn't rock and make sores. The remainder of the harness was put on. The leather was new and rather stiff and he moved around the patient horse for some time making adjustments. When he was satisfied that the harness fitted correctly, Culvato whistled, clicked his tongue and called encouragement as he backed the horse into position between the shafts of the vardo. It only took a moment or two to fasten the shafts to the harness saddle.

"You chose a right name for the horse; 'Hector'. It used to mean swaggering fellow, you knows," Mr Watson said. He laughed with everyone else at the joke. They knew what he meant; the horse did walk with a swagger, as though he was proud of his new role.

"If he's smart enough to be trained for it, in the future I plan to use him as a performing horse. When he learns some tricks he'll swagger even more," Culvato chuckled. He gave the harness one last check before climbing into the driving seat and taking hold of the reins.

The caravan turned slowly to face the lane. He let the horse get the feel of the harness and the weight of the vehicle before driving out of the wood yard. When he reached the lane, he brought the caravan to a halt. Peering around the side of their new home, he grinned at Ursula, who was still standing with the others in the yard.

"Want to ride with your rom?" he called.

As nimble as a young girl, she scrambled onto the seat. Her face glowed with excitement and she held onto his arm with both hands as he slapped the horse's back with the reins.

"Walk on. Walk on there" he called.

The caravan rocked from side to side as it lifted in and out of the ruts in the lane.

"Better than using two feet, ain't it?"

"Oh, Culvato, it's just as I dreamed it would be. It's lovely. I wish we could just keep on driving."

"We can't. Not yet. We've got to wait till Tawno gets here and Synfye's vardo is finished. And I've a bit more work to do on the ride."

"Don't matter, it'll give me time to make another rug and finish the new quilt."

"Dadrus! Dadrus, me legs are tired."

Culvato looked down to see Hugo trotting along beside the wheel of the caravan.

"Come on up then, my tikni. Put your foot on the iron step and hold your dai's hand."

Hugo didn't need telling twice. Ursula took hold of the little boy's hand and he settled between his parents and watched with interest how his father handled the reins.

Piramus walked beside the horse, ready to grab the bridle if it took it into its head to bolt, but the horse was comfortable with the load and moved at a steady pace along the lane.

***

Synfye noticed how her son had watched Hugo climb onto the caravan and understood how disappointed the child would be at not being invited to join his cousin. She put her hand on Seth's shoulder, and said: "Our own vardo will soon be finished. Mr Watson said that by the end of the year it'll be ready to move."

"Will it have chickens in a coop on the side and a box for my new ferrets, dai, like our old vardo?"

"It'll be smarter than the old one and better than your Kaka Culvato's vardo. Ours will have somewhere for your dadrus to come home to," she said with an edge of bitterness in her voice. She was missing Tawno, but she knew full well that he would only turn up if and when he wanted to.

Culvato had already widened the entrance leading into the campsite, and carefully driving over the grass, he parked the caravan under a line of beech trees. The bender tents were close by, for when the weather worsened, one tent would be used as a stable for Hector and the young donkey that they had bought for Hugo.

By the end of the week, Culvato and Ursula had settled into the caravan, but Ursula still preferred cooking by using the fire outside.

One evening, everyone gathered in the caravan to discuss future plans. The men sat with Synfye at the table. Ursula made herself comfortable next to the stove, and although she listened closely to what was being said, her fingers were busy making lace.

"I've been thinking that we need more than just the ride. We have talked it over and Ursula has suggested a side show of stuffed birds and small animals. It might draw more folk to the fair," said Culvato. "I've found a man living near Eastwood who's very good at taxidermy. When I went to see him he showed me three tableaux of wild animals and birds. Each one is arranged in front of a picture, and they're covered by a glass dome to keep off the dust."

Ursula gave Culvato a nod of support. They had gone together to see the man's work and were both more than pleased with his artistic skill and his imagination with fur and feathers.

"We could display all three arrangements on tables inside a bender tent. The glass will protect them and keep them clean as people look at them. Someone can stand at the doorway and take the money off folk as they go inside. There will be hardly any outlay - a tilt won't cost much, and the rest will be profit."

"Sounds good! They could travel on the wagon. Be safe enough if we put them in wooden boxes and strap them down," Piramus said.

"Your peepshow will draw in the crowds, and with me and Ursula reading palms and telling fortunes, we should all make a comfortable living," Synfye said. As she spoke, she wondered what Tawno would say when he found his romni and son working in a fair. *I've no choice*, she thought. *He said that we must stay with Culvato until he finds us, and that's what I'm doing.*

***

Synfye's bow-top caravan, its canvas roof covered with snow, was brought to the campsite in December. It was smaller than Culvato's vardo, but certainly large enough for Synfye and Seth. A tiny stove sat near the door, and a ledge with match boarding fitted to shoulder height behind, made an internal seat. Synfye had already made cushions to fit the ledge, and matching curtains were tied back with ribbons at the window above the bed. She disliked sewing, and she was more than pleased when Ursula offered to help. A pegged rug, made in colours to match the cushions, was lying on the floor, and when the stove was lit, the interior was snug and cosy. Synfye looked forward to the time when she could show the vardo to Tawno.

The weather worsened. Her mule, Hugo's donkey and Hector were comfortably stabled in the largest of the old bender tents. Ben was grateful to have the warmth of the animals, and, wrapping himself in an old blanket Ursula had given to him, he burrowed beneath the straw each night.

Culvato, Ursula and the children were in their caravan when the door suddenly opened and a flurry of snow blew inside. Ursula blinked with surprise as the cold air hit her and Piramus entered the vardo. He threw four pigeons on the floor before pulling the door closed.

"Brought you these for dinner. I took some to Synfye, but all she did was to grumble about the mess I was making with me boots," he said, unwinding the scarf around his neck.

With a twinkle in her eye, Ursula said: "Do you remember when she was first married? I found her trying to pluck some pigeons like fowl. I told her you don't pluck pigeons. Disembowel them, cut off the head and feet, then plunge the bodies into a bowl of hot water and wait. They're ready when you can peel the skin and feathers all off together." Ursula exchanged a roguish look with Culvato. "She was that mad with herself for letting me find out that there was something I knew and she didn't."

With a grin, Piramus began replacing his scarf.

"You had best stay and eat these with us. Is Ben wanting to be fed as well?" Ursula asked. She hadn't seen the boy for a couple of days, and wondered how he was managing to keep fed and warm with only the old man as company.

"The boy's well enough. He spends a lot of time with the horse and mule. Says Hector is learning to say yes when he offers it some hay," Piramus said. Hugo leaned against his knee and Piramus closed his arms around the warm body of the child.

"How's that?" Culvato said.

"The horse nods. The chavvi seems to be good with animals. I seem to think he'll stay with us when we move on. He'd be useful and company for me." Piramus hung his coat on a hook beside the door and continued: "He's grown fond of you, Ursula. The lad is still of an age to miss his mother."

"He can travel with us if he wants to. Can do as he pleases," Culvato said with a shrug.

Ursula smiled and nodded.

"The boy is easy to like, and I'd miss him if he left."

The Gypsies remained snowbound for the next month, and after that came frost and weeks of heavy rain.

***

In the stinging freshness of an April morning, the Gypsies dismantled the bender tents. The field was cleared of rubbish and Piramus replaced the piece of turf on the scorched earth where the fire had been. When everything in the field was as tidy as possible, the Gypsies began their journey. The caravans were followed by the flat wagon, pulled by the donkey. It carried the child's ride, the sideshow and also Piramus' peepshow, all covered by oiled canvas and lashed down with ropes.

Leaving Eastwood behind, they travelled through Awsworth on their way to Ilkeston.

A week or so earlier, Culvato had ridden to Ilkeston. When he was returning home, he had noticed a field. It lay fallow, flat and well-drained, with a wide entrance; an ideal place to set out the fair. He made enquiries at a cottage nearby, and he met the owner. For a small fee, the man was pleased to give Culvato permission to use the field for his fair. The Gypsies had quickly become expert at fitting the sections of the ride together. When they arrived at the field, it didn't take long before the ride and the sideshow were ready for use. The weather was fine, although it was damp underfoot, and word quickly spread around the small community that a band of Gypsies were staging a fair. People began to arrive in family groups to stare, and as soon as the children saw how the painted animals whirled round, they begged their parents for a ride. Because of Mr Watson's skill, the roundabout, when on level ground, spun around with very little effort. The children squealed with delight, and Ben was kept busy collecting coins in an old hat of Culvato's.

When the adults saw the show tent they were more interested in seeing the peepshow and the lifelike glass-covered animals. They didn't seem to mind paying a farthing to Synfye or Piramus to enter and gape at each spectacle.

Ursula had put up her pole with its caged linnet beside the show tent and began the business of telling fortunes. Soon, a queue formed as people waited to hear what the future had to offer them.

As the sun set over a row of trees, the people drifted homeward. The Gypsies, tired with their efforts, sat together in Culvato's caravan. He sat at the table and counted out the day's takings. Dividing the money into three piles, he pushed the smallest amount towards Synfye.

"You'll need to take more than this, Culvato. I can earn better money dukkering from door to door and selling clothes pegs," she said, though she didn't refuse the money, and quickly pocketed her share.

He gave her a sharp look. "You're lucky to be getting that! Don't judge too soon, early days still. The hawker's licence is paid for until the end of the summer, so we've plenty of time to earn more." Not for the world would Culvato admit to being disappointed with the takings, or let Tawno's wife know that he was having doubts about his enterprise.

Piramus stared at the table and pushed some coins around with a finger. "What we could do with is to find more attractions to draw the crowds. Maybe stilt walkers, a few clowns or someone with a caged wild animal. You would have to pay them, but it might be worth while if it pulled folk in to look around."

The old man saw a glow of enthusiasm lighting up his nephew's face. As the work had progressed at the wood yard, Piramus had seen some money changing hands, and he thought privately that the outlay for the ride and sideshow had been far more than Culvato had envisaged. He so wanted the fair to be a success, for the young couple's sake.

There was a short silence broken by Culvato.

"I've been thinking of a children's up-and-down machine, or another sideshow maybe. An open-fronted show-tent where a ball can be thrown into a bucket, if it stays inside, the Gaujo would have a prize. Money back, maybe? The outlay wouldn't be much, and we could use Ben to take the money."

"Good idea! And I think folk should know that we are coming to their town or village. Call at an inn or tavern and tell the landlord and customers about the fair the day before we arrive," Piramus said.

Sitting quietly, making her bobbin lace on a cushion, Ursula watched Hugo losing his fight to stay awake. The triplets and Lionel lay wrapped in blankets. They looked like contented cherubs as they slept.

Seth and Hugo, back to back, snuggled under a quilt. The excitement had tired them out. Seth, already fast asleep, would stay there until his mother fetched him in the morning. Ursula listened intently to everyone's suggestions, but she made no attempt to join in the conversation, until Piramus suggested that Culvato should stand on a box and shout to the crowds about the wonders of the galloping animals and the marvellous sideshow.

"I'll make you a costume to wear if you like. A bright red coat with gold braid trimming the sleeves, and a silk shirt set off by deep lace on a cravat. Maybe you could hold a whip to crack, with ribbons matching the coat?" Ursula offered.

Culvato rubbed his chin with his fingers. He hadn't shaved since that morning, and the rasp of his stubble sounded loud in the silence. He wasn't sure if he liked the idea of making an exhibition of himself to advertise his fair. The new concept would need to be thought about.

Chapter 10

Synfye thought about Tawno sometimes, but mostly she was unconcerned about his whereabouts. Occasionally she would meet a man whom she liked well enough to have sex with, but there was always the thought that Tawno would one day return and they would live together as before. Having the security of being with Culvato and Ursula, she was content to travel with them until she met up with her husband again. Ursula had asked, as tactfully as possible, how she could afford to pay for a vardo and mule. Synfye had turned her questions away with a careless laugh. She never breathed a word about the purses stolen by the urchin, although she smiled to herself when she remembered finding that one of the purses was filled with gold coins and there was more than enough to pay for the vardo. When questioned by Culvato, she replied in a haughty manner, that it was Tawno's money she had spent, and that he would want his family to travel in a vardo.

***

After his whipping, Tawno Ardry had been escorted to the boundary of Melton Mowbray Town with his two dogs and set free with a stern warning never to return. No one told Tawno why he had been arrested and punished in such a manner. Because Gypsies were constantly hounded by so called 'civilised' folk trying to discourage travellers from settling in their towns, Tawno had thought he had just been unlucky. But when he had seen Brandy-Joe Lincolin standing with his cronies in the crowds, he guessed from the man's laughter that he had been somehow responsible.

Smouldering with resentment and stiff and sore from his whipping, Tawno trudged for the next few days in the general direction of Nottingham. On the third day he met a vagabond he knew. The man was travelling in the same direction as he was and so the two men shared their meagre supply of food and a bottle of whisky. The dogs, keeping guard, stayed nearby. Sitting in the light from the fire, the vagabond brought up the subject of Tawno's humiliation. The man had left Melton Mowbray in a hurry when he heard the rumour that the authorities were seeking a Gypsy with a similar description to him. Now, listening to his companion, he realised that the search had not been for him, but for Tawno.

"I did hear how it was Brandy-Joe Lincolin set the tale around town that you was a villain, and it was him who gave out your description. That's probably why the constables were looking for you. The rumour was that you had stripped and robbed a rich merchant coming into town, and you're well known up north as a highwayman."

Tawno ground his teeth with anger.

"I've never done such a thing in my life. I've known others who do it, and they make a good living, but I've always stuck with buying and selling grais," he said. Once again his anger was white-hot. Tawno vowed to get more than even with any member of the Lincolin clan, if or when he met them.

The following morning, Tawno bade the vagabond farewell

and they parted company at the crossroads. When he met a travelling family who were not known to him, Tawno told them he was looking for his brother, Brandy-Joe, a tall man with a big moustache. He asked if the family had seen or heard of him. He learned that a Gypsy fitting the description had been seen on the previous day, travelling south, and his heart quickened.

For the next three days, Tawno thought constantly about Brandy-Joe Lincoln and fantasised about how he would treat him or any member of his family the next time they crossed his path. He cooked and ate small game that he caught in his snares or that was brought to him by his dogs. Fruit and berries he found along the hedgerows were a welcome treat. More than once he had seen the unmistakable signs of recent campfires made by Gypsies, and he had a feeling that Brandy-Joe was not far in front. There was no need to hurry.

When Tawno arrived at a gently sloping grassy bank, he rested by the roadside. After some time, his eyes began to sting and water. Wood-scented smoke swirled and wreathed through the trees and the thick undergrowth on the other side of the road. Wiping his eyes with the back of his grimy hand and commanding his faithful dogs to stay, he tied them to a bush. There was a mossy path leading into the wood. Moving stealthily, he stopped every few minutes, listening for any sound that might reveal a human presence. A cooking fire had to be nearby, as he could smell hotchi-witchi and other food aromas mingling with the smoke. His mouth watered at the thought of eating a plateful of well-cooked hotchi-witchi baked in clay. Whenever he snared a hedgehog he would always take it home; it was a meal that Synfye excelled in cooking.

As silent as possible, Tawno pushed his way through the undergrowth and followed a narrow stream until he heard the sound of a woman singing a Gypsy melody. Pressing himself against an old gnarled tree trunk, he peered around it, through a leafy bush. The sight that met his eyes made him gasp. Clamping his teeth together, he thanked his lucky stars he'd been so careful in his approach to the camp. Stretching to get a clearer view, he grimaced. His back still ached, and was sore from the whipping.

In a large clearing stood two Gypsy men with long moustaches, one was Brandy-Joe Lincolin. The other man had similar features and the same sturdy build as his companion, but he was a stranger to Tawno. The ground around their feet was littered with branches, twigs and leaves. A young woman, perhaps the wife of one of the men, was dragging the larger branches away and throwing them on a bonfire at the far side of the clearing.

The men stood by a rough table heaped with a great quantity of sloe, ash, alder and other green leaves mixed together. Tawno watched as the men chopped the leaves to a fine consistency.

Brandy-Joe took handfuls of a white powder from a hessian sack and scattered the powder over the leaves. His voice carried clearly as he called to the woman.

"Hurry up and bring me those boxes from the tent, Curlanda."

Standing back, Brandy-Joe watched as his companion plunged his hands into the leaves and mixed everything together.

Tawno stood transfixed, staring at the proceedings. At first, he wondered what the men were making. He immediately understood when the woman placed some small wooden boxes on the table and they began filling them with the mixture.

"How many have you got?" the man asked, picking up one of the boxes and examining its painted decoration.

"A dozen. They ain't all that big, but if we can sell these,

I can make some more caddies. Always find a buyer for mutterimengri," Brandy-Joe said, with a grin.

Tawno pursed his lips in a soundless whistle. *Takes nerve, that do. If them's caught with counterfeit tea, them'll hang higher than any gypsies before them,* he thought.

With a few wire tacks, the lids were fastened down and the men turned to the woman.

"Don't you want to finish the hotchi-witchi before you go?" she said.

"No. We'll be off. The Gaujos will be wanting their china cup of hot mutterimengri."

The other man, Cemake, gave a chuckle and a knowing wink to Brandy-Joe who was busy putting the tea caddies into a sack.

The Gypsy's lurchers were tied to a tree at the far side of the clearing, and were lying down. To mask his scent from animals, Tawno daily rubbed a secret concoction of herbs on his skin; he didn't care that it turned his skin a darker brown. The dogs had so far failed to recognise a stranger near the campsite, and Tawno's dogs were too far away to be heard barking. Fortunately for him, the water flowing near his feet had masked any sounds he'd made on his approach to the camp.

"Best we get along, Cemake," said Brandy-Joe, throwing the sack over his shoulder. Playfully, he slapped his wife's buttocks. "Stay here in the camp, monushi. Clear up this mess and tend to the tikni until we get back. We'll not be more than a couple of days."

Tawno dodged back behind the tree as Brandy-Joe turned in his direction.

The pretty Gypsy girl followed them to the edge of the clearing, and she watched as the men untied their dogs. She gave a farewell wave as they left by a path leading away from

Tawno's hiding place.

Staying where he was, Tawno kept the woman in sight as she threw the remainder of the branches on the bonfire. As she worked, she hummed a tune. He saw her fetch water from further along the stream and fill a kettle hanging on an iron prop over her cooking fire. Her movements were tantalisingly seductive. It had been some time since he had used a woman for pleasure, and he licked his lips in anticipation. Waiting patiently behind the tree, he let his thoughts dwell on the gratification of raping that comely young woman, the woman who was married to his sworn enemy.

An hour or so passed and Tawno judged that the two men were well away and unlikely to return. Moving silently through the trees, he reached a path near to the one used by Brandy-Joe and Cemake. He was unnoticed by the woman until he stepped into the sunlit clearing.

With a frightened squeal, the Gypsy woman pulled a well-honed knife from her belt. Holding it at arm's length, she stood with her back to the larger of two bender tents, ready to defend herself and her baby.

"No need for that," Tawno said, waving a careless hand towards the knife. "Come to meet Brandy-Joe. I'm a friend, and I want to talk business with him." Tawno gave his best attempt at a warm smile, but only succeeded in showing his dirty yellow teeth. He had not bothered to shave for several days, and he looked villainous. "May a didikai rest by your fire?"

Although Tawno had spoken in the Romani tongue, Curlanda Lincolin bit her lip nervously as she watched him swagger confidently across the clearing. She stepped back, still holding her knife in a purposeful manner and looking at him with suspicion.

Tawno threw his bundle on the ground. Rubbing his foot over the scattered twigs and leaves on the ground, he gave her a knowing look.

"Looks like you've been busy?"

"If you follow the path yonder you'll catch up with my rom. He hasn't been gone above an hour."

Deciding that she had nothing to fear from the stranger, she moved nearer to Tawno and replaced her knife in its sheath – though she pulled it to the front of her belt, ready for use.

She was a little older than Synfye, and much prettier. Curlanda's olive complexion was clear, and she dressed her lengthy dark hair with bright green ribbons, matching her long skirt. As she bent over the cooking pot, Tawno saw the swelling of her breasts over the neckline of her white blouse. Wiping his mouth with the back of his hand, lascivious thoughts flooded his mind. With eyes narrowed, he wondered how Brandy-Joe had managed to ensnare and marry such a beauty.

He crouched beside his bundle whilst his mind raced with ideas of how to get the most from the situation. He took a clay pipe and a small tin containing tobacco from his waistcoat. Rolling a few strands of tobacco in the palm of his hand, he made a pellet and pushed it into the bowl, pushing it down with a thumb as hard as leather. With his eyes on Curlanda, he lit his pipe with a stick taken from the cooking fire.

Tawno knocked the ash out of the bowl and put his pipe away. The girl realised with some disquiet that he was in no hurry to leave.

"I can give you some hobben, but you must eat it quickly then be gone," she said. Passing him a pewter plate of hotchi-witchi stew, she asked, "Is your woman near?"

"A mile or so back down the road. She's been calling and hasn't caught up with me yet." His eyes stayed on her white blouse, imagining how her breasts would feel and wondering what excuse he could give for spending the night with her. The stew was good - as good as, if not better than Synfye's cooking.

"The day has been long. I'll stay a while and rest me bones under yonder tree." Smiling into her eyes, Tawno placed his empty plate on the ground. "Your rom's lucky to have a woman who can cook a hotchi-witchi so good. Best I've tasted for years," he said, rising to his feet.

Pleased by Tawno's compliment, she flicked back her long hair with both hands. The movement brought her breasts up high. Her earlier mistrust had vanished, and she smiled.

"My rom wouldn't like me to be inhospitable to his friend." She gestured towards the bender tent, built under a tree at the far side of the clearing. "Rest in there if you want, it's coming on to rain, I think."

As Tawno turned to look at the tent, he brushed against Curlanda. Quick as the spring of a tiger, he put his arm around the girl and pulled her to him. Lifting her onto his shoulder took only a heartbeat. He clutched one arm and her flailing legs tightly. She gave a piercing scream and struggled. Her fingernails raked the back of his coat and she tried to catch hold of his hair, but his scarlet bandanna covered most of his greasy locks.

He carried her inside the nearest tent and allowed Curlanda to slide to the ground. In a quick movement, he lifted her skirt and long petticoats, twisting them so that they were tight over her head. He took a length of cord from his coat pocket and swiftly wrapped around the girl's neck. He then knotted it around the skirt hem over her head. That rendered the girl powerless to use her hands to defend herself and partly stifled her screams as she tried to draw breath. She kicked at where she thought he was standing.

Curlanda was naked from the waist down, and with a vicious movement, Tawno pulled her to the ground and straddled her. He parted her legs and his breath came in quick, loud pants as he rhythmically rose and fell over her desperately struggling body.

Somehow, Curlanda felt the handle of the knife among her clothing and managed to remove it from its sheath. She repeatedly attempted to stab through her clothing at the man above, but was hampered by his weight. Tawno felt a sharp pain in his arm, and his eyes turned red and narrowed with hate when he saw the red stain on his sleeve.

"You bitch! You Lincolin, chikli whore. I'll have my revenge on all your kin for what they did to me and mine."

At each word, Tawno hit the hidden face of the girl with his fists until she lay quiet and still. Not content with his brutal actions, Tawno fetched a piece of firewood from the bonfire and began beating the unconscious girl until blood seeped through her garments and made a dark pool around her head.

Sweating and panting heavily, he stepped back and shook back his black hair from his eyes, then noticed his scarlet bandanna lying on the ground. When he saw that a corner was lying in the pool of blood surrounding the girl's head, his mouth twisted in distaste and he quickly stuffed it inside his pocket.

Keeping his eyes on the still body, Tawno backed towards the tent opening. He stopped when he thought he heard a movement and a soft moan. Staring at the still figure on the ground, Tawno hawked and spat.

"You'll not be cooking hotchi-witchi for anyone else. You're corbed!" he shouted before turning and leaving the tent.

Taking a deep breath, he looked around the clearing. He threw the piece of wood he'd used onto the cooking fire. The only sign of his presence was the empty pewter plate. Putting it under his arm, he retraced his steps around the camp, his eyes searching for any signs that might give Brandy-Joe a clue to the murderer. Only when Tawno was satisfied nothing in the camp could be found identifying him, he picked up his bundle and rejoined his dogs.

***

Brandy-Joe Lincolin and his cousin Cemake were astonished to find the cooking fire out, and no Curlanda hurrying forward to greet them with her usual welcoming smile. The men began to worry when their calls got no reply. When they noticed their dogs were acting strangely, standing close together, trembling and whining, the men looked at them in curiosity.

"Drat the woman. Where is she?" Brandy-Joe growled. He threw an empty sack on the ground and looked along the paths with a face like thunder. Women were supposed to be waiting for their husbands' return, willing and ready to attend to their needs.

"You did say two days. She's perhaps gone calling at them cottages we went past."

They turned towards the bender tent when they heard the thin cries of an infant.

"Listen. What's that? It's our tikni." said Brandy-Joe, striding towards the tent. The roaring sound he made when he found Curlanda's body terrified Cemake, his face drained of colour when Brandy-Joe staggered out of the tent holding his baby son, Jem.

"What is it? Is the tikni hurt?"

"She's mullered! Someone's done her in. Killed her dead. Yesterday, by the looks of the blood." Brandy-Joe's eyes bulged with shock. He trembled so badly that Cemake rushed forward to take Jem from his arms, fearing that the yelling baby might be dropped.

"What you mean?"

"Look for yourself."

With a hand that trembled, Cemake lifted the flap and

peered inside the tent. He saw something that, at first glance, seemed to be a bundle of rags on the ground.

"Strewth!" Still holding the baby, he backed away and joined Brandy-Joe in the clearing.

"You need a drink. We both need a drink. Come and sit under that oak tree," he said. Taking hold of his arm, Cemake led the dazed man across the clearing and made him sit facing away from the tent. Leaving the protesting baby on the ground next to his father, he hurried to where he had left his own few belongings, partly hidden under a bush. He always kept a bottle of whisky and he gave a sigh of relief on finding it still in his bundle.

Taking a mouthful of the spirit, Cemake wiped the bottle top with his hand before handing it to Brandy-Joe. The shocked man poured a generous amount down his throat. They sat a while without speaking. Brandy-Joe took another drink.

"Is... Is she in there alone? Any signs of who could have done it, or why?"

"I'll go in and have a proper look if you want. Stay there. I'll call if I want you."

At the sight of numerous beetles feeding on the congealed blood, Cemake's stomach heaved. Trying to ignore the stench of death, he pulled a blanket from a makeshift bed, and then half rolled and half pulled Curlanda's body onto the blanket. With tender care, he cut away the cord and pulled the stiffened garments from the girl's face. When he saw the damage done to her once beautiful features, he wished he hadn't looked. It was only when he pulled Curlanda's skirts down to cover her legs that he noticed the knife. After prising it from her fingers, he laid it on the ground beside her. A folded blanket was nearby, and he used it to cover the naked limbs before stumbling from the tent. He was just able to reach the bushes behind the tent before vomiting. It was a moment or two before he felt enough in control of himself to walk across the clearing and join Brandy-Joe.

"Any left?" Cemake said, pointing to the whisky.

Without a word, Brandy-Joe gave him the bottle.

Dropping to his knees, Cemake lifted it to his mouth and almost emptied it.

"She fought like a mad thing. The man must have been well marked. She had her knife out." Cemake spoke in short bursts, staring into the distance.

"She would. H-how?"

"Blows. I noticed a piece of partly burnt wood half in the ashes. Looks like it could have blood on it. Don't think owt's been disturbed. Just wanted her." Cemake nudged Brandy-Joe and passed the bottle back when he saw tears running down the man's face. "Tikni Jem must have been asleep. Good thing."

Brandy-Joe placed a hand gently on his son's head. At his father's touch, the baby began crying again.

"He must be hungry. Will you see if there's owt to feed him with? Good thing I've got you to help me look after him. I know nothing about small tiknies."

"We'll have to find the rest of the clan. The women will take care of him for you." They sat in silence until Jem's crying could not be ignored any longer. "Can you think who? Anyone been around her lately? Though I must say she never flaunted herself like some women do," Cemake said, rising to his feet.

With a shake of his head, Brandy-Joe covered his face with his hands and started sobbing. Cemake, finishing the last drop of whisky, threw the bottle to one side. Giving Brandy-Joe a sympathetic glance, he went to search for food suitable for a baby. There was some stew in the cooking pot, cold and congealed. Adding a drop of water, Cemake made a fire and heated the stew. He wondered who could have murdered Curlanda. Remembering her smile and wave as they left the camp yesterday, his emotions overcame him and he wept.

As gentle as a mother, Cemake fed Jem and dressed him in clean clothes. As he finished, Brandy-Joe rose to his feet and for a few minutes he stood looking at the baby. He spoke in a shaking voice.

"I'm going to bury her in the woods. She'll like that. Stay here with Jem and I'll come and fetch you when I'm ready."

Dazed with shock, Cemake picked up Jem and, cradling the baby in his muscular arms, he watched Brandy-Joe striding away among the trees carrying a short shovel.

"Your dai was a very special person. We'll never forget her. When we meet up with the family we'll tell them about all this and they'll find out who did it. Don't you worry, my little tikni, Kaka Cemake will look after you," he said.

Brandy-Joe dug Curlanda's grave under the branches of an elm tree, his rage giving power to each thrust of the spade. He took a long time to carve her name, Gypsy-fashion, deep into the bark of the tree that would shelter her.

With the birds singing an anthem, the two men buried Curlanda in the woods she had loved so much. They stood together with the baby lying on the ground at their feet. Shoulders shaking with their sobs, they gave silent prayers before returning to the camp. It was Cemake who gathered Curlanda's few belongings together and, his face an angry mask, Brandy-Joe set fire to them.

"I'll find out who did this if it takes all my life," Brandy-Joe said, watching the fire as it died into ashes.

It was Cemake who noticed that a pewter plate, which had been made by Brandy-Joe, was missing.

"Thought you had three plates," he called.

Brandy-Joe looked at his cousin with vacant eyes.

"Don't know. Curlanda sees to all that." Suddenly realising what he had said, he put a hand over his mouth and rubbed his stubbly chin.

"Don't matter. We have three cups so the tikni can be fed," Cemake said with a shrug. He dismantled the tent and packed their belongings into a wooden barrow; as usual, the Gypsy's barrow was covered over with an oiled canvas tilt tied securely in place with string.

They travelled south in easy stages, Cemake and Brandy-Joe took it in turns to carry Jem and reached the main campsite of the Lincolin tribe. When they arrived, their sombre expression spoke for them. The women gathered round, and loving arms took the baby from Brandy-Joe. The men then went to the chief's vardo. Brandy-Joe's knock brought the chief's romni to the door, and he told her he had sad news to tell. They were invited in, and, pulling a shawl over her head, the woman left them so that they could speak with the chief in private. They discussed Curlanda's death for some time before the chief, lying flat on his bed with a broken back, was carried from his vardo by his sons and set down near the fire. The elders were called together, and everyone offered condolences to the widower.

The chief lay so that the flames lit up Brandy-Joe and Cemake's every expression. As usual he was in charge of the family meeting. Brandy-Joe had asked for the baby to be returned to him, and sat holding Jem in his arms, leaving Cemake to relate the facts to the elders.

"Have you any idea who would do this? Do you have enemies? A Gaujo perhaps? You found no traces of a stranger?"

Brandy-Joe shook his head.

"I have thought and thought, but no one comes to mind. There was one person who might have done it, but the last time I saw him he was having a whipping, and if they didn't hang him he'll be in gaol for at least a year. I'd done no horse-trading anywhere near where we camped. Before we left, we both searched everywhere. We did find a bush near the road with a broken branch, but that could have been done by anything. No. Nothing. It's my fault; I broke the rules of the clan. I should never have left my romni without someone else there with her."

There was a long silence as everyone searched for some comforting words.

"You have a fine son, Joe Lincolin. Let him be your solace, and together make a fresh start," the chief said, gently.

Brandy-Joe looked down at the sleeping baby and sniffed back his tears.

"My Jem has the look of his mother. We will travel the roads together and I will care for him. Curlanda and I often spoke of his future. We'd planned for him to be an acrobat. When he's older he'll perform at country fairs, like she would have wanted." As he finished speaking, Brandy-Joe lifted the infant high in the air, before covering his little face with kisses.

Some of the younger women exchanged glances. Brandy-Joe was a strong and a good-looking man and had been an excellent husband. They thought that at some point, when his pain had healed a little, he might consider taking another wife. After all, they whispered to each other, a tikni needs a woman to care for it.

"I'll join you, Joe, if you'll let me." Cemake Lincolin placed his hand on Brandy-Joe's shoulder as he spoke. "I'm as much to blame as you for what happened to Curlanda."

"You are a true friend, cousin, but you have your own life. A woman is waiting to wed you, and you'll soon have tiknies of your own. No. When Jem is a little older we'll take the road together. But never will I give up the search for the one who did this foul deed. However long it takes I'll avenge my lovely Curlanda."

Chapter 11

Tawno felt no more remorse at killing Curlanda Lincolin than he would have felt at snaring and killing a bird or rabbit.

After leaving the woods and collecting his dogs, his only thoughts were of how he could leave the neighbourhood without being seen, either by Brandy-Joe Lincolin or any other Gypsies who might be in the area - or indeed by anyone who would remember his face.

At first, Tawno travelled in the direction of Stamford, after which he skirted around the market town of Newark. Sleeping by day and travelling at night, he moved stealthily but swiftly through woods, farmlands and villages. If he saw a pedlar or Gypsies of any clan, he hid until they were gone. Upon reaching the old Roman road, he planned to travel to Grantham and see if he could find some kind of work before making his way to Nottingham. He had a friend living near the town of Grantham whose line was house breaking and petty thievery. Although Tawno could not supply him with urchins on his visit, he thought his friend would probably be pleased to use his devious talents in some way that was profitable to them both.

When he reached the outskirts of Grantham, Tawno left

his dogs tied under a hedge and ordered them to guard his bundle. He walked with a swagger into the centre of the town and headed for a beer-house known for its tolerance towards people who made their money by illicit means.

It was a market day, and the pungent stench of animal waste rising from the penned beasts in the market place made many people's eyes water. Ignoring the stench and shouldering his way through the crowds, Tawno's eyes were never still; he peered constantly into shopping baskets, and was on the lookout to steal an unattended purse. He was unfortunate.

With his foot already on the doorstep of the beer-house, Tawno heard his name called in a husky whisper. Out of the corner of his eye, he saw Toby Selwyn's half crouching, half running movements as he hurried towards him. Placing a claw-like hand on Tawno's arm, Toby swiftly guided him inside the cobweb-trimmed beer-house, putrid with rat droppings and stale ale.

"Well met, friend," he croaked, fingering his scrawny throat. As child he had been half throttled by his father in a drunken rage.

They sat facing each other across a rickety and stained table. Eventually, Toby caught the attention of the busy serving wench and called for two tankards of ale.

Tawno scowled at his friend and said: "I was coming to find you, Toby. But I ain't used to having me name yelled out across the market place for everyone to hear."

Wiping his nose on his coat sleeve, Toby eyed the other people in the bar.

"Sorry friend," he muttered.

As the men waited to be served, Tawno's eyes shifted to the strangers in the smoke-filled room, hoping his presence had not been noticed. It had, but none of the other people there let it show, for they too were hoping to remain anonymous.

Ale was placed in front of the men and paid for by Toby, and then, with heads almost touching, they spoke in whispers.

"I hope you've brought me some more of your boys. The last lot were real good. Small, quick and didn't need a lot of victuals," Toby chuckled into his tankard.

"No. I 'as come..." Tawno's words broke off in mid-sentence as he felt his coat collar seized. At the same moment his companion's wrists were shackled and both men were lifted from their seats.

They both began to fight, but it was useless to struggle against the competent and professional parish officers who had been sent to arrest Toby and those associated with him.

Tawno was strong, but the constables were stronger. At three to one, the odds were stacked heavily against him escaping once his wrists were enclosed in manacles. He was affronted at being so roughly handled, and shouted abuse and threats when the men gripped his arms and dragged him outside. They bundled him into the waiting horse-drawn wagon and locked the grilled door. Tawno screamed obscenities at them, but the constables, used to such language, ignored him. Toby Selwyn had crawled across the dirty straw which covered the floor of the wagon, and lay in a corner moaning. Kneeling by the door, Tawno peered through the grills in an attempt to see where he was being taken. He grabbed hold of the bars. The horses lurched forward at the crack of the whip, and his head made sharp contact with the bars. He cursed out loud.

To avoid grinning urchins clinging to the outside of the wagon and poking sticks at him, he shrank into a corner and stayed next to Toby. His hands covered his head and he moaned aloud until the wagon stopped. Ignoring the shouts of 'Get a move on Gypsy, we ain't got all day,' he slowly crawled towards the door. Bile rose into his mouth when he saw the size of the building and the words 'County Gaol' set in stone above the strong iron gates which led to the prison yard. Tawno had heard grim stories about the magistrates in that place and the harsh punishments they handed out for minor offences.

Inmates jeered as Tawno and Toby, protesting loudly, were dragged across the exercise yard, through an arched doorway and into the debtors' cellblock. Stumbling up a flight of stairs, the men found themselves in the governor's office. Pushed forward, Tawno fell on his knees in front of an imposing wooden desk.

"Who have we here?" The man behind the desk wore black, which drew attention to his thin, pallid face. His stick-like fingers dipped a quill into an inkwell.

"A Gypsy sir; arrested in the company of Toby Selwyn."

"What have you to say for yourself, Gypsy?" the governor asked without lifting his eyes from the ledger in front of him.

Tawno shook his head in bewilderment.

"I don't know, I… I c-cannot think," he stuttered.

"I suggest you start with your name, fellow."

"Ardry, sir. Tawno Ardry. Why have I been brought here? I was having a quiet drink when this man came to sit with me. I don't know him. I was arrested with him and brought here."

"You will be detained until the facts of the matter can be resolved. Place the Gypsy in a lower cell. Food once a day."

As Tawno was hauled to his feet and taken from the governor's office, he tried to explain that a mistake had been made and that he was an honest tradesman, but the men holding him only grunted, escorted him down the stairs and pushed him inside a cell with a low ceiling.

Since the prison had been built, detainees using the smoke from lighted candles had written names, dates, and short messages on the ceiling. The light from the gaoler's lamp revealed one name overhead which was dated 1696.

Enough light filtered through the semicircular and iron-barred window for Tawno to be able to make out that he was in a narrow cell. A dozen or so men sat or stood chained to rings set into the walls at regular intervals.

As two gaolers held the struggling Tawno, a chain was fastened to the manacle on his left wrist and threaded through a ring on the wall; it was then attached to an iron fetter placed on his left ankle. The gaolers stood back examining their handiwork, and without speaking, left the cell.

For someone who was born as free as a bird to roam at will, to be locked in a small, stinking cell was the stuff of which nightmares are made. He could endure to be detained a day or so before a whipping, or to be placed in a set of village stocks, but the situation was different; it was serious.

Wide-eyed with panic, Tawno looked around at the other inmates. Everyone was filthy. They had obviously been there for months. The floor, treacherously slippery with slime and algae, was strewn with wisps of straw that did nothing for the comfort of the prisoners. The stench of the filth made him retch.

His fellow inmates looked dejected, and were silent apart from the occasional moan or a plea to God for release. From time to time, Tawno heard shouts and even laughter coming from somewhere outside, but those sounds were muted. He wondered where they had taken Toby, and thought it strange the man had not been brought to the same cell as him. Tawno was to hear later that Toby had been taken to the condemned cell and hanged the following week for his part in a robbery.

A wooden pail stood on the ground just out of reach of Tawno. He watched as a rat climbed up and balanced on the rim before falling inside. The rat reappeared. Sitting on the side of the pail, it shook droplets of water from itself and nonchalantly rubbed its whiskers with its front paws before scampering away.

"Anyone know you're here?" The man to the left of him turned his head as he spoke. Tawno was repulsed when he saw the man's eye sockets were empty.

"No," said Tawno. After testing the strength of his chains, he tried to ease himself into a more comfortable position as he crouched against the wall.

"Why do you ask?"

Tawno thought the man had not heard and opened his mouth to repeat himself when he spoke.

"If no one knows you're here, they can't pay to make you free," he chanted.

The hair on Tawno's neck lifted as he realised the man was probably insane. *Thank God he's chained and can't reach me,* he thought.

Allowing the back of his head to rest on the ring fastened to the wall, he closed his eyes, desperately trying to think of some way to get out of that dreadful place. A deep groan escaped him as the realisation of his terrible plight sank in. No one, not one person, friend foe or family, knew of his whereabouts.

The day dragged and gradually the dim light faded into darkness. Tawno was pleased when a couple of the prisoners lit a stub of tallow candle, which gave off a comforting glow.

"When do they bring us food?"

Giving a chuckle, the blind man turned his head towards Tawno.

"They will bring whatever you wish for, but only if you pay."

"I've nothing to pay with. The turnkey kept my coat and emptied my pockets as soon as they brought me through the inner gates. His excuse was that it would pay for my transport."

"You were lucky. Some are whipped through the streets or put in the pillory first." The statement came from the other side of Tawno. Turning, he saw a man wearing the shreds of a silk shirt.

"My name is Rafferty, sir. Pleased I am to make the acquaintance of another gentleman of the road, such as yourself." The man spoke in an exaggerated and cultured tone, which at any other time would have made Tawno spit with irritation. Gypsies thought of those travellers as socially below them, a nomadic group made up of various vagabonds and thieves.

Giving a nod to the skeletally thin man, Tawno settled back to listen to his story. It was sad. During the following hour or two, between bouts of coughing, Rafferty related how it was that he had come to be in the prison. With a sinking heart, Tawno realised that the man's situation was similar to his own. He turned to face the blind man.

"How long have you been imprisoned, old man?" Tawno said, taking the long, white beard to be a sign of advancing years.

"When I was arrested I was twenty-two, and I was desperately ill with a fever when I arrived here. Not long after I arrived, the rats took my eyes as I lay chained and helpless. Now I'm thirty and pray for death, but my body is strong, for others go and I stay."

Tawno had no words of comfort to offer to a man whose sorrows seemed to be greater than his own; he knew that he would eventually face a court hearing and be able to plead for mercy.

"Bread is brought to us each morning. Eat a little and save some to barter with, unless you know your visitors will bring you food. That way you will keep your strength. The water in yonder bucket must last us the week. Visitors bring it to us."

"I saw a rat go into it, then run off. No one should drink it now."

134

Gilded Wagons

The blind man grinned widely, showing toothless gums.

"Gypsy here won't drink after a rat has had a pee in the water," he called out loudly.

Laughter rippled around the cell as they enjoyed the thought of a dirty Gypsy turning up his nose at drinking the life-giving water. A man chained at the far end of the cell called,

"You'll be pleased to lick the slime from the floor Mr Gypsy, if this new gaoler takes you in dislike. Don't do to cross this one. Call him sir. Give him whatever he asks for, and for goodness sake don't answer back. If you can get to your feet, bow." Chains clanked on the stones as the man added, "Look out, here he comes."

Tawno made no reply. He knew from past experience how to conduct himself in the presence of gaolers. He looked towards the solid, metal-studded door and heard the rattle of keys and squeaking bolts. The prisoners remained silent and kept their eyes lowered until the gaoler, swinging a whip, had passed them by. They watched intently as the man made his way to where Tawno was crouching.

"Well, gentleman Gypsy, what can I do for you?" Removing a shapeless cloth cap, the bandy-legged man sketched a bow then stood with his head tilted on one side. He held a candle lamp in such a way that the light made Tawno screw up his eyes and turn his head. The man, pleased he had made the Gypsy uncomfortable, grinned through his unkempt beard.

"How long will I have to stay here?" Tawno remembered the other prisoners' advice, and quickly added, "Sir."

"Are you trying to tell me that you haven't been locked up before, Gypsy?"

When he saw how Tawno hung his head, the gaoler added. "Until a person has been brought before the court no one leaves. If they are lucky they're found not guilty. Ask this lot here." The gaoler jerked his head in the direction of the other prisoners, who quickly lowered their eyes. "If you want something, Gypsy, I might be able to get it for you."

"I've no money," Tawno said in a flat voice.

"Your waistcoat will buy a blanket and a nice piece of cheese for your supper. Yer neckerchief will buy a pint of ale."

Keeping his gaze fixed on the gaoler; Tawno slowly undid his neckerchief and handed it to the man. It had been rinsed in a stream and the bloodstains were no longer visible on the red cotton.

"I would like to keep my waistcoat tonight, sir, if you please."

Unsure if Tawno was being sarcastic, the gaoler gave him a hard stare.

"I'll bring your ale - later."

Letting out a long breath, Tawno watched the gaoler move away. The cell door clanged shut and a babble of voices began calling out advice.

'Get him to take your chains off! Tell him you want a room upstairs! You can have more than one visitor when you have a room next to the yard! Spend some time in the day room! It is better to live in that part of the prison!' Waiting until the men had finished calling suggestions to Tawno, the blind man spoke in a soft voice.

"Only buy and sell what is a necessity. Better rooms will not fill your belly or quench your thirst."

Laying his throbbing head back against the wall, Tawno closed his eyes in order to consider what action or story would benefit him most. He thought about Synfye and the children, and wondered if she had found Culvato. His brother was his only hope, but if he could not get a message to him, there would be no help from that quarter. Perhaps he could strike a deal of some sort with the gaoler; or maybe a prisoner who was allowed outside the prison during daylight hours would help him in return for his boots. Suddenly, his hand went to a concealed pocket in his waistcoat. He relaxed when he felt his pack of cards, but then looked with dismay at his wrists, which were already raw from the chafing of the manacles. It would be difficult to cheat at cards without his usual dexterity.

***

Three weeks later, Tawno wore only his breeches and shirt. His body was filthy, and the sores on his wrists were swollen with puss. He had grown a beard that was as wild as his unkempt hair. When he moved, the chains attached to his ankles rattled on the stone floor. So as to be ready for court the following day, Tawno had been moved to a different cell, and the wall behind him was green with damp. The slime on the ground had stained his breeches beyond recognition.

Through half-closed eyes he saw a young woman walking towards him. With an expression of distaste she lifted her skirts to prevent sullying them.

"I was told my brother was in here, perhaps you know of him? Jonas Bigsby?" she said in a voice soft with concern. "He was playing cards with some friends in Grantham when he was arrested."

"Food. Have you brought food?" Tawno asked, holding out both hands and giving her a pleading look.

She took an apple and a piece of cheese from her basket, and silently handed them to him. She watched Tawno bite into the apple. Her eyes widened as she noticed he only ate half the cheese, putting the remainder inside the waistband of his breeches. Glancing at her, he gave a slight smile.

"I can sell that for water. They put the bucket too far away for us to help ourselves."

"Can I get you some water? Have you a cup?" The girl

stared and stepped back as Tawno gave a bitter laugh.

"You have to pay for everything here, even for a loan of a cup."

"I… I have a farthing. Will that be enough?"

"Give it to me, girl."

Passing it to him and then quickly stepping back, she stared wide eyed as Tawno placed the coin inside his mouth.

"What did you say your brother's name was?"

"Jonas. Jonas Bigsby."

"And what's your name?"

"Soult. Charlotte Soult. My husband is waiting outside."

"They carried a dead fellow out of here yesterday. Think his name was Bigsby. Said he'd play cards with the gaolers. Teach them new tricks."

Tawno closed his eyes. He was too tired to explain why the man had been beaten until he had died, but at least the apple and cheese would keep him alive for another day.

Three weeks in a stinking prison had done nothing for Tawno's temper, and he presented a sullen figure when he was brought in leg irons and chained wrists before the justices. He stumbled up the few steps to the courtroom and stood looking towards those he regarded as being pompous, legal bureaucrats. His heart sank. Not one friendly face.

"Name?" a clerk called across the courtroom.

"Tawno Ardry. A travelling merchant, your honour." Bowing low, Tawno's eyes roved over the seated men facing him.

Silence fell in the courtroom as the judge studied the papers on his desk.

"You say you know nothing about the man called Toby Selwyn, but you were in his company drinking when he was arrested."

"I had only just arrived in town Monday midday and

was quenching my thirst before making my way towards Nottingham, your honour."

Wringing his hands, Tawno tried to convince the judge of his innocence, but he looked a sorry figure; unshaven, with shabby clothes and unwashed, shoulder length hair. His waistcoat had been exchanged for a crust and a cup of ale when he couldn't ignore his hunger pangs any longer.

"A silver snuffbox was found on your person. Where was that from?"

"It's mine. I won it in a card game. Years ago, it's always with me." Biting his lip, Tawno silently cursed Ben the urchin for stealing the snuffbox.

"Was the box claimed by the person bringing the charges?" The judge asked, turning to others in the courtroom. When he heard no one had laid claim to the snuffbox, the judge coughed. He looked sternly across the crowd of sweating people at the back of the court and shook the feather end of his quill pen at Tawno.

"You are a villain, fellow. Although you lay claim to the snuffbox, you also had a pipe and tobacco in your possession. I notice you give me no good reason why you are in this town. I order you to be transported to the colonies for ten years."

Tawno clutched hold of the nearest thing, which fortunately was a stout rail, to steady him and prevent his legs from giving way.

"But, sir. I have nothing to do with the man called Selwyn!" he yelled, in despair. "You haven't heard what I have just said. I'm innocent of the charges. You can't send me away, I'm no choramengro, you stupid rokkeramengro."

Tawno's face was red with rage, and he shook his fist at the judge. He thought it so unfair to sentence him for something he knew nothing about. A constable held Tawno's left arm tightly as the Gypsy leaned over the rails surrounding the dock. Although the judge didn't understand everything Tawno shouted at him, he certainly knew that it wouldn't be complimentary.

"I give that man two extra years for disrupting the court. Put him down for twelve years in the colonies. Hard labour," the judge said. "That will rid the town of one vagabond," he muttered to a learned gentleman on his right.

Yelling and struggling to free himself as he was led away was futile. The gaolers returned him to his old cell, but this time they shackled him to a wooden post in the centre. They left with Tawno sprawled on the ground with his head singing from a well-aimed kick.

***

A while after he had left them, a family of travellers found Tawno's dogs still guarding his bundle. They recognised the faithful animals, but couldn't find anyone who had seen Tawno in the town. After a few days, the family travelled on. They took possession of the bundle with the intention of giving it to Synfye when they next met up with her.

Within a month, Tawno was led onto a sailing ship. Before going down to the stinking hold, he took one last look at the sky over England.

"I'll return. When I do I'll get my revenge on you mochadi, riffli Lincolin tribe. The musgros have got me now, but I'm not corbed with you yet not by a long way. Just wait and be atrashed!" he yelled, before the man shackled to him from behind pushed him down the steep wooden steps.

Chapter 12

For years, people remembered the spring of 1796. Culvato's two show booths and his tents were torn to pieces by the gales. His gathering of stalls and amusements included a caged lion and other supporting acts, and he always employed a local casual workforce to help his small travelling army of tent men.

The fair was set out on a village green on the outskirts of Doncaster. Whirling leaves and twigs danced in the storm. Ursula and the children were in the vardo, listening to the sounds outside. They relaxed a little when they thought the wind had dropped and the worst was over, and then, there was an almighty crash. A gnarled tree had fallen on top of the largest wagon; its impact spread, rocking nearby vehicles. They listened to the cracking and lashing of the trees and the pounding of the rain on the roof and windows, and they cried out and clung together as their vardo shuddered.

"My goodness, what a storm it is! We must get out of here or we'll all be killed! Hold each other's hands tightly, keep your heads down and follow me!" Ursula ordered. It took only a moment to close the doors of the vardo. She did her best to protect the children as they leaned into the wind and battled their way to a thick beech hedge. They crouched in its shelter under the flailing twigs.

The caged lion roared, but the noise was lost amidst the general turmoil. Strings of coloured flags fluttered wildly along the peaks of the grey tents and show booths, before breaking free and disappearing across the field.

The tent men glanced at the low clouds scudding across the leaden sky as they battled to stay upright, they were grim and apprehensive. The storm threatened to destroy everything; the canvas tents repeatedly bellied, resembling ships' sails.

Against the wind, Culvato called to men who were unable to hear properly, but they saw his frantically waving arms, watched him mouthing words and understood his meaning.

"Don't bloody stand there looking daft! Shift yourselves! Everything will get blown to bits if we don't do something quick! Get more ropes fixed to those tents over there, and peg them other ropes down better or they won't hold!" Culvato yelled.

Every man on the campsite joined in the frenzied attempt to anchor the tents securely. For a while it seemed the ropes would hold, but the canvas continued to billow and creak alarmingly. Suddenly, the largest tent gave way.

"Bloody hell, get out of it!" The men sprang to safety, as the ropes broke free and snapped. Razor-sharp whip-lashing ropes missed them by inches and explosive retorts made them flinch. Almost immediately, support beams and rafters gave way and the other tents collapsed. A huge piece of torn canvas sailed across the field.

"We ain't paid enough to be heroes!" one man shouted as he raced away across the field.

Standing in the driving rain, hair and clothes dripping wet, Culvato watched helplessly as one by one the tents ripped apart and collapsed, some onto important and expensive equipment. Through angry tears, he saw the children's ride lifted and blown over.

"We can't take any more of this. We'll have nothing left." Culvato could hardly keep his footing in the wind, and it spun him round. In a state of despair he fought his way across the field and saw his family crouched under the beech hedge. Ursula didn't speak as he threw himself down next to her and the children. More than an hour passed, and then, clutching the lapels of his coat together, Culvato rose to his feet and stared at the ruined fairground that used to be his thriving business.

"The wind isn't so strong now. At least you're all safe and both the vardos are still standing. I wish I could say the same for the bloody tents. I heard some poles snap. Good thing Big Bill didn't break." Culvato was referring to the main pole set in the centre of the largest tent, thick as a ship's mast and painted sealing-wax red. Without Big Bill there would not be an indoor arena. "Not a damn tent left standing. Everything's ripped to shreds. Nowt can be done here, we'll have to leave. I don't think anyone's been hurt, thank goodness. I'll get the men to clear up what we can, and in the morning we'll move on. We can stop a while on the Doncaster campsite. I should be able to buy enough new canvas in the town."

"Look at our chavvies' ride. It's ruined, Rom," said Ursula, tearfully.

"Don't be upset, Dai," said Lionel. He stood close and held his mother's hand tightly to his chest.

"We'll help Dadrus build another one," Hugo said, pulling on her sleeve.

Culvato pointed across the field to where a group of men stood together, gesturing and staring at the devastation around them.

"Go and tell the tent men to catch them silly grais and tether them over there, you chavvies. They'll bolt and be lost to us if they ain't soon caught and tied up safe."

Once the worst of the storm was over, it felt like a great adventure to the children. Both boys, with the triplets close behind, ran with bare feet sliding in the mud to join the fairground men.

Culvato moved closer to Ursula. His expression was grim.

"We didn't have a very good night's takings with the weather being so bad. If we aren't careful we'll lose all our fortune, and more besides," he said.

"I've still some of the old gold jewellery and a bit of that money. That'll see us through bad times if we need it."

"Ah. Well, we'll see. Keep everything safe, Romni. Maybe I'll be able to manage without spending it. I've still got some money we've earned hidden behind the panel."

Ursula and Culvato were so intent on their conversation that when Synfye and Piramus walked up to them, they were startled.

"This is a fine state of affairs. Nothing left," said Synfye.

"Don't be stupid, woman. Only needs a bit of new canvas and a bit of wood. Your trouble is that you would rather be off travelling than earning an honest penny," Piramus said, throwing Synfye a look like thunder. "Allus got a down-turned word to cheer a body up," he grumbled.

Ursula turned away so that the others wouldn't see her tears, and Synfye called over her shoulder that she was going to see if the fire was still alight. Tossing her dishevelled hair back off her face, she hurried in the direction of her vardo.

The old man had seen the agony on his nephew's face and he put his hand on his shoulder in comfort as they walked across the field together. "Shame her rom doesn't get here and take her in hand. A hazel switch across her backside would soon curb her tongue," he muttered.

Together, the men walked around the site and surveyed the

damage. Noticing how the workmen were finding it difficult to round up the animals, Culvato went to help them. His boots squelched in the mud and he nearly lost his footing as he struggled to grab hold of the reins of a couple of mares which were rearing up with eyes rolling. Around the edge of the field, some women were tugging tilts into place over their bender tents, searching for washing blown off the hedges by the wind or trying to make order inside their homes.

With a quick look at the children's ride as she went past it, Ursula returned to her living wagon and found Synfye on her knees, blowing on the embers to try and rekindle their cooking fire. Ursula sniffed back tears.

"Is there any fire left? I'd have thought it would have gone out," she said.

"I put that big flat stone over it before the worst of the rain came down," Synfye replied. She nodded towards a flat boulder with a hole in the centre, which she used as a brake when her caravan had to negotiate a steep hill. "This should burn now. We'll be needing plenty of warm water to wash the mud off the chavvies, and the men will be grateful for a hot meal when they've finished packing the wagons." Rising to her feet, Synfye jerked her head to where Culvato and children were watching the ride being pulled upright. The two women stood a moment, waiting to see if Culvato needed their assistance, and then, with a sigh, Ursula collected a bucket and went to fetch water from the overflowing stream. She frowned when she found the stream cloudy with silt; the water would need to be sieved through fine muslin before they could use it. *The triplets can do that when they come off the field. It will wash some mud off their legs and feet,* she thought.

On returning to the cooking fire, Ursula was cheered to see that flames were beginning to lick around some dry wood. The women always stored a small amount of kindling and wood in their vardos for an emergency such as this.

With the weather turning the roads into quagmires, Culvato knew the importance of beginning their journey no later than five o'clock the following morning. They were able to make a temporary repair to the wagon damaged by the fallen tree, and it was usable for carrying light items, if driven carefully. After standing overnight loaded with equipment, most of the carts and wagons were up to their axles in mud. It took nearly four hours and a great deal of shouting and cursing, in several languages, to persuade teams of horses to pull each vehicle onto firmer ground and out into the lane. Slowly, the field emptied.

On their arrival at the Doncaster campsite, they found only a small number of Gypsies living in bender tents. That left plenty of room for Culvato's entourage. He chose the firmest available piece of ground to park his caravan and wagons.

Piramus guided his pair of horses, which were pulling the largest flat wagon, to a halt beside the caravan. The horses were tired and sweating after pulling not only their own load, but extra equipment from the wagon which had been broken in the storm. Yelling encouragement and with a great deal of slapping of reins on the backs of their horses, Ben, with Hugo seated beside him, brought his wagons up. They formed a semicircle, with Synfye's vardo parked at one end and Culvato's vardo at the other.

Ursula drove the wagon containing the lion and parked it behind their caravan, making sure to leave it far enough away for the stench of the animal not to be a problem. By the time the camp was established, the rain had ceased but it was mid-afternoon before Culvato returned for a meal.

"I'm going into Doncaster when I've finished eating. Uncle Piramus and Ben will come with me. I'll have to buy miles of new rope and sheets of new canvas to remake the show tents. We'll take the big flat wagon to carry everything," he said, taking a plate of broth from Ursula and making himself comfortable on the caravan steps.

"Will they be able to sell you enough canvas and rope?" Ursula asked as she ladled broth onto other plates and handed them to the children.

"If there's not enough in Doncaster, I'll go back to Chesterfield tomorrow and buy what I need from there. I'll tell some of the men to cut down a tall tree or two whilst I'm away. Some poles snapped during the storm, and they will need replacing. Good thing Big Bill and the bale ring didn't get damaged. Would have been months before we could get them replaced. As it is, it will be weeks before the tent men can get the canvas stitched together and oiled."

When Culvato had left for town, Ursula and Synfye wandered around the campsite. They found people that they knew living in the bender tents, and both women indulged in a good gossip and caught up with news about relatives and events.

As usual, Synfye asked the question: Had anyone heard anything of the whereabouts of Tawno? They listened politely but they shook their heads and looked at her with pitying eyes. Although years had passed, they remembered Tawno's reputation, and guessed that he had either been hanged or lay buried somewhere with his throat cut. With a careless shrug, Synfye glanced across the field. She stared with interest to where a bald-headed man with a big moustache had set up a portable smithy. Lifting a heavy iron bar onto the anvil, the blacksmith hammered the red hot metal until its two ends met. With eyes half closed, Synfye watched his big shoulder muscles ripple as he worked. Moistening her lips and tugging her bodice down to emphasise her breasts, she felt the stirring of curiosity and wondered who the stranger could be - and, more importantly, if he had a romni.

Ursula was deep in conversation with a friend, and so Synfye nudged her to attract her attention and pointed towards the half naked blacksmith.

"You know him?"

"No. Never seen him before," Ursula said, after a cursory glance at the man.

The other woman, frowning at Synfye's rudeness, shook her head and turned her back on her.

Ursula noticed that even though Synfye had moved away, her attention was still fixed upon the blacksmith. Ursula did not intend to get involved with whatever Synfye was planning. She finished her conversation, headed back to the vardo, and called the triplets to join her.

"Get your baskets, girls, and we'll go and gather some herbs," she said.

Ursula took the girls to a piece of common land where she knew an assortment of wild herbs grew in abundance. They spent a happy hour or so gathering them. She would dry some and keep them in small, decorated boxes; the remainder of the herbs would flavour their evening meal.

After leaving Ursula, Synfye watched the man from a distance for a while before walking to the far side of the field. As she moved nearer to the man, she swung her hips in a provocative manner, and, keeping away from the smoking furnace, she gave the blacksmith a flirtatious smile.

"We haven't met before," she said, in a throaty voice.

The man glanced briefly in Synfye's direction. Many women had thought they could charm him with a smile. Without answering, he grabbed hold of a trailing rein and helped his young son, who was having trouble bringing a piebald mare to a halt.

"Whoa! Whoa there, rakli. Come on, then. Quiet there. No

need to fret. Whoa." With a practised hand, the blacksmith calmed the mare and stood stroking her nose. He threw a stern look at Jem, who had grown into a self-confident boy.

"Too big for you to handle, I've told you before to fetch me when big grais like this need bringing in."

Jem smiled into his father's face.

"Feet are a mess, Dadrus. The man said can you do owt with her?"

Running a hand down the mare's leg, Brandy-Joe placed each hoof in turn between his knees and cleaned out the accumulated muck before examining it.

"Right. They are a mess. Take a lot of working on." Letting the mare put her foot to the ground, Brandy-Joe stood back, assessing her. He had seen the mare before. The family who owned her loved and treated the mare like a valuable member of their family. "Worth doing. Few weeks rest, new shoes, yes. Tell him yes."

With a click of his tongue, the boy led the mare away. Brandy-Joe paid keen attention to the way it walked.

"I've got a grai," said Synfye with a smile.

"Good for you." Brandy-Joe didn't look in her direction.

"It needs shoeing." Synfye fluttered her eyelashes.

"Get your rom to bring it over. What's his name?" Brandy-Joe moved towards his anvil and picked up a hammer.

"I haven't got a man now. I was married to Tawno Ardry."

The hammer dropped to the ground. Brandy-Joe's thick eyebrows met as he frowned at Synfye, who tried to look sad. *Wait long enough and you'll find an answer to everything,* he thought.

Trying to look unconcerned, Brandy-Joe picked up the hammer.

"Where was he when you last saw him?"

"Melton Mowbray, years ago. Should have met us in Eastwood, but he never turned up and we ain't seen or heard from him since."

"Us?"

"Me chavvi, Seth. We travel with Tawno's brother, Culvato." Synfye pointed to the gilded caravans and the covered lion cage, upon the side of which was painted 'Ardry Menagerie'.

Brandy-Joe's face was expressionless as he looked across the field. He had met Culvato. *Who would have thought a nice man like that could have a rotten brother like Tawno.*

"I'll see to your grai later. I've other things to do first," he said putting down his hammer. Brandy-Joe, using a large pair of leather bellows, intensified the heat of the fire.

Synfye waited until the coals glowed in the hope that he would speak to her again. When it became obvious he was too preoccupied to spend time in idle chatter, she tossed her head and turned on her heel. Hoping the blacksmith was watching, she swung her hips as she returned to her caravan. Lifting her skirts high to show a narrow band of lace on her petticoat, she climbed the steps and seated herself next to Seth.

"Who's that, Dai?"

"Petalengro. He's coming over to see our grai later."

"What's his name, Dai?"

"Don't know. Seems nice enough, got a chavvi about your age." With a smile playing on her lips, Synfye moved inside the caravan and began to comb her hair.

***

Now the triplets were older, they were allowed to play with other Gypsy children as long as they stayed within Ursula's sight. The girls never walked when they could run and enjoyed doing acrobatics to impress other children.

"How do you do it?"

Heather did a back flip, and, showing off, followed it by

doing a number of flick flacks. She ended up standing in front of the Gypsy boy who had asked the question.

"We are cricked every morning by our dadrus."

"What's that? Cricked?"

"He puts my chest to his chest and pulls my legs up. My heels have to touch me head."

"Ner," the boy said, his voice filled with scorn.

Hugo and Lionel, who were never far away from their sisters, pushed Heather to one side and stepped forward.

"We'll show you, look."

Placing his hands around his brother's neck, Lionel allowed Hugo to lift his feet up so that they rested on his shoulders.

"Me dadrus does it to us every night before bed," Hugo said.

"Do it hurt?" a little girl asked.

"Not now, used to," Rose called from her perch on Lilly's shoulders.

"Why is your hair that colour?" another Gypsy boy asked. All the children had dark hair like Hugo and Lionel, in sharp contrast to the triplet's wheat-coloured locks.

The other children stared at the sisters who jumped to the ground and stood close together, holding hands. Hugo and Lionel were shoulder to shoulder in front of the girls, facing the boy who had spoken.

"They are like that so they can do acrobatic tricks better than anybody else." Hugo and Lionel clenched their fists in readiness for a fight. On seeing their combined defiance, the boy backed away.

Thinking the children were playing happily together, Ursula had returned to her vardo. After cleaning and putting some of her fresh herbs into the cooking pot, she sat on the top step of the vardo with a cushion on her lap, twisting and spinning the threads on her bobbins to make lace. Suddenly,

151

she became aware of shouting and laughter coming from the far side of the camp. She craned her neck to see who or what could be causing such a commotion.

"Hello those in the camp! May we enter?"

Ursula gasped in surprise when a man, dressed in a shabby blue velvet coat and a tricorne hat trimmed with nodding feathers, walked towards her on stilts. A woman wearing extra-long skirts accompanied him. She was also walking on stilts. Behind them came a young girl, leading a donkey laden with panniers and wearing a battered straw hat with holes for its ears to poke through. All the children in the camp and most of the adults had gathered and surrounded the strangers. From where she sat, Ursula noticed Synfye leaning against her caravan door, watching every move the new family made and eying them suspiciously.

The couple on stilts stood looking at everyone for a moment.

"Make room! Make space for me to come down," the man called. He lifted first one leg then the other to scatter the children. Dogs ran around barking, and everyone stepped back and watched the man and woman leap gracefully to the ground. Holding his stilts and grinning broadly, the man swept his dingy hat from his head, turned on his heel and bowed and winked at the children.

It was clear from her expression that the excited questioning from the children pleased the woman. Lifting her extra-long skirts, she draped the folds over her arm. The woman answered the children in a melodious and cultured voice. Ursula viewed the woman with interest, for she had been thinking for some time about hiring a person to tutor her children - especially the triplets, whose future was unpredictable.

She was concerned about the triplets; their skin had none of the swarthiness of the Gypsies. In spite of living out of doors, their skin, although honey coloured, remained soft and smooth. Their fairness could not be hidden, and they were showing signs of an inborn sophistication, noticeably when they ate. She knew Culvato had no intention of liberating them to a different life. He looked upon them as his daughters, and in fact he was overprotective. With a start, Ursula realised she was being addressed.

"We are looking for Mr Culvato Ardry. We heard he might be here," the man said, in a booming voice. He had guessed rightly that the imposing gilded caravan belonged to the showman. He was looking across the heads of the children, and as his eyes met those of Ursula, he gave her a candid smile.

"Who are you? What do you want with Mr Ardry?" Hugo asked. When his father was away from the camp, he was the eldest male in the Ardry family and in charge. Hugo would not reveal whether his father was in the camp or not until he knew who the strange people were and was sure that they hadn't brought trouble to the family.

"We heard Mr Ardry was looking for a good stilt-walking entertainer," the man said, holding his carved wooden stilts away from the fingers of the curious children.

"You are welcome in our camp, stranger. State your business with us." Standing on the top step of her vardo, Ursula looked at the stilt-walking family, and with a quick glance at Hugo, inclined her head.

"We are the Lovells, lady. I heard from a traveller that Mr Ardry could use a class act on stilts. We juggle and do acrobatics." Removing his hat again, Mr Lovell gave a low bow as he finished speaking. Ursula judged him to be about thirty. His wife, much younger, rose from a graceful curtsy. Holding his hat over his heart, Mr Lovell continued: "We'll be on our way to the town, to perform in the streets there if we have been incorrectly informed. But my child, Belle, is tired, and before we go, we beg your permission to rest where no one can steal our few belongings."

Ursula studied the family. They were not Gypsies and were both well spoken. They didn't appear to have anything but their donkey worth stealing.

"Times are hard, Mr Lovell. 'Tis the only way some can keep from starving in these difficult days. You may camp, friend. My man will be back directly. He is chief here and will decide if you stay or go."

Exchanging a warning glance with Synfye, who had moved nearer to listen and was quite capable of speaking out roughly to Gaujo strangers, Ursula settled herself down on the step again. Replacing her cushion on her lap, she continued working on her lace.

Although her fingers were busy, Ursula was fully aware of the Lovell family making themselves comfortable.

Sitting on the thick roots of a gnarled hawthorn tree, Mrs Lovell spread a cloth over the grass. She had taken food from one of the panniers and set it out on plates while her daughter, Belle, carried a jug to the riverbank to fetch water.

After the family had eaten their meal and were rested, Mr Lovell took hold of Belle and began to crick her. He took hold of the child's arm and bent it back until she cried out in pain. Each limb was treated in the same manner. When he had finished, Mr Lovell pulled the weeping child to him, and with her chest resting against his stomach, he took hold of the child's ankles and pulled her feet up until they touched the back of her head. He did that a dozen times before he let the child rest.

Weeping bitterly, Belle moved slowly to her mother's open arms where each painful muscle was massaged with scented oil. The Gypsy children had gathered around the Lovell family to watch. The Ardry girls, ignoring Belle's cries, did flick flacks and turned cartwheels. At the same time, Lionel and Hugo juggled and tossed four hoops to each other in a rapid succession. When Belle stopped crying, the triplets drew her away from her mother and sat rubbing her joints while telling her about their own training. Some Gypsy girls who had been watching began to weep in sympathy, and a young boy ran to tell his mother what was happening.

Watching from the caravan steps, Ursula nodded with approval. Her own children had had to suffer the same treatment since babyhood in order to become supple enough to do tumbling acts gracefully.

***

The sun lay low in the sky when Culvato returned home. Ursula hurried to remove his hat and coat, and, placing food on the table in the vardo, she waited to hear whether or not his hunt for new canvas and ropes had been successful. Culvato had almost finished eating when he jerked his head in the direction of the Lovell family. He seldom missed anything unusual happening in the camp, and he had noticed their small campfire.

"Who are they, Romni?"

"They arrived looking for you, not long after you left. Their name is Lovell. Strolling players; stilt walkers with a rakli. Said they would work their act in the town if you couldn't use them. That's all I know, Rom."

As she finished speaking, the couple heard a knock on the door. Piramus smiled broadly when Ursula's eyes widened in amazement. The bald, broad-shouldered man with a drooping moustache was beside him, dwarfing the old man. It was the blacksmith Synfye had admired across the field. Culvato invited both men into the caravan as Ursula slipped outside to find her children.

***

A wisp of smoke rose from under a tin can containing dye made from mint roots. Lilly and Rose knelt beside Heather as Hugo and Lionel used a bunch of crushed twigs to stroke the dye onto Heather's hair.

"If you don't keep still it'll show light streaks and look a mess," Hugo warned.

A mutinous glint shone in Heather's eyes and her bottom lip stuck out. "Don't care. I'm not having folk say we ain't Romani," she muttered.

All the children sprang to their feet when they heard Ursula's gasp of horror.

"What on earth?" She pulled Heather towards her and lifted her soaking tresses with trembling fingers. She knew immediately why the children were trying to change their appearance.

"They said we wasn't Romani because we weren't black like the others, but we are, ain't we, Dai?" said Heather.

"You are what God made you, and trying to change yourselves by doing this is wicked."

With dismay, Ursula saw the dye was running down Heather's face and staining her clothes. Both the boys' hands were stained brown. She glanced at Rose and Lilly and gave a sigh of relief. They hadn't yet been in contact with the boiled herbs.

"I should whip you all for doing such a foolish thing! Hugo, you're the eldest and should have known better. Get over to the river you boys, and wash it off your hands. I shall whip you both later. Heather, you come with me. We'll go to Synfye's

156

vardo and try and wash it out of your hair before your dadrus sees you."

Ursula and Synfye used soft soap on Heather's hair and face until the child screamed with pain, but the dye was stubborn, and refused to be washed away.

"I had best go back to the vardo or Culvato will wonder where I am," Ursula said, looking at the tearful child. "I don't know what he'll say to you, chai."

Synfye grinned.

"Leave her here tonight. We'll have another go at getting rid of the stains tomorrow."

"Bed." said Ursula, firmly catching hold of Lilly, who was trying to hide behind Heather. Rose held onto Hugo and together with Lionel, who walked on his hands, they followed their mother across the field and into the caravan. The four children sat silently in a row as Ursula was introduced to the bald-headed stranger. If Culvato missed Heather, he made no comment.

"This is Brandy-Joe, Romni. He's joining our band, travelling as a strong man, fire-eater and petalengro. His chavvi, Jem, will work with him. He's outside with their forge."

Spitting on his palm, Culvato slapped Brandy-Joe's upturned hand. This would be a binding agreement for Culvato to employ Brandy-Joe until they broke up by mutual consent.

Ursula warmly welcomed the man, who was the same height as her when he was seated. A blacksmith would be a very useful addition to the fair and for him to have a young son was an added bonus.

"I work alone when I practice my fire eating, safer that way. My Jem helps me work the smithy, and he's a good acrobat." Rising to his feet, Brandy-Joe peered through the window into the near darkness. "Getting late to build a bender tent."

'You can share the space under my flat wagon. It's dry

and I've put down clean straw. Plenty of room for everyone," Piramus said, opening the door of the vardo.

***

Following both men outside, Culvato called good night before walking across the field towards the hawthorn tree.

Mr Lovell sprang to his feet and wiped the palms of his hands down the side of his trousers when he saw Culvato coming towards him. He had seen the Gypsy chief return from the town, and had watched the three men leave the caravan.

"Good evening, sir. Name is Lovell, sir. We, that is I, wondered if we could join your band. We are stilt walkers, with gay costumes. We bring smiles to faces young and old." Rubbing his sweating hands together, Mr Lovell smiled nervously at Culvato, then glanced at his wife, who stepped forward.

"The people who owned the last travelling fair we worked in were thieves. Took all we earned. We don't mind paying for a concession to perform in safety, but they wanted everything we owned. They even wanted to use our child as a beggar. I said no, you're not taking my pretty Belle." Mrs Lovell stood with her chin high and her hands clasped together on her chest as she spoke.

Culvato glanced at where Belle lay fast asleep under the hedge. He realised how much the family needed the security of other fair workers. When performing their act they were at the mercy of anyone who wished to disable them.

"I might be able to use you. Have you got a licence?"

The couple nodded.

"You will both need to turn your hand to other work - maybe drive the new wagon I've ordered." Culvato gave Mr Lovell a keen glance when the man continued nodding with enthusiasm.

"See me in the morning and show me what you can do. I might be able to use your girl with my own family, especially if she can ride a horse and is willing to learn trick-riding."

Husband and wife exchanged a delighted glance at the prospect of working permanently with the Ardry family. Culvato's reputation for treating the artists employed by him in a fair and honest manner was becoming widely known. The couple stood hand in hand as they watched the showman walking back to his caravan.

"A settled home for Belle, and the opportunity to do our new act, Mr Lovell."

The happy pair snuggled down under the hawthorn bush. That night, Ursula fell asleep before Culvato did. He lay beside her with both hands behind his head, plotting a new route. He had managed to buy all the new canvas and ropes he needed, and wondered if some Gypsies on the campsite would be pleased to earn a small wage by helping the tent men to rebuild the tents. He began thinking of ways to expand and develop what he now called the 'Ardry Travelling Fair'. Culvato was a happy man. He had caught his rainbow and it had not dissolved in his hand. His dream was to have the largest and best travelling fair in Britain.

Chapter 13

The Ardry Travelling Menagerie arrived on the outskirts of Nottingham Town during a heat wave. It was late summer, and a high brick wall on one side of the lane partly shielded the coffle of colourful wagons and gilded caravans from the strong sunshine. The creaking of leather and wood and the clatter of painted wheels, together with the clip-clop of horses' feet were sounds which soothed Ursula. During the past fifteen years, the couple had found it helpful in their business dealings to speak without using Gypsy cant and to behave in a majestic manner. Culvato was deeply respected by the fairground folk and Ursula loved to be called the boss's wife.

Although she continued to do her comedy act on stilts with her husband, Mrs Lovell met the Ardry children each day in order to teach them basic schooling and a semblance of refinement and propriety. During their lessons, Ursula had watched, listened, and learned how a well bought-up Gauji woman spoke and behaved. Giving the excuse that she was helping the children, Ursula also used their schoolbooks and could now read and write and she had a natural gift for reckoning up numbers.

One day, Culvato had wanted the girls to work with a new

horse he had bought for the show ring. He wasn't pleased to be told that the triplets and Belle would only be able to join him when they had finished their lesson in one hour's time.

"I see no need for the girls to talk and behave different to the rest of us," Culvato complained to Ursula.

"Mmm." She looked at him. "Have you forgotten how we used to tramp around the countryside pushing a wooden barrow, and how folk scorned us? When our children are talking to folk, even to the gentry, they'll be able to hold their heads high and speak properly with anyone. That squire last week thought he could cheat our Hugo about the rent of his field. He thought he was a common Gypsy youth until he started speaking."

"Well, I think it's daft," Culvato muttered under his breath, as he slammed the door of the vardo and stomped across the field.

However, Ursula had her own ways of wheedling what she required out of Culvato, and the lessons continued.

***

Ursula sat in the driving seat of the gilded showman's lead vehicle. She looked a splendid figure with her black hair swept high, the heavy tresses held in place with tortoiseshell combs. Gold earrings hung down, touching her shoulders and glinting in the sun.

Heaving on the reins, she pulled up the grey horse, which was as tired as Ursula herself. "Whoa, whoa there, Warrior," she called. As the brightly painted caravan rolled to a halt, Ursula called over her shoulder: "This is it - the Astwood Estate."

Putting down her sewing, fifteen-year-old Lilly moved nimbly to sit beside Ursula.

"I hope that they have a large lake; we'll be needing plenty of water," she said.

"When your dadrus met Lord Astwood in Nottingham, he invited him to bring the fair here. He thought it would entertain his sons and the servants. If we please them, the family might tell their friends, and we could be invited to other country houses."

Lilly clutched the side of the door to steady herself when Ursula shook the reins and the caravan began to move through the high ornate iron gates. The girl looked at the gilded coat of arms which embellished the centre of each gate. With a sigh, she wondered why she felt a strange feeling of nostalgia whenever she entered a large estate or an elegant house with servants.

"I could live in a place like this," she murmured, and then quickly glanced at Ursula, worried that she had heard. She had not let her secret longing be known to anyone, not even her sisters whom she loved dearly. She dreamed of being the mistress of a large establishment with servants at her beck and call. Also, despite her Gypsy upbringing, Lilly had a yearning to dress in the latest fashion and possess beautiful things.

Ursula's attention was on the horse, and she misheard Lilly. She had been looking for a secret marker, lying on the road, which would have been left by Culvato; she thought that Lilly had asked if they were in the right place. Nudging her, Ursula pointed at a small pile of hay arranged in the shape of a crescent moon.

"There is the patteran; this will be the way."

The women saw a stony driveway running between mature horse-chestnut trees. Clicking to the horse and slapping its back with the reins, Ursula drove the caravan at walking pace along the drive. In the distance, behind a spinney of dark yew trees, they could see part of a slate roof and some tall, twisted brick chimneys.

"Where's Dadrus? I thought he said he'd be here to meet us," said Lilly.

"He's over there in the shade of that oak tree. I can see him talking to some gentlemen." Ursula pointed with her whip towards a tree which had thick spreading branches.

As the caravan approached the men, a group of Shetland ponies, running free, galloped past the vardo and the wagons. Suddenly, they stopped and began grazing on the rich grass beside the drive. They were the most recent addition to Culvato's fair, and he hoped that after training, they could be used in the show ring. Already, they'd caused trouble. The ponies enjoyed themselves. They were free spirits, going anywhere and eating anything within reach of their greedy mouths.

On the previous day, they had raided a cottage garden, trampling down plants and eating the cabbages. A few coins turned frowns into smiles, but Ursula intended to have stern words with Culvato about the wayward animals - and if possible persuade her husband to sell them.

Rose and Heather were in the wagon that carried the merry-go-round. Rose held the reins and carefully guided the horse between the tracks made by the vehicle in front. They eyed the coat of arms displayed on the entrance gates and Heather sighed longingly.

"Must be nice to be rich and live in a house like this, to have servants to cook your meals and wash your clothes," she said. "I wonder what it would be like to have a maid to do everything for you?"

"You had best not let Dai or Dadrus hear you say such a thing. You wouldn't be able to sit on a horse for weeks."

With a sniff and a scornful toss of her head, Rose glanced at her sister. "Not find me gaujified. Couldn't stand living in a settled house and seeing the same thing day after day," she said.

Noticing the marker, and keeping to the tracks made by Ursula's vardo, Rose brought the wagon onto the drive. They were followed by Piramus and Ben, with Lucky, the mangy camel attached by a chain to the back of the tenting wagon. Following them, driving the wagon carrying the lion cage, came Mr Lovell and his family. Hugo and Lionel brought their heavy wagons through the gates. They both wore red neckerchiefs tied loosely around their necks with white shirts unbuttoned to the waist. They both took pride in keeping their riding boots highly polished. Synfye and Seth came next in their vardo, followed by Brandy-Joe and Jem driving a long wagon piled high with the main tenting poles - including Big Bill.

Behind them came the remainder of the entourage. Mostly, they were on foot and carrying packs or pushing handcarts.

With a quick bow to the gentlemen, Culvato hurried to join Ursula. Standing on the wheel and facing the people driving behind, he cupped hands to his mouth and shouted.

"Everything is to go to the lakeside! Follow the drive and turn to the right at the stables. A road leads down to the waterside."

Taking the reins from his wife, Culvato sat down. Both Ursula and Lilly hurriedly moved inside the caravan when a gentleman climbed up and joined Culvato on the driving seat.

A second, younger gentleman walked to the next wagon driven by Rose. The hem of his long three-caped cloak was dusty and flapped against his high leather boots. He disregarded the sun as he removed his tall hat and gave a bow.

"Do you wish me to show you the way, ladies?"

"No, sir, we follow the vehicle in front." Rose spoke sharply, she felt sticky with the heat, and was tired and in no mood to dally with a stranger, however handsome.

Hiding her bare feet under her skirts, Heather looked into a pair of hazel eyes which twinkled with suppressed laughter.

"Of course, how remiss of me not to realise - one vehicle follows the next."

His murmured reply brought a curve to Heather's lips, and a dimple appeared in her cheek. Glancing over her shoulder, she saw him step away from the vehicle as Rose cracked the whip and the wagon lurched forward.

William Astwood stood by the drive as the vehicles made slow progress towards the lake. Silently, he thanked his father for allowing Culvato to bring his menagerie and the most beautiful girl he had ever seen to Astwood House, and he wondered why they had never thought of having a fair in their grounds before. He knew other families allowed show people to entertain their guests. He kept his eyes on the wagon driven by Rose until it turned a corner and was hidden by trees.

As soon as the vehicles reached the meadow next to the lake, the heavily laden wagons sank in the soft ground. Men cursed as they squelched through the mud and removed some of the bulky loads to reduce the weight. The strongest of the horses were harnessed together and used to pull the lightened wagons into another meadow, on higher ground. The living wagons were sheltered at the back by high bushes and the wagons formed a semicircle, with the lion cage at the far end.

When the vardos and bender tents were in position, the travelling women spread straw on the ground in the hope that it would prevent most of the dust, mud and stones being carried into their living quarters.

Thank goodness it's the end of the day. Maybe it will grow cooler when the sun sets, Lilly thought, as she helped Ben round up the Shetland ponies. As they tethered them, she noticed Ursula releasing the fowls from a coop which was permanently fastened to the back of their caravan. The birds ran around, clucking and picking over and eating anything edible around the campsite and in the hedgerows. To protect them from foxes they would be rounded up and placed back into their coop at nightfall.

The fair was assembled as though by magic. Poles and tons of canvas turned into show tents. Wooden structures were fitted together and the merry-go-round was put together like a jigsaw puzzle. That one was far larger than the round-a-bout made by Mr Watson in Eastwood Town fifteen years ago. The brightly painted farm animals, each with polished leather saddles and bridles, revolved dizzily and galloped as though alive.

Lucky the camel was led to the water's edge by Brandy-Joe. He was fond of the supercilious beast and had found the knack of making it obey him. They were followed to the lakeside by two spaniels and a mongrel bitch called Nipper. The dog was well named, and would receive a kick from Lucky if it came too close to his back legs. Hugo loved the little dog, and had taught it to do tricks; he dressed it with a frill around its neck as part of his clown act.

***

Piramus walked past Heather and Rose carrying his peepshow, which he gave a new coat of brightly coloured paint each year. The girls smiled at the old man who in turn gave them a saucy wink.

"Where are you off to, Uncle Piramus?" Rose called.

"I'm going to change the pictures in my peepshow. Never seen them look so shabby," he said, resting the contraption on the ground.

"You want some pictures of horses, or of the pretty bathing

belles at Scarborough?" Heather said, with a laugh.

Rose nudged her sister with a sharp elbow and frowned a warning at her. There was no need to comment, for Heather blushed, embarrassed at her forwardness.

"Your dai was looking for you both. Best get over to your vardo, sharp." Piramus gave a chuckle as Heather wrinkled her nose at his advice. The old man knew the girl had no love of domestic chores. He groaned a little as he picked up his peepshow. *Getting old*, he thought, *or this thing is getting heavier*. He made his way to the bender tent that he shared with Ben. The youth had made it high and had placed plenty of stones around the base to keep out the draughts. Piramus noticed with approval that Brandy-Joe and Jem had built their tent next to his; they would be able to share the cooking fire. He gave a low chuckle. *Bathing Belles indeed. Those girls are far too young to know of such things.*

When he reached his tent, Jem was standing nearby, practising juggling with flaming batons. *The boy has no fear of fire. I dare bet that he will be a fire-eater like his dadrus one day*, the old man thought, smiling at the concentration of the young man.

***

"I thought you girls were going to help me with this food. Your dadrus will be good and ready to eat a decent meal. The hobben served to him in those inns he stays at is only fit for Gaujos and curs," Ursula spoke crossly, worrying about her husband. She thought he had looked tired recently. "You young ones disappear across the fields as soon as I turn my back. I never know where any of you get to nowadays."

"We wanted to practice our tumbling. Heather can stand on her head and hold out her arms now when she's riding the rosinback in the ring, Dai." As she spoke, Rose took a knife from her belt and began peeling turnips. "I've practised it times many, but I can't seem to get my balance like her," she said, sighing.

"You are all showstoppers in the ring. I can hear the applause, even when I'm sitting in the vardo. Look how well you can leap on and off the back of Warrior. It seems to me that you fly, not jump."

Rose gave Ursula a grateful look. Her confidence had been shaken a little by her sister's prowess and Ursula's encouragement was just what she needed.

"I'll have to find time to do more practice," she said.

"Remember that I need help with feeding all of you. I can't expect Synfye to keep helping me like she did today, she has her own meals to prepare," said Ursula.

Before the fair closed and the family gathered for the evening meal, Ursula saw Synfye walking towards her. *She looks smug. Wonder what she wants. I hope she doesn't expect to borrow my best kettle again,* she thought.

"Come to ask a favour. Can I bring Brandy-Joe, his chavvi Jem and my Seth to supper tonight?" Synfye asked; she looked sly.

Ursula stared at her without speaking.

"Brandy-Joe wants to talk to Culvato."

"What for? I mean, what would he want to talk about over supper? They see each other every day."

"We might be getting married."

Ursula's mouth dropped open.

"But you're married to Tawno."

"Been almost fifteen years since I last saw him; I feel nothing for him now."

Ursula's eyes widened when she saw Synfye put her hand on her stomach, and then she frowned.

"You're not pregnant, so don't come making out you are.

Brandy-Joe is too honourable for that. I do see a baby, though, but it won't be for a year or two."

Synfye shrugged and then looked sulky. She had no intention of telling Ursula that she had enjoyed many hours in Bandy-Joe's arms, and if she wasn't pregnant it wasn't from the lack of trying.

"Joe has asked whether my rom will ever come back to me. I've told him that he died. No need to say owt else. After all these years, nobody will remember finding that bundle of clothes or giving me the pewter plate. Anyway, it might not have been Tawno's pack." With a toss of her head, Synfye looked defiantly at Ursula. "Since his wife died, Joe has been lonely, and after all these years..."

"Well, I don't know what Culvato will say. We haven't heard anything from Tawno and know nothing about him except what those travellers said. They recognised his dogs and they really thought that they were guarding his things. The last time you say you saw him he was in Melton Mowbray. I think that it'll be best if you wait and see what Culvato says tonight."

"Don't you go blabbing to him first, I don't want you putting your posh ideas into his head before Joe has had a word with him."

Ursula didn't bother to answer. She turned back to her cooking, her mouth set with disapproval, and she felt a little embarrassed. She had thought no one had noticed her emulating Mrs Lovell and speaking in a more refined way.

The fairground was quiet, and the animals had been fed and bedded down for the night. Wood smoke and steam from various cooking pots permeated the air. Seth followed Brandy-Joe and Jem and they joined the Ardry family around their campfire. They were made welcome and Brandy-Joe sat down on a wooden box which had been placed ready for him beside Synfye. They chattered about nothing in particular as the food was handed around.

"Give the audience your new performance tomorrow afternoon, girls," Culvato said. He smiled at the triplets; he had watched the girls for months as they worked to perfect their new act. "The tent's ready. All the floorboards are in place, nice and taut for working on." He winked at Ursula when she handed him a plate of steaming broth and a chunk of bread.

In between mouthfuls, he continued: "I've had a ring fenced off for you to practice on. It's on a level part of the far meadow. If we put some sand down and run the ponies on it for a while it should make it firm enough for Warrior to trot round in safety."

"Make the ring really flat, Dadrus." Lilly was worried the horse would stumble and break his stride. The last time she had done her voltige act on the rosinback she had slipped and thought she had put out her hip.

"No need to be bothered, my flower. Warrior is the quietest rosinback I've ever had. He's like a moving mountain. It will take more than a yapping dog or screaming chavvi to make that one shy and put a foot wrong." Beaming, Culvato lit his briar pipe and leaned back in his seat.

Heather looked up from polishing a snaffle bridle.

"Warrior will soon need some new tack, Dadrus. The girth slipped at least an inch when I did a handspring the other day, and the stirrup leathers are both stretched about three inches now."

Everyone around the campfire glanced towards Hugo as he walked into the light from the fire. He stood a moment looking at his father.

"Can you examine Copper, Dadrus? His right foreleg feels hot. I've spent the last hour sponging it with cold water, but it doesn't look too good. It might be best if he rests it for a day or so." Hugo smiled his thanks at his mother as she handed him his dinner. Rose moved to make room for him, and he seated himself on an upturned bucket next to her.

"It seems everyone has a problem tonight. Let's forget our troubles for now and get Lionel to play us a tune," Ursula said.

"First, I have to make an announcement," Culvato said. "Our friend, Brandy-Joe, and my Romani-pen, Synfye, are to join hands the Romani way. They will be known as man and wife from this day."

A round of congratulations followed Culvato's words. Brandy-Joe was blushing deeply as he sat holding Synfye's hand. He was happy working in the fairground. He liked the people, and had won Culvato's respect by working hard and being constantly good humoured. At first, the intrusive thoughts of Tawno made him distance himself from Synfye, but as he got to know her he found she had many qualities. Now they were man and wife, Brandy-Joe would move his possessions into Synfye's home. The vardo and its contents were now his property to do with as he wished.

Brandy-Joe had never mentioned to Culvato that his last name was Lincolin, nor had he talked of the fate of his first wife. He still hoped to find her killer.

Staring at his feet, Jem scowled. He couldn't understand why his father should want to rommer that woman when there were others who were younger and prettier and certainly better tempered. He also disliked Seth, and the thought of having to call him brother made him cringe.

Rising to his feet, and with a brief bow towards the happy couple, Lionel began playing his Pandean pipes. Within minutes the three barefooted sisters sprang to their feet and collected their ribbon-trimmed tambourines. They began spinning around in a dance which sent their colourful skirts and long blond hair flying. Clapping high in time to the music, Hugo and Ben joined them. The triplets, holding out their tambourines, encouraged the boys to kick a rhythm on the taut skins. Lionel played the music faster and faster. Soon, the dancers were breathless with laughter.

***

No one noticed the two riders sitting on horseback under a tree, watching and listening to the merry group.

"You were right, William. The girls are lovely, but remember, they are Gypsies. If my knowledge of such people is correct, they have many rules. Their code of behaviour is far stricter than our own. You will have your throat cut one dark night if you even smile at any of their women. They will certainly not tolerate any of their woman folk being defiled."

"Who's talking of defiling them? No one could convince me that those three girls are true Gypsies. Look at that pale hair and sun-kissed skin. Their faces are as finely boned as any I've seen. Their hands and feet are well formed and dainty. I am certain they are gently born. I wonder if they were stolen as babies. That young lady wearing the green skirt is beautiful, Henry. I can't stop thinking about her. Just look at her dimples when she smiles."

As William was speaking, Henry Astwood looked at his brother in some alarm. His claims about Heather's beauty were made in such glowing terms, and he had never known William to be so smitten by a pretty face.

"Just remember you are gentry; and also remember Papa's horsewhip cuts through hide. If you ever brought the wench home, no decent woman would acknowledge her as your bride. She would face a very lonely existence," he said

With a snort of derision, Henry turned his horse and rode away. *The lad is a besotted fool. He certainly isn't listening to me, he* thought. With a sense of shock, he realised William was twenty-two and no longer a lad. He could, even though she was a Gypsy, legally marry Heather without permission from his father. *I suppose the girl is attractive in a dirty kind of way,* Henry thought, with a shrug. *Thank goodness it is me who is heir to the family estate. That Gypsy girl will never become the mistress of Astwood Hall.* With those comforting thoughts, Henry dismissed Heather from his mind.

After a lingering look towards the girl, William followed his brother back to the stable block. He knew without doubt where his future happiness lay. As the second son of the house of Astwood, he would need an occupation to earn his bread. *When the gypsies leave I'll travel the country with the fair. It will be the only way that I can get to know and win my beautiful Gypsy love,* he thought.

Chapter 14

There was a festive air to the campsite. The dancing flames from the campfires and the candle lamps fixed outside and inside the vardos and bender tents gave a warm glow. The wedding celebration for Synfye and Brandy-Joe was over. They had decided to stay with the fair instead of travelling off as newly married couples usually did, and were settled in their caravan.

The scraps from the meal had been thrown to the dogs, and someone in the darkness began humming a refrain. It was steadily taken up by some of the young folk. Hugo fetched his violin from the caravan, and began to play. The music somehow tugged at the heartstrings.

Culvato sat on the caravan steps, leaning against the door and smoking his pipe, at peace with the world.

"We'll be staying here until the end of the week. Mr William has persuaded his father to allow us to perform for a party of their friends tomorrow afternoon." Culvato was pleased to be able to stay in the district; he had another engagement booked near Nottingham in two weeks' time. The weather was still fine and calm and the site at Astwood was perfect for the performers to put in extra practice without townsfolk and their children coming to stare. Very often they would taunt them if they spotted a mistake, which would make the performers very nervous and liable to make a fatal error.

"Oh, good! It will give us time to work out a new routine with the horses," Heather said. Her eyes sparkled at the thought of seeing William Astwood the next day. They had exchanged a few shy words earlier when they had met unexpectedly in the stable block. Remembering the way he had looked at her, and had bowed low as though she was a lady, she felt hot and excited. She examined her hands so that Ursula would not see her flushed face and suspect that she had an interest in the young gentleman. Ursula was strict about the girls going anywhere without a sister or someone to act as a chaperone. Heather could expect a whipping or worse if anyone saw her speaking to William and mentioned it to her mother.

At daybreak the following day, the triplets and Belle threw buckets of sand and straw down in the roped-off enclosure. They gave it a good raking before rounding up the Shetland ponies. They drove them at a full gallop round and round the enclosure, until the girls thought the ground was firm and safe to work on. Hugo, Lionel and Ben arrived just as the ponies were leaving and galloping back into the meadow.

Hugo was testing the state of the new arena by stamping on it. When he saw a clump of grass sprouting through the layer of sand, he shook his head.

"I'd get them back in again, girls. They haven't left a wide enough path, and the ground is still very uneven to run on. If you trip you'll be in trouble!"

"It will be flat enough when we've worked for a while!" Heather shouted back. She was checking that the tack was safely buckled into place on the broad back of her favourite voltige horse, Warrior.

"Let's hope so. We don't want any more accidents. Seth is still limping from his fall last week," Lionel said.

"He shouldn't have been showing off, then. Anybody knows you can't jump down from a horse like he tried to do," Rose gave a tart reply.

The troupe preferred to practise early, before anyone or anything could distract them from the dangerous work of acrobatics on horseback. The rosinback they had chosen for the workout was a steady, dependable creature, fifteen hands high, and looked very much like a dappled rocking horse. He could trot around in a circle for as long as the girls required.

The horse wore a working tack of a long checkrein and a leather pad, called a roller crossing his back. The checkrein held the horse's head in position as he moved. Piramus had made the tack and checked it regularly to see if the stitching had become loose. On either side and on top of the roller, the Gypsy had sewn firm leather handles. A lunge rein connected to the bridle was used by the trainer to keep contact with the horse as it worked. The girls and anyone working with the horse always checked that the roller was secured properly behind the withers and that the buckle was tightly closed under the horse's belly before rehearsing their riding tricks.

Warrior moved around the ring at a controlled canter with short, even strides. Hugo stood in the centre of the ring, holding the lunge rein, with a whip in each hand. He turned in a tight circle, always facing the horse.

"Get a longer run before jumping, Lilly! You don't give Lionel enough room. Get closer to Heather, and get your chin up and look forward!" Hugo ordered. The three standing on the horse's back moved closer and stood with arms outstretched, swaying to the easy lolloping motion whilst waiting for Rose to join them.

"I can't take a longer run when all we've got is half a ring," Lilly muttered into Heather's neck.

"Now, Rose. That's it. Up, and balance, and now count: one,

two, three, four, and down, down, down. That's better. Now Lionel. Good. Now try it again, but get those arms out straight next time. And for goodness' sake smile."

Belle ran, and missed her footing.

"Not on your knees for God's sake! Don't grab at the roller. No half leaps from your knees, neither. Jump clean to your feet and stand." Still holding the lunge rein, Hugo cracked his long whip while pointing his short whip towards the horse. Warrior pricked his ears, but carried on trotting at the same steady pace.

After practising for more than an hour, the performers dismounted, leaving just Heather on Warrior's back. She stood relaxed, moving in rhythm with the horse. She was very slim and straight and her face glowed as she composed herself. The girl was a lovely sight. After a small practice jump, she made a backward somersault. She balanced a moment, and then, holding the roller, she dropped to her knees before leaping to the ground. Holding one of the side handles, she ran beside Warrior whilst turning a laughing face towards her sisters.

"How's that? Did it look messy?" she asked.

"If you stand a minute or two longer, and give a wave to the audience before kneeling, it will look better. Let me try it!" Rose shouted, as she ran and took her sister's place on Warrior's back.

"No, Rose, it's too dangerous! Let Heather break her neck if she wants to!" Hugo shouted. He ran to the horse's head, and pulled hard on the check-rein, he brought the animal to a halt.

With some surprise, Rose noticed that Hugo's face had turned chalk white.

"I'll be able to do it. We've been practising while you've been working with Dadrus." Rose spoke softly when she realised how upset he was. Sliding from Warrior's back, she stood close to him. "You mustn't worry so much about me. I'm always very careful," she said.

Hugo gave her a long, searching look before turning away. Cracking the whip, he shouted," Come on, do it all again - and properly this time!"

Although he should have been working, Ben stood near the ropes watching the troupe. He became aware of someone standing behind him. Glancing around, he was amazed to see William Astwood so early in the morning. He thought that all rich gentlemen stayed in bed until midday.

"They are extremely good," William said, without taking his eyes from Heather's figure.

"You've no right to be here. I know it's your field, but if they see you watching you'll be sent off," Ben growled.

Whether it was William's little spaniel running into the practice ring, or the girth on the horse slipping to the side, no one would ever know, but as Heather took a leap into the air, Warrior missed a stride. His broad back was sideways on when Heather came to land. She wobbled for a moment with arms flailing, trying to regain her balance. William dashed forward just in time to catch her in his arms. They landed inelegantly, sprawled out together.

William lay winded, his head buzzing from its contact with the ground. Heather lay with one leg bent under his body, her face grey and twisted in pain.

Flinging down his whips, Hugo ran to them.

"Good God, Man! Why on earth did you rush forward like that? She's used to falling and knows how to land without hurting herself!"

William opened his eyes. To his astonishment he saw that everyone looked more angry than concerned with him.

"Sorry," he managed to say, before losing consciousness.

As soon as he knew that Heather was hurt, Ben ran towards the show tents, waving his arms and shouting at the workmen.

"Get Mr Ardry. Tell the boss that Miss Heather is hurt."

A number of tent men heard Ben's shouts, and, snatching up some spare canvas, they raced to the enclosure. Laying both the injured on a canvas sheet, the men quickly carried the couple to where Culvato's vardo was parked, and placed them gently on the ground.

Kneeling beside Heather, Culvato examined her leg. Although his touch was gentle, she screamed in agony. With a face pale with worry, he looked up as Ursula bent over them.

"The boy has cracked his head, Romni. Heather has broken her leg, which means no more work on the horses for a fair number of weeks." Culvato spoke with a bitter edge to his voice. Heather was, in his opinion the star performer. The act would lose a lot of sparkle without the girl's vitality.

"I can see to Heather. A stick will keep her leg straight, and I'll give her a dose of my herbal remedy to lessen the pain. But it will be best to get Mr Astwood back to his home quickly. His family will want him seen by their own doctor. They won't thank me to meddle," Ursula said. Without looking at William, she turned her full attention to the groaning girl.

When the housekeeper saw William being carried to the house by a group of Gypsies, she became hysterical.

"Sir, sir! The Gypsies have killed Master William. They are bringing him home, dead."

Doors flew open and people rushed to see what the commotion was all about. Lord Astwood, standing on the top step under the porch, took in the situation at a glance, and swiftly organised footmen to carry William inside.

"What happened?" he said, curtly.

Removing his hat, Culvato bowed.

"A fall, in the field, sir. Hit his head on a stone and knocked himself out cold."

The Lord stared hard at Culvato. Without a word he turned and followed the footmen into the drawing room.

William was dazed, but able to stagger a few steps. He was helped through the entrance hall and into the drawing room, and was lowered onto a red velvet-covered chaise-longue. As he settled down, the housekeeper, who by now felt a little more in control, placed cushions behind his head and covered his legs with a blanket before sending a maid to fetch a tray of tea. At a sign from his master, the butler poured a measure of whiskey into a glass and handed it to William.

"It was a mistake to let those vagrants through the gates. I'll send them all packing, forthwith." Lord Astwood was just about to send for the head gardener, when William lifted himself from his pillows, and hand reached a hand out towards his father.

"No, Papa. This was not of their doing. I happened to trip and bang my head on the ground. Could have done the same thing anywhere, and might not have been found for hours. Good thing they were there."

"Mmm. That so?"

"Yes, Papa. They treated me very well. They were placing cool cloths on my brow when I regained my senses. They waited until I felt more like myself before carrying me home."

"I suppose the servants and villagers would be disappointed if the fair left without giving a performance. I'll keep my word to the ruffian. Let them stay and put on their show."

"Thank you, Papa." With a sigh, William leaned back and closed his eyes, remembering Heather's graceful movements and the feel of her hair on his face and her body in his arms. William took a deep breath, and thought that he could still smell her flowery perfume lingering on his jacket.

***

It wasn't until the doctor's fifth visit that William was allowed to leave the house. He had been desperate for news of Heather, but he had not dared to ask his brother, and dared not risk sending any of the servants to ask how she fared, in case word got back to his father.

Immediately after the doctor had declared that he was fit and had left the house, William made his way to the stables. He ordered a horse to be saddled and, refusing to be accompanied by a groom, he rode as quickly as possible to the Gypsy encampment. On his arrival at the campsite, it seemed everyone was busy working, and no one was available for idle conversation. Tethering his horse to a bush, William walked to the largest of a group of caravans. He saw a woman sitting alone on the vardo steps making lace. Ursula had seen the arrival of the young man, and was fully aware of William walking towards her, but she kept her eyes lowered until he spoke.

"Please, would you be able to tell me how the young lady fares, the one who fell from her horse?"

As he spoke, Ursula felt a tingling on the back of her hands. *This young man will be important to Heather in the future*, she thought. Looking into his hazel eyes, she saw a change come over William. An older man stood looking at her; a man tanned by the wind and sun, with laughter lines around his eyes.

"Could you give her a message? Please, will you tell her that I am so very sorry. It was my fault, you see. Her accident… I didn't know. I'm…" William turned away from the woman who stared at him so strangely.

"The girl's leg will quickly heal. She is strong and healthy."

With a sigh, William began walking towards his horse. How could he possibly express his regret to someone who looked at him with such amusement?

Rising to her feet, Ursula called: "I will tell her you asked about her, but from this day you are not to speak with her! She is a Gypsy, and not of your world!"

As she watched William's shoulder droop despondently, Ursula shook her head. *I might just as well have told the moon not to shine,* she thought. *But then again, Heather isn't a true Romani, and if the circumstances had been different, Heather would have been of his world - and who knows if fate would have brought them together.*

On their last evening at the Astwood Estate, Culvato and his family relaxed around the campfire. They sat talking about their journey, and the route they would be taking to Nottingham Town.

After catching Heather's eye, Hugo rose to his feet and faded into the shadows. Whispering to Heather that they would not be gone for long, Lilly, Rose and Belle also left the campfire.

"Thought we was never going to get away. Dai was talking to you girls non-stop all night," Hugo said. Annoyed by the delay, he tapped a whip against his boots. "Come on. Hurry up. The light will have gone before we have chance to get the horse ready. I want us to be perfect when we show Dadrus the new act we've put together."

The four young people set off at a run to where Warrior stood cropping the grass. The girls watched as Hugo caught hold of the horse by the rope bridle and they followed as he led it into an adjoining field. The triplets and Belle were fifteen, but where the sisters were flaxen-haired and had blue eyes, Belle had black curls, and her eyes were a tawny brown - they twinkled an invitation at Hugo, which he ignored. The girls were of the same height, and ran bare-foot across the grass.

They waited at the side of the practice enclosure until Hugo had the horse trotting around in a circle. His eyes never left the animal as he used his whip to command its attention. As Warrior moved at a steady trot, Belle, followed by Rose and Lilly, sped across the field and sprang onto the horse's back. They stood and balanced as the horse continued moving in a circle, Hugo holding the lunge rein.

"Good girls! That's the way! Now! One at a time! Up and over!" Hugo called.

He gave a groan when Rose and Lilly performed near perfect somersaults but landed on their backs on the grass. When he saw that Belle was still sitting where she had landed and had begun weeping, Hugo yelled at her in disgust.

"You fools! Call yourselves acrobats! You are supposed to land on your feet. Belle! You're worse than them two. None of you are as good as our Heather." In the heat of the moment, he forgot to keep his voice down.

Sniffing back tears, Belle joined Lilly and watched Rose gracefully leap onto the horse, but instead of landing astride, she lay across its back. As she tried to stand, the horse broke its step, and Rose had to scramble in an undignified manner to stay on.

Hugo threw down his whip in frustration.

"We'll never have a new show if you don't do it better! Come on, do it again, proper this time."

Unknown to the young people, Culvato was standing behind a thorn bush. He had been watching the group of young acrobats at work for a number of nights, and, knowing that they were doing it for his sake, he felt very proud of their achievements. Turning away, he grinned when he heard Hugo yelling fresh instructions.

"You get on with it, chavvi. Those girls will jump far higher for you than for an old 'un like me," Culvato chuckled. He was still grinning when he returned to the campfire and seated himself on the steps of his caravan.

Ursula had also missed the young folk and gave an inquiring glance at her husband as he sat down next to her. She relaxed when he lit his old briar pipe, his eyes twinkling.

The morning dew still lay on the grass as the tents were dismantled. William heard shouting, and saw the activity from the window of his bedchamber. He could no longer put off facing his father and telling him of his decision. He found Lord Astwood seated at his desk in his study.

"Good day, Papa."

"William?" His father looked up with some surprise. He seldom saw his sons so early in the morning. He put his paper to one side. "Come in, boy, and close the door."

William thought wildly of how to speak of his future, and found he could only concentrate on the scratch on the desktop. He cleared throat.

"I have to tell you, Papa. That is..." William found it very difficult to meet his father's eyes. "I... I wish to travel."

"So you will, my boy. So you will. I have plans to send you on a tour of Europe, starting with France and going on to Italy later in the year."

"I mean to travel with the fair. I wish to..."

Lord Astwood's eyes suddenly became like the points of bayonets.

"Never."

William's mouth became very dry. "But, Papa."

"I said no! No son of mine is going to go gadding around the country like a vagrant." Lord Astwood had risen to his feet, and stood pointing his finger at William. "It's the fall, that's what it is. The blow to your head was far worse than the doctors thought."

"No, Papa. I..."

"Say no more, it's just a whim. Dreams, a flight of a young man's fancy. Forget we had this conversation and I will never refer to it again. Next year you will come into your inheritance and travel abroad with your brother and me. By then you will have forgotten all this nonsense."

"I have made up my mind, Papa. I am leaving with the fair people."

There was an ominous pause while father and son, both with reddened faces, regarded one another.

"If you go, you will never return here. You will never have a groat of my money. Everything will go to Henry."

William swallowed and nodded. "I was hoping that you would let me leave with your blessing, Papa, but so be it."

"Take nothing from this house. Only what clothes you wear," Lord Astwood cried, as William turned to leave the room.

As he reached the door, William hesitated for the briefest moment. Without a backward glance, he walked through the entrance hall and through the portrait gallery filled with paintings of his ancestors, and then out of the house. He didn't see his father peering out of the study window with tears rolling down his cheeks and clutching his chest, or notice his brother standing on the porch steps with his hand covering his mouth.

"Henry. Henry!" The cry came from the study.

Quick as a flash, Henry Astwood ran to where his father was standing. Seeing his father stagger, he helped him to a chair.

"Go after him. Bring him back, dear boy."

"It's the Gypsy girl, father. She has bewitched him. He can't think of anything but the wretch," said Henry.

With a groan, Lord Astwood put his head in his hands. After a moment, he said: "If that is the case, all we can do is wait until he comes to his senses and returns home. And remember this, my son: he will always have a home here on his return."

"Yes, Papa. We will keep his room just as it is, constantly ready for him." Henry put a hand over his eyes. "Oh, I wish he had never set eyes on the girl. I shall miss him, Papa."

"One day he will walk through those doors again. Wait and see, Henry."

Chapter 15

After the stormy interview in his father's study, William Astwood straightened his shoulders. He went to find Culvato Ardry; he was in the big tent, supervising the removal of equipment. William stood a moment or so until Culvato noticed him, then asked, with eyes downcast, if he could work and travel with the fair people.

"I've all the performers I can use," Culvato said in a curt manner, and turned away. He hadn't forgiven William for Heather's accident.

"Anything! I'll do anything. I don't expect to have a big wage, just enough to buy my food," William pleaded.

Culvato heard the despair in his voice and weakened. William was not the first young gentleman who had asked to join the fair. It seemed a romantic life to most young men until the rough weather and hard work brought a dose of reality in the form of calluses, and then they remembered home comforts and family.

"Can you go without sleep?"

William nodded. He would work day and night and do anything asked of him if it meant he could be near Heather.

"Can you get soaked to the skin without catching cold and

returning back here to your comfortable home when you tire of our rough way of life? There will be no servants to fetch and carry for you in my camp."

"I'm very strong and healthy, and seldom catch colds. I am fascinated with your fair, Mr Ardry, and I want to be a part of it."

Culvato scrutinised the young man's face and saw firm determination in his jutting chin.

"Can you drive a wagon?"

"Yes. I can drive all kinds of vehicle, and take good care of horses too."

"If you travel with my show you'll have to muck in and do any odd jobs that come along; drive, clean out the animals, help with the stakes and poles, roll up the canvas - everything," Culvato said.

"I will turn my hand to anything you say, Mr Ardry. I'll not give you cause to regret hiring me."

Culvato jerked his head towards a group of men dismantling a show booth.

"Give them some help," he said.

William joined the casual work force and by the time night fell, every muscle in his body ached.

***

As the fair travelled to the next venue, William walked behind the last wagon in the company of some of the tent men. They were unshaven, shabby and raffish looking, and most of them smoked blackened clay pipes. As the men discussed their work they used terms that were incomprehensible to William.

On reaching the town, William's heart sank. Standing on the side of the road stood his brother, anxiously watching as the travellers filed past. Henry moved forward and put out his hand when he saw William.

"I am not returning home!" William's voice reflected his determination.

"Don't worry. I'm not here to ask you to do that." Henry put a hand under William's elbow, and walked along with him, speaking in a low voice. "I've come to give you some money and a change of clothes."

With a snort of exasperation, William stopped to face to his brother.

"I don't need money. We live off the land, and I shall earn enough for my wants."

"You'll need a pair of good stout boots, William. It's not always warm and sunny. You walked out in house shoes and silk hose, and you'll have to have a hat and coat."

Looking down at his light shoes, William smiled reluctantly. In the few miles he'd walked, the soles were almost worn through, and every pebble seemed to feel like a boulder. They had stopped outside the Rose and Crown, and William's mouth watered when the smell of food wafted through the inn's open door.

"I have rented a room here. Come inside and see what clothes I've brought."

With a glance at the disappearing convoy of wagons, William followed his brother to the most comfortable bedchamber the inn provided. As he passed the dining room, hunger pangs reminded him that breakfast, which had consisted only of a cup of water, had been at five o'clock that morning. The idea of living off the land was fine until such time as the farmer caught you stealing his turnips. Culvato had yet to pay him for helping to dismantle the show booths the day before.

"I asked the landlord to serve a meal in here so that we can eat and talk in private. Will you join me, brother? It could be the last meal we share for some time." As he spoke, Henry sat down at the table, which was already set with platters of cold fowl, beef and fruit tarts, and gestured towards the chair facing him.

"I am not used to the way of things yet. Some of the men are rough fellows, but good hearted, I think. They offered me some dinner last night, but when they said it was squirrel boiled with potatoes, I told them that I had already eaten," said William, pulling a fowl apart and eating hungrily.

Henry shuddered at the thought of eating a rodent, but didn't remark on it.

"We all want to have you back, William. Father said to tell you that you will always be welcomed back home when you have had your fill of roaming. If you can get word to me where you are I could perhaps meet you and we could share a dinner. Just now and again," he added hastily, as he saw a flash of irritation on William's face. He waited a moment or two, before saying softly: "The girl? Is she your reason to leave?"

William eyed Henry warily, and reddened as he saw his brother's perplexity.

"I know that to you and father it must seem illogical, but however long it takes me, I must get to know her better," he said. Wiping his mouth with his napkin, he continued: "I need to find out how and why she purports to be a Gypsy. Although there are three of them, and they are all lovely, it's Heather who stirs my senses. I have only to catch a glimpse of her and I am filled with a throbbing happiness. If I find out that she is not Mr Ardry's true daughter, I shall make her my wife."

"Well I can't say that I understand, but if that is the way of it," Henry shrugged, and then drained a glass of wine before rising to his feet. "I have brought your most sturdy boots, and I've a good wool coat and breeches which belonged to John, the land agent. The hat is an old one of yours. Take care the coat is not stolen, for I had the housekeeper sew coins into the seams. If you do have a problem in the future, at least you will have the wherewithal to make the journey home in comfort."

William, touched by Henry's thoughtfulness, blinked back tears. He had not expected such kindness from his father and brother.

"Whenever possible I will try to keep you informed of my whereabouts. Tell Papa not to worry about me too much, and give him my love. Tell him… Oh tell him that I wished that things could have been different," William said in a voice filled with emotion. The brothers hugged and, with William promising to take care, he took his leave. He strode confidently along the street in the direction the fair had taken, and didn't see Henry standing at the window, watching him and sadly shaking his head.

***

For more than two years, William travelled around Britain with the fair. From time to time he let his family know that he was safe and happy, but he didn't return home. Every task allotted to him he completed in a willing and cheerful manner. He helped with the animals and, together with the other men, he erected and dismantled the show tents and rides. Eventually, he became proficient enough to teach newcomers how to do the work.

William never made any reference to Heather, neither by look nor word. When other travelling men discussed the sisters, or spoke about any other women associated with the fair, William would walk away. One day, a tent man hastily collected his belongings. He bore a bleeding cut running from his mouth to his ear. Rumours flew around the camp that the man had been caught in the woods with a Gypsy woman. Neither the man nor woman was seen again. William's brother had been correct when he had said the Gypsies tolerated no interference with their women folk.

***

Their eyes met across the meadow. William was holding a handful of wild strawberries warmed by the afternoon sun and his lips were stained red with the juice of the sweet fruit. Swallowing nervously, he glanced around but the couple were alone. Heather slid gracefully from the back of her horse and stood stroking its glossy neck. She let the reins trail on the ground and allowed the horse to crop the grass.

"Miss Heather, you are alone, where are your sisters?" William was stunned. His golden girl was almost near enough to touch. A sudden breeze lifted Heather's skirts and he almost saw her knees. Her blouse was made from fine linen gathered along the neckline which curved to reveal her smooth shoulders. With a quick movement, she held her skirts against her legs. It was the first time the couple had been alone or had an opportunity to speak freely, and they were both a little shy.

"Lilly is sewing costumes, and Rose has gone with Hugo to the farm to help him pick out a new puppy from a litter of Jack Russells. He wants to train one to work with the horses."

His eyes devoured her. Heather had been aware of William's interest for a long time, but she was startled by the intensity of his gaze. She couldn't look away. She didn't want to look away. They moved closer to one another.

"Do you like strawberries, Miss Heather?" His voice was low, as though he was scared of breaking the spell.

She is like a ripe strawberry, he thought, *pink and fresh and glowing with health. Untouched. Virginal. Sun kissed limbs and sun streaked hair that flow around her face like a curtain of liquid gold.* He had fallen in love with her more than two years ago. With a

191

young man's passion he had given away his inheritance to be near her, and the more he saw her, the more he loved her. They were never able to speak more than a few words - mostly about his work, for she was always chaperoned - but the couple's eyes spoke volumes.

"Oh, yes, I've always enjoyed eating strawberries." Her heart was pounding, and her throat was tight and dry. She flicked back her hair and her tongue wetted her top lip.

He looked into her blue eyes and marvelled at the way her eyebrows curved delicately to frame them.

Within moments, they were sitting close to each other, sharing the fruit. He reached out for more strawberries, picking the ripest and popping them one by one into her mouth.

"You are not eating any," Heather said, in a breathless whisper.

"I want you to have them all; I want to watch how you bite off each stem so daintily. Has anyone told you that your teeth are beautiful? White and perfect."

She smiled a woman's smile, and with a trembling finger she touched the skin at the open neck of his shirt. She felt him shudder as he drew in a deep breath.

William noticed a spot of red juice at the side of her mouth, and he longed to kiss it away. Slowly he reached for her, pulled her to him, and watched how her eyes closed as he brushed her lips with his own. Her arms snaked around his neck. They were smooth and warm, and he savoured her womanly perfume.

"You are so lovely," he murmured, as they fell back onto the soft grass.

He entwined his fingers in her thick golden hair. With his tongue moving lightly over her lips, William tantalized her until she opened her mouth, and then he explored the strawberry-flavoured softness. Heather responded to his kisses with a passion that she didn't know she possessed. This was how love should be. It was right. True and good.

"Love me, William. Make love to me," she whispered.

He felt her heart beating as her body arched to meet his. With a loud groan, William rolled off her and sat up.

"We mustn't. One day. When the time is right, I will ask your father if we can marry, but I'll not spoil our love by taking you before we are wed."

"No, William! Dadrus will never agree. It's hopeless. He wants us all to marry Romani men." With lips swollen from the passion of their kisses, and her eyes swimming with tears, Heather pushed back her hair. She wanted him, wanted more of that passion. She wanted to feel his body pressing against hers. Wanted...

William was fully aware of her desire, and it took all of his willpower to lean away from her.

"If we are patient, something may change his mind. You are only just seventeen and who knows..."

Heather, crying out in distress, jumped up, and that brought William to his feet. He watched helplessly as she ran across the field and jumped on her horse.

"It's not fair!" she cried. "Others marry who they want and no harm comes to them. Why should we be any different?"

***

He watched as the horse leaped gracefully over the low fence, and listened until the sound of its galloping faded. William glanced at the flattened grass and sighed. One day that golden girl would be his. The pleasure they had felt would become intensified as they taught each other the ways of love. He had to be patient for a while longer, he told himself, and he had the strength to do so now he knew she loved him in return.

As he made his way back to the fairground, his mind spun

193

with ideas. He could return home, taking Heather with him. If they were careful and timed it right, her family would not prevent her leaving. *But then, my father would not accept her; and seeing his attitude, all the servants would be insolent,* he thought. That would be no life for such a vibrant girl. Her gaiety, only one of the many things he loved about her would be dimmed and would eventually disappear.

He could buy a caravan and they could travel the byways, but he knew that her brothers would get revenge by killing or maiming him - and what would become of Heather then?

Eventually, William came to the hedge surrounding the showground. His legs felt weak, and for a moment he leaned against a tree. He wondered if he was strong enough to carry on with his work as though nothing had happened. *I've no choice,* he thought. *If I leave the fair now I'll never see Heather again.* No. Anything was better than that. He remembered her sweet warmth and the feel of her. She wanted him. It was no use to make plans; they had to hope that one day her family would let them marry.

***

Heather was grooming her horses when she saw William return. The hotness between her legs flooded through her body. She was trembling so much that she almost dropped the grooming brush. She shook her head with dismay. It was awful, if that happened each time she set eyes on him, someone would be sure to notice her interest in William. Somehow she must stifle her feelings and try to behave as though their wonderful meeting had never happened. *I'll speak to him in private, and say, it was a mistake to let you kiss me. A silly girlish weakness let me be carried away. I've come to my senses now. I know it was wrong and it must never happen again. If you attempt to speak to me I will have my dadrus dismiss you.* Could she say that to William? Heather continued to brush the horse, angry tears running down her face. *How can I tell him that? He'll know I'm lying. We love each other too much.*

The whistling of a groom came closer and a cheerful, 'Do you want me to finish that job for you Miss Heather?' made her turn away and wipe her face with the back of her hand.

"No. I've nearly finished. Go and make a start on the horse at the end of the row," she said.

I must look a mess. I can't let anyone see me in this state, she thought. Catching sight of a water bucket near her feet, she bent over and quickly dipped the edge of her skirt in. She splashed cold water on her flushed cheeks, and held the sodden cloth over her eyes for a long moment. When she stood up, she felt calmer and ready to face people.

During the following months, the couple deliberately kept out of each other's way, although they watched each other from a distance. William worked like a man with double strength, and even Culvato passed an approving comment or two about him. Heather used up her energy by creating a new way to jump higher on and off the back of the horses, and even her sisters marvelled at her prowess.

It was a long time before the couple had an opportunity to speak privately. William saw Heather heading towards a stream carrying a bucket. He waited behind a bush, glancing around to see if anyone had followed Heather. She was alone, she had not noticed him.

"Hsst, Miss Heather."

With a little squeal, she dropped the bucket, blushed deeply, and trembled at being so close to him.

"I need to speak with you, Miss Heather. Not here; someone may see us. After everyone has finished their meal tonight, I shall be behind the big tent."

He noticed Rose making her way towards the stream, and,

quickly moving to the other side of the bush, he walked away.

If her sister noticed Heather's heightened colour when she returned to the vardo with the water, she made no comment.

***

It was dark as William made his way to the largest tent. His black shirt made him almost invisible. He sat in deep shadow for some time and although people passed by, no one noticed him. Hearing the swish of bare feet on the grass, he rose to his feet and saw a woman's figure coming towards him.

"Miss Heather. I'm so pleased you managed to get away," he said, in a low voice.

There was such longing in his tone that her heart felt as though it was tearing.

"What do you want, William? Hurry, I dare not linger. I will be in such trouble if I am found here." As she spoke, Heather glanced around nervously, but was satisfied that for the moment, they were alone.

"I am going away. I've had word that I'm needed at my family home. Please believe me when I say that I love you. As soon as my business is done, I will return."

"Will you be away for long?"

"Something is amiss at home, but it will not prevent me from hurrying back to you, Miss Heather."

The soft rustle of a skirt was loud enough to make the couple jerk apart. Rose was only a few feet away from them. She saw a shadow melt into the darkness.

"Have you taken leave of your senses, Heather? What if it had been Dai or Dadrus who saw you here?"

"Oh, please, Rose. William had to see me. He wanted to say that he is going away."

"And a good thing too. How long has this been going on?"

"Some weeks ago we met, and it was by chance, really it was. We love each other, but we know that it's hopeless. Oh Rose, I'm so unhappy."

"We had both better get back to the vardo before we are missed," Rose said quietly. She also had a secret love that could not be.

Heather caught hold of her sister's arm.

"Are... are you going to tell Dadrus?" Her eyes were huge with fright, and her hand covered her mouth.

Before Rose could answer, a voice boomed out.

"What are you two doing skulking behind here? Waiting for a lover?" Seth stood peering past the girls into the darkness.

For a moment the girls were speechless. Suddenly, Seth gave a spiteful laugh.

"Is that the best bit of manhood you can get to meet you?" he said.

An old and very smelly pedlar had come into view. He was heading for the tent.

The girls exchanged relieved glances.

"We don't tell you our secrets - and what about you, why are you out here? Is another girl going to claim you are the father of her baby?" Rose said in a haughty voice.

This comment hit home, and he reddened. "No one asks where a man goes at night," he said. Without another word he turned, and stalked away with his lips tight, the mean look on his face so reminiscent of his father, Tawno.

The girls held hands for comfort as they returned home.

"Man? He's never going to be a man like..." Rose didn't finish the sentence, but her voice was filled with scorn.

"Rose?" Heather's pleading tone was unmistakable.

"Don't worry. I'll not tell anyone, but please be more careful in the future," Rose said, and wondered if she dared reveal her own heart-rending secret to her sister.

Chapter 16

William Astwood was away from the fair for three months. On the day of his return, Heather saw him speaking with Culvato before going to muck out the horses. No one asked why Heather glowed with happiness and smiled so much, but Rose told her in a sharp tone that if she didn't change back to her normal self, people would soon be asking questions.

One afternoon, William stood at the back of the crowd in the smaller of the show tents during the performance, all set to lead the clapping and whistling. He was also there ready to rush forward and protect the girls if there was any sign of malicious or amorous intent coming from the people in the audience. It had been known for some wag to release a mouse to run across the stage in the hope of disrupting the show.

Enthusiastic applause reverberated around the tent as the three Ardry sisters and Belle Lovell brought their act to an end. Performing acrobatic feats, their supple bodies tumbled and leapt in high twisting somersaults. They followed each other around the stage in a colourful, spellbinding display. All four girls wore their hair threaded with white and silver ribbons. Belle's black curls were a sparkling contrast to the triplets' shimmering platinum locks which they had braided into high crowns.

As the girls received their well-earned applause from behind smoking candle lamps, Heather, breaking ranks with a wide grin, danced across the wooden boards of the minute stage with her hands held high to encourage an extension of clapping and approving whistles. She had caught sight of William when she first ran onto the stage, and she had blushed under her makeup. Whenever she happened to catch sight of him during the day she would always try to catch his attention and give a sweet smile.

Rose copied her sister as she moved forward on the stage, but with less passion, for she had made a mistake halfway through the act. Culvato usually watched every show; she knew that he would scold her and probably give her some extra practice to do when she left the show tent later.

Lilly turned from side to side, facing the audience with her teeth-clenched smile fixed from habit; she hated working in the show tents. The stench of the unwashed bodies of the audience, combined with smoke from the cheap candles made her want to vomit. Belle stood beside her, waving a hand gracefully, although perspiration ran down her face and she was breathing heavily, her dark curls appeared unruffled by her exertions.

Behind a curtain and out of sight of the audience, Hugo waited with his white and brown terrier, Nipper. They wore matching ruffs and conical hats, topped with a pom-pom. Hugo was unrecognisable in his guise as a laughing clown. His eyes had never left Rose throughout her performance, and when she curtsied and ran to where he was standing in the wings, he caught hold of her arm.

"Dadrus didn't watch tonight, he was outside talking to a gentleman," he said as she was about to push past.

Throwing a cloak around her shoulders and giving him a

grateful smile, Rose stepped closer.

"I've got a new idea for the act. We'll use Nipper with the horses in the show ring. We can practice it together when you've finished here. I'll meet you after supper," she whispered.

With a bound, Hugo was in the centre of the stage. Watching the self-assured young man cartwheel and leap across the pliant boards with swift ease, Rose put her hand to her mouth with fear. That was the man she loved more than any other. She had always admired her big brother, but recently those feelings had changed. She no longer followed him around as she had when they were children. She loved her sisters and Lionel, but somehow she knew deep down that it was a different kind of love. Rose longed for Hugo to hold her close, to fondle and kiss her like she saw Culvato kiss Ursula. She had wicked and dirty thoughts about her brother, and she knew that they were very unnatural. She tried to stifle her feelings, but she cried herself to sleep most nights.

Gales of delighted laughter came from the audience as Nipper jumped through the paper-covered hoops held high by Hugo. The merry sound followed the girls as they hurried across the field towards the parked caravans and wagons. Rose's miserable expression went unnoticed.

Ursula spoke with unaccustomed sharpness when Belle and the sisters entered the vardo.

"Come along in, you girls! Where have you been? Get changed out of those spangles and get into your riding habits. Quick, now, Dadrus wants you ready to work in the ring when Hugo has finished in the show booth. When you are ready, one of you must carry some more wooden balls out to Synfye for the bucket stall. You'll find her working the merry-go-round. I'm going over to the lion cage. With the noise it's making I think someone's teasing it again. I'll box their ears if I find that it's children poking sticks again."

Closing both the top and bottom door of the vardo, Ursula left the four girls to change into their riding costumes in private, and she walked swiftly towards the lion cage.

Glancing through the vardo window, Heather watched Ursula walking across the grass.

When she was safely out of earshot, she said: "I dare say that Dai will go and see Beebe Synfye again. Kaka Brandy-Joe slept in Jem's tent again last night. It's been weeks since he lived in the vardo. It's as though they're not married anymore."

"Don't talk such rubbish! You're always thinking the worst, Heather." Lilly said. Then she turned to Rose with a pout, "You forgot to catch me!"

Lilly's accusation made Rose pause whilst pulling off her spangled tunic.

"It's you, you're too fast with the movements, Lilly," Heather said. "We can't keep up when you launch yourself into the air at that dreadful speed."

Moving away from the window and throwing a pair of discarded shoes in a corner, Heather frowned at her sister. "I wish you would stop showing off, Lilly. We all know you think that it's below you to do a performance in the show tent, but Dadrus won't let you sit sewing all day with Dai, or just do riding acts, however hard you try to coax him."

"Dadrus brings in the crowds by showing off freaks like us, and with our ability to work on the boards and the horses..." Rose shrugged her thin shoulders. She sounded far sulkier than she had really intended. The girls looked at Rose in astonishment. No one had ever suggested that the three lovely sisters were freaks, although they were fair skinned and identical.

Pulling on a figure-hugging riding habit trimmed with gold lace, Heather decided to ignore Rose's comment, and perched a tall, veiled hat on her head before nodding towards her sisters. "I like doing the act we do now, and I enjoy hearing and seeing the audience applauding, but lately I've thought it would be nice to do something a bit different. Make some changes here and there."

Rose was just about to speak of the changes which she had thought about when Belle, looking across from the space allotted her for changing her clothes, let out a mocking chuckle.

"If you don't stop your squabbling, we'll all be doing something different. Mr Ardry will be using his whip on all four of us if we don't get to the arena on time and mount our horses," she said.

As Belle turned to pick up her own riding hat, the triplets forgot Mrs Lovell's teaching of deportment, and that they were now young ladies. Every one of them pulled a face and stuck out her tongue.

"Yes, Belle dear." They said in unison.

Heather carefully closed the doors behind them as they left for their performance.

***

Three months before, a group of drunken men had entered the caravan belonging to Brandy-Joe and Synfye. Unaware of the intruders, the couple had been working in the fairground. When they returned home they found the vardo almost wrecked. Most of the china and glass had been smashed. Only tin plates, cups and an old pewter plate survived the men's attention. After the event, Synfye looked very unhappy and her arms and face were badly bruised. No one was told why, and they didn't dare ask, but they guessed that it had something to do with Synfye's sharp tongue.

The truth was that as Synfye was clearing up the mess, Brandy-Joe had picked up the pewter plate, and, after examining it, he held it out towards his wife.

"Where did this come from?" he growled.

"Tawno, it must have belonged to him,' Synfye whispered. It was the first time since their marriage that she had seen Joe look so furious.

"How did he get it?"

"I don't know. Years ago some travellers found his dogs guarding some things, and somehow they thought that they were belonging to Tawno. When they looked in his pack, that plate was among his clothes. They must have thought I would want his things, and they passed everything on to me."

"Why haven't I seen it before?"

"You... You like me to use china plates. I've never needed to use that one and it's been kept in the back of the cupboard."'Synfye cowered under the evil look he shot at her.

"See this marking on the back, woman?" Brandy-Joe held the plate out towards her. "I made that. This plate was used in the camp on the day my poor Curlanda was murdered. The person who battered my wife to death stole this plate." The plate was thrown across the caravan and clattered to silence in a corner.

Shaking her head wildly, Synfye backed towards the door. She was seven months pregnant and clumsy, and wasn't quick enough to prevent Brandy-Joe from seizing her by the hair and dragging her across to the bed. Squirming, she tried to avoid blows raining down on her face, and attempted to protect her swollen belly.

"I didn't know! We haven't seen or heard anything from him in years. The last I saw of him was when he was being whipped in Melton Mowbray Town," she cried in terror.

Brandy-Joe stood back.

"I bet you knew all about it. Been laughing at me and my Jem with that idle son of yours?"

It all came flooding back to him. Curlanda's bloodied body lying in the tent, digging her grave, burning her things. He also remembered the good feeling he had had when, because of his treacherous whispers to the authorities in the town, he saw Tawno's back running with blood.

"To think I've been sleeping with a woman who was married to the murderer of my beautiful Curlanda! You disgust me. I feel defiled just looking at you. The day we burnt your vardo, you all should have been inside it. Fire is the best way to get rid of vermin," he said.

Synfye stared.

"The… The vardo? It was you who burned it. You? Oh!"

Still cursing, Joe staggered from the caravan, leaving Synfye holding her stomach and sobbing on the bed. It was the first time Brandy-Joe had deliberately hit a woman and hurrying to the back of the caravan, he vomited. Vowing never to take her as his wife again, he also swore aloud that if he ever found Tawno he would have revenge.

The shock of the assault brought on the premature birth of their daughter. With the help of Ursula, the child was born, but she was very tiny. Synfye called her Isopel after her grandmother.

Jem always made his own bender tent. He didn't encourage Seth to join him, preferring that young man's absence to his presence. On the night his father arrived smelling of drink and asking if he could share his tent, Jem didn't enquire why. Nor did he question why the married couple continued to live apart; he marvelled that the couple had stayed together for so long.

When his mother asked him to return home, Seth quickly moved his few possessions into the caravan. The new arrangement suited him very well, for he disliked sleeping under the wagon with Piramus, and he was too lazy to make a tent for himself.

***

Carrying the basket of wooden balls, Rose made her way across the field to where Synfye was supposed to be turning the merry-go-round. It was a new ride, two feet wider than the last one. It had eight carved farmyard animals painted in bright colours for children to enjoy, and to them it appeared to spin as though by magic.

Earlier that day, Synfye had thought that Isopel looked rather unwell and wanted to stay with the baby in the vardo, so Seth had taken his mother's place and was turning the handle of the ride in a steady rhythm. When he saw Rose approaching, he stopped the ride and jumped to the ground. He stood with both hands on his hips, his dark eyes narrowed. His gaze gave every indication that he was mentally undressing her. As she drew closer, Rose turned cold and paled under her stage make-up. A few days earlier, she had overheard a conversation between Ursula and Culvato. They were both agreed that Rose would be an excellent match for Seth when she was a little older.

Looking at Seth's sharp features, Rose shuddered as she moved towards him. *Nothing will make me marry that bully*, she thought. Once, she had come across Seth whipping his little dog until the animal was dead. The sight had sickened the tender-hearted girl, and she had wept and been disturbed for days afterwards.

"You took your time, girl! Get the ride moving while I take those balls to my mother! She's with the baby in the vardo. There's plenty of folk waiting to give their children rides, and we aren't turning good money away," he said, in a sulky voice.

She thrust the basket at him.

205

"Don't you order me about! I've to do my act in the arena now. Work the ride yourself."

Turning smartly on her heel, Rose walked away, but with a sudden flame of anger, Seth caught hold of her arm. She was spun around to face him with such force that she staggered.

"You three think you're better than us. Let me tell you something, my lady. I'll get you on your own one of these fine days. You won't be such a high and mighty..." Seth stopped what he was going to say when he heard Synfye call him.

"Bring the wooden balls over here, double quick, Seth."

"One of these fine days..." Seth said, with a finger pointing at Rose. He gave her an insolent look, and aimed a stream of spittle at Rose's feet before walking towards his mother's caravan.

Standing at the entrance of the arena and holding Warrior by his bridle, Lilly had seen the couple facing each other, she shouted as loud as she could.

"Rose. What the deuce are you standing there for? Give him the balls and get over here! We must mount up and start the performance!"

Beyond Lilly, Rose saw that crowds were turning out of the show tent and had begun to wander across the field towards the roped arena. Rubbing the mark Seth had made on her arm, she gave a sigh. A crowd like that meant a late finish, and she wanted to work on her new act with Hugo before it became too dark.

Wearing a plain red and green clown costume and a painted face, Ben led a couple of ponies close to the roundabout. The animals were saddled and ready to give children rides. He noticed that Seth was holding Rose's arm as he was talking. He saw her stagger, and Ben stepped forward. Rose had mentioned to him on the previous day that she had not felt well. But when Ben heard Lilly shout and saw Rose turn and hurry towards her sister, he stayed where he was. With narrowed eyes, he watched as Seth walked across the field to his mother.

Ben didn't have much time between rides, but when he had a moment to spare he watched Lilly, and spun a dream. He saw her ride with the other girls, round and round in the arena. He held his breath with apprehension each time Lilly leapt from the horse and her brother Lionel caught her in his arms.

"One day I will be the one to catch you," he said, but only the ponies heard his promise.

Chapter 17

When the 'Ardry Menagerie' came to Nottingham, the streets of summer in 1836 were enlivened by vivid advertisements pasted on walls and fences. Culvato had commissioned artists to portray a variety of acts in bright colours including the menagerie, horseback riding, and the children's rides. It was one of the posters that caught the attention of twelve-year-old Beatrice Soult.

"Nanny! Nanny Grant. Look at the picture," said Beatrice as she tugged at Nurse Grant's hand and pointed to draw the elderly woman across the street.

"Miss Beatrice! You must refrain from showing vulgar curiosity in public," Nurse Grant said in a severe tone; but her eyes twinkled as she looked down at her charge, she was as beautiful as her mother had been at her age.

Ignoring her nurse's stricture, the child looked in rapt wonder at the astonishing sight: a roundabout displayed in each corner of the poster; a fiery lion in the centre; and three ladies in skin-tight costumes standing on the back of a horse. Turning to her brother and Peggy, their maidservant, Beatrice pointed to the picture.

"A fair is coming to Nottingham, Richard. Look at those

ladies. I am sure that I could ride my pony in that same manner."

"Don't you dare try such a thing, Miss Beatrice. You would break a leg, or worse," said Peggy, in alarm.

The two women looked at each other with dismay when they saw a mulish expression settle on Beatrice's face. The little girl could be very difficult to manage if she didn't get her own way.

Nurse Grant tried to distract Beatrice's attention by guiding her around a muddy puddle and pulling her across the road.

"If we don't hurry to buy your new pencils, the shop will be closed. Your governess will not be pleased if you cannot write in your schoolbooks," she said.

"I would like to go to the fair, Peggy," said Richard. He scanned the poster with wide eyes.

"I will ask your mamma about it when we return home," Peggy promised, taking hold of his hand.

"Fairs are rough places, and only the lower classes attend such functions." Nurse Grant's nose was tilted high enough to dislodge her bonnet as she spoke.

Walking with Richard behind Nurse Grant, Peggy heard what the older woman said, and, without her noticing, she grimaced.

"Have you ever been to a fair, Peggy?" Richard asked.

"Hush now," Peggy whispered, bending down. "Once, when I was a little girl, I went with my brother. We rode wooden farm animals on a roundabout and had a wonderful time. They went round so fast that I was breathless for an age afterwards."

Richard's face beamed. He thought Peggy was the best nursemaid in the world, for Richard had been told it was Peggy who had passed him to his mamma for a cuddle when he was born.

It was the custom each afternoon, whilst sitting in front of the nursery fire, for Nurse Grant and Peggy to have a cup of tea. Meanwhile, the two children sat at the table and were served bread and butter and a glass of milk by a younger maid. Both Nurse Grant and Peggy were under the impression that the children couldn't overhear them.

"I see no harm in taking the children to the fair, Nurse Grant," said Peggy, once she saw the children were busy eating.

"Pickpockets and vagabonds hang around such places, and Gypsies are always ready to make folk part with their hard-earned money. No place for people such as us." With a dismissive sniff, Nurse Grant rose to her feet. "I must go about my duties now. Mrs Bigsby's gown needs to be pressed. And she wants me to dress her hair in ringlets and curls in plenty of time before dinner tonight."

"How is she? I heard Mrs Bigsby has kept to her rooms for the last week," Peggy asked. She wanted to find out about the health of old lady, but she knew if she asked Nurse Grant a direct question she wouldn't be told anything which could be repeated in the servants' quarters.

Nurse Grant replied in a lofty voice.

"Mrs Bigsby has had a cold in the head, but, thanks to my ministrations, she is now fully recovered."

Peggy hung her head in silent acknowledgement of Nurse Grant's superior standing in the household. Seeing the young girl's cheeks were flushed, and believing that it was Peggy's thoughtless question which had made her feel embarrassed, Nurse Grant seated herself again and began fanning her face with her apron. Peggy darted a glance at the older woman and risked speaking again.

"If we were to be accompanied by male members of the household, the master might let us go to the fair," Peggy murmured, hopefully.

Nurse Grant smoothed her apron over her knees and adjusted her skirts.

"I shouldn't think so. The last time the mistress attended a fairground the doctor had to be called in. She was unwell for weeks."

"Why was that, then?" Peggy stared at the nurse; her eyes were wide and sparkled with curiosity. That would be something to tell the other servants about when they had their bedtime cocoa.

"How should I know? If I did, I wouldn't tell a rumour spreader like you," Nurse Grant said, tossing her head. It was not for her to say that her mistress had met a Gypsy fortune-teller at the fair. The woman was wearing an amethyst necklace, and Charlotte had thought that it was the necklace that had once belonged to her mother, the one that had disappeared when her triplet girls were born.

Peggy had asked one question too many and Nurse Grant shot an icy look of disapproval towards the young nurse and then left the room with her skirts rustling.

The children had finished their meal. They watched the departure of Nurse Grant in silence and saw that a spark, which had jumped out of the fire and onto the pegged hearth-rug, was distracting Peggy.

"I shall ask Mamma if we can go to the fair when we are taken downstairs," Beatrice whispered.

"What if she says no?" Richard whispered back.

"Then I shall ask Papa."

Peggy dealt with the smouldering spark and moved to take away the children's empty plates.

"But what if...?"

Richard yelped as Beatrice gave her brother's shin a kick.

"All finished. Milk cups are empty? There's good children," Peggy said, beaming. "It's almost six o'clock. Go wash your hands and face and I'll brush your hair. It's time for you to go downstairs."

211

Seeing their parents each evening was something that the children enjoyed. Their governess would have already reported their progress and Charlotte would question her children about their lessons.

It was an unusual occurrence that George Soult had returned early from his office, and sat with his wife in the smaller drawing room. Softly draped curtains hung at the windows, and well-filled bookcases and cosy furniture made it a room to relax in.

The couple smiled with approval when Beatrice executed a graceful curtsy. Richard, not to be outdone by his sister, gave a splendid bow that rivalled his father's elegance.

Placing an arm around her son, Charlotte drew him close and dropped a kiss on the top of his head. Beatrice took the opportunity to snuggle up to her dear papa.

"What have you been doing today, Beatrice?" George asked.

"This morning I practised my scales on the piano. After that, I had a drawing lesson. This afternoon we went for a drive into the town with Nurse Grant and Peggy, and we bought some pencils..."

Richard leaned forward, and received a disagreeable stare from Beatrice when he interrupted.

"We saw a picture of a lion, Mamma!"

"Really?" George and Charlotte exchanged amused glances over the children's heads.

"It was a poster, not a picture, Richard." Beatrice turned back to her father and took hold of his hand, as she said: "There is a fair somewhere in Nottingham, Papa. Please could we go and visit it? Oh, please, Papa?"

"A fair?" George was startled. He hadn't noticed the advertisements proclaiming the arrival of Culvato's menagerie.

Across the room, Charlotte beckoned to Peggy who was sitting on her usual wooden seat by the wall. With flushed cheeks, Peggy stood in front of her mistress and curtsied.

"Why did the children see this poster?"

"It was very large, mistress. It had been stuck on the wall outside of the shop which we went to," Peggy said, nervously.

"George?" With a raised eyebrow Charlotte looked at her husband.

"We must discuss the matter. Tomorrow, Nurse will tell you both what we have decided," George said.

With that, the children had to be content and they dutifully said good night to their parents before they were led from the room.

***

The noise of the fairground could be heard from streets away. The carriage halted at Friar Gate near the centre of Nottingham, and because of the amount of traffic, it was unable to proceed any further.

"For goodness' sake, stop jumping around, Beatrice! You will make yourself sick. Richard, come here! If you move away from us you will be lost in the crowds forever," Nurse Grant scolded. Pulling Richard towards her, she took him firmly by the arm. Holding herself very straight and tall, she faced the three male servants and Peggy, who had caught hold of Beatrice just in time to prevent the child from being trampled by a wild-looking carthorse.

"We must keep together at all times, and as you were told by Mr Soult, never let Miss Beatrice or Master Richard out of your sight," Nurse Grant said to the servants. "If one of you is unfortunate enough to be separated from the rest of us, we will meet back here at four o'clock. That will give us two hours. Plenty of time to see what there is to see."

As they reached the first show booth, Ben, dressed as a clown with a painted smile juggled a set of brightly painted balls. The children and servants laughed at the antics of a little dressed-up, sad-faced monkey that was begging for coins. They couldn't resist putting a farthing into its tiny fist. His elderly master, turning the handle of a hurdy-gurdy, tipped his hat with its bobbing feathers, and winked at the ladies. Nurse Grant allowed herself a small smile as she drew Beatrice away.

"Look! Oh!" Richard shouted. His eyes were huge as he stood watching a woman standing on a platform, sensuously weaving a snake around her body until the serpent's head lay against her cheek.

Both women averted their eyes. Somehow the act seemed immoral, and yet strangely beautiful.

"Throw a ball! One ball in a bucket to win a prize," Seth called, beckoning the party closer. He was also dressed as a clown.

"Let me, Peggy! Let me try. I shall win, I know I will," Richard said, tugging Peggy's hand.

No one was more surprised than Richard when he won a china mug. His face glowing with excitement, he showed his fairing to Peggy and the others. Beatrice pouted. All of her balls had jumped out.

"A grand show to be seen! A show to amaze everyone young and old," Culvato, complete with whip and top hat called to the crowds who obediently flocked inside the show tent. He had noticed the way the adults were grouped protectively around Beatrice and Richard, and experience told him that the children would chatter about their outing to their numerous young friends.

Giving a shrill whistle, he caught William's attention. "Get those people inside and put them on seats near the stage," he said, pointing to the entrance of the tent with his whip.

The adults in the party were not sure how it was that they were so swiftly guided through the crowds, but Nurse Grant and Peggy found themselves seated on red plush chairs, with Beatrice and Richard between them. The man servants were grouped just behind.

The gasps of the audience masked that of Nurse Grant when the triplets ran onto the stage. She knew immediately who they were. Hadn't she brushed their mother's platinum hair a million times? Hadn't she washed that beautiful face, faithfully reproduced in triplication? The expression they wore was just like their mother's. The young women tilted her heads as they watched each sister move gracefully across the stage. Charlotte tilted her head in the very same way. Nurse Grant glanced at Beatrice, again, so like her mother at that age. Nurse Grant didn't know whether to laugh or cry. To see the three babies grown; knowing that they had all survived and were so beautiful made her want to weep with joy. She went hot and cold and hot again. What was she to do? Tell Charlotte? Mr Soult? Mrs Bigsby? Return home and say nothing?

"It has finished, Nurse Grant." Peggy saw the older woman was flushed and using a fan to try to cool her face. "Are you unwell? It's a trifle warm in here," she said, concern showing in her voice.

Nurse Grant took a deep breath and tried to bring herself under control.

"It's the heat. I will feel better once I am in the fresh air," she said. Taking another deep breath, she held Beatrice firmly by the hand as they mingled with the crowds heading towards the exit. Once free from the press of people, she let Peggy take hold of the child, and she stood for a moment, looking around.

"Over there! They are performing on horseback," Richard cried, setting off with a manservant in close pursuit.

"No! The merry-go-round! I want to go on the roundabout," Beatrice shouted, anxious to climb onto the back of a red rooster.

Everyone was breathless by the time they had caught up with Beatrice and Richard. They allowed each child to climb on to a wooden animal, but with strict instructions to hold tight and to stay where they were when the ride stopped.

"We will find you and help you down," Nurse Grant said, eying the height of the platform. At that height, a lady would be sure to show an ankle or a great deal of petticoat - maybe both. She glanced at the man servants and beckoned them forward so that they could assist the children.

As the roundabout spun, Beatrice threw her head back, laughing. Her bonnet was caught by the wind and was lost among the crowds. It took three rides before the children could be persuaded to leave the exhilarating experience and to look at other attractions.

The roped-off enclosure was surrounded by the public. Mouths gaped open and sighs of wonder were heard as Hugo strode into the ring carrying his whips. The triplets and Belle, who were now wearing riding habits trimmed with sequins, followed him. Dressed in that way, the triplets resembled their mother even more. Holding a handkerchief to her mouth, Nurse Grant wished she hadn't been persuaded to accompany the children. That had been the main condition Charlotte had laid down before she agreed to them going, and Nurse Grant couldn't find it in her heart to disappoint the children.

As they were leaving the fairground, Ursula Ardry passed close to the Soult party and noticed Beatrice and Richard. She felt a tingling on the back of her hands. Ursula saw immediately how much the children resembled the triplets. For a moment, her eyes met those of Nurse Grant. An unspoken message passed between them. The Nurse turned and hurried away to catch up with the others. Ursula gave a sad shake of her head. *No use fretting, my dear. Nothing will prevent a meeting between them if the stars foretell it,* she thought with a resigned sigh.

Chapter 18

Synfye wasn't sure what awakened her in the middle of the night. It could have been a brushing of clothing catching against the outside wood of the vardo. Perhaps it was a familiar perfume, that half-remembered concoction of herbs which, when rubbed upon swarthy Gypsy skin, made dogs and horses obey the wearer's commands.

When the vardo rocked and the door opened, she was curled up in bed, and straining to see through the darkness.

She was afraid. Brandy-Joe wouldn't enter the caravan and use her, even if he was blind drunk. Although, by Gypsy law, the vardo was legally his, he hadn't been inside it since their quarrel; not since he discovered the truth about Tawno's involvement in his wife's murder. She was alone with the baby. Seth was with Culvato in a neighbouring town, negotiating a new site for the fair. Synfye expected them both back about midmorning. Stealthily, her hand moved under her pillow, where she kept a razor-edged knife. Before she had time to draw her weapon, a strong hand clamped down hard over her mouth. Iron-like fingers cruelly pressed her cheeks, making her teeth ache. The pressure stifled her scream.

"Dub yer mummer, it's me."

Recognising the whisper, a shudder shook Synfye's body. Her eyes, accustomed to the faint light, stared wide with fear at the dark shape of the intruder.

"Mullo. Tawno's mullo has come to haunt me," she said, hardly moving her lips. Her voice shook with terror.

Relaxing his grip a little, Tawno's sour breath blew on her face.

"I'm no mullo. I've come back to join my loving family. Word got to me of my brother's success, and I want to be with you, my romni," he whispered.

"But how? We all thought you were dead. Where have you been? How did you get here?"

"Dead. Yes. For thirteen years I've been in a land where death was better than living. First I had to find a passage home to England. It took more than a year to save up enough money for the fare. Then I had to make me way up north and find you all. But now I'm back, my romni."

"How have you been living? Why did you have to leave us so long?" Synfye's voice still shook, but her fear was now about something else.

"Got picked up by the constables. They transported me. Said I'd been thieving. Twelve years they gave me." Tawno stood back from the bed, but kept his eyes on Synfye. "All those who travelled over to the colonies with me died. Couldn't stand the outdoor life and they all got sick. I got to know a seaman and he 'elped me get back to England. Been back a while, watching you."

"I'll light the lamp.'

'No! No. I don't want anyone to see me yet. Talk about you. Where do you fit into me brother's fair?"

Synfye swallowed.

"I've a sideshow, balls in buckets. Pays well. Seth helps around the fair. He's a good chal."

Tawno could just make out Synfye's figure lying under the blankets. His looks had changed. His hair and beard had flecks of grey, though he was still fit and lean. During his last year in the colonies he had earned and stolen small amounts of money. Carefully saving each coin, he had managed to make his way to the coast and buy a passage on a clipper sailing to England. Since his return to his home country he'd made a precarious living by stealing and selling horses to individuals often shadier than himself. Spells of imprisonment, whipping, starvation, and days in the stocks did nothing to change Tawno's thieving ways, although as he travelled through the countryside he had become far more cautious.

"I've brought some grais for Culvato. Tethered them in the woods. Perhaps I'll give a couple to the chal."

Synfye smiled and nodded.

"You must be miles away from your friends."

"Friends. I never trust them that call themselves friends." Tawno gave a sharp laugh. "I've not forgotten those so-called friends in Melton Mowbray. Brandy-Joe and his pals informed on me, and blamed me for a job that they had done. I saw them standing in the crowd. They were grinning like the fools they are when the gaolers whipped me. I was more than lucky that day not to have had me neck stretched."

He rubbed his hand across his face, and Synfye heard the rasp of his stubble.

He knew. He must know that Brandy-Joe works in the fair if he's been watching. Does he know about him and me being married? she thought. Swinging her legs out of the bed, she went to the food cupboard. Cheese, bread and a plate of cold fowl was placed on the table. Tawno eyed it hungrily.

"Drink?" he growled.

"I've ale and a bottle of whisky."

"Ale."

Returning to the bed, and sitting with her knees drawn up to her chin, she watched in the dimness as Tawno gobbled up every piece of food on the table. When he'd finished, light was just beginning to streak the sky. Suddenly a whimper brought Tawno's attention to the baby.

"The girl. Mikailia?"

"She died on the journey to Eastwood. Fever took her."

Synfye held her breath. If Tawno asked to know more, she intended to tell him the same story as she had told Ursula. Even after all this time she would find it impossible to explain her dreadful act of abandoning their daughter in a wood to starve to death. For all his faults, Tawno had loved his children.

"The big boy?"

"Oh! Seth. He ain't rommered yet. Out tonight with Culvato, be back later today."

"So, where's this tikni from?"

Synfye had no time to answer. She cowered back with her hands covering her cheeks, when, springing to his feet, Tawno leaned over her. He looked three times his size to the terrified woman.

"You. You have a new man."

"We thought you were dead. We had no word from you. It's been years, Tawno."

Synfye cowered lower when he lifted his fist. Suddenly, his red-rimmed eyes narrowed and he put his face close to hers.

"Why? Why would you sleep here, and him, your man, sleep somewhere else?"

"We... He found the plate you took. He had made it and knew you were the one. His woman, Curlanda, was killed most horrible," she whispered.

Snatching a hank of her loose hair, Tawno yanked Synfye to her feet.

"What's... his... name?" he growled, with a tug of her hair

punctuating each word.

"Joe."

"Joe. What?"

"L-Lincolin,"

Synfye found herself flying across the caravan to sprawl on the floor. She fell awkwardly and heard the bone crack in her arm.

"Out. Get the mochadi beng in here."

With a scream she rolled over, and Tawno aimed a kick in the small of her back.

"Wait." With his eyes bloodshot and mouth dribbling spittle, Tawno smiled an evil smile. "What does this man of yours do for a living?"

"F-Fire. Fire e-eater and juggler. He's a f-farrier and l-looks after the camel," Synfye sobbed, holding her arm.

"Sit down, woman. I've decided to wait until everyone's awake. Then I'll go and see this new rom of yours. I've a score to settle with 'im. Not only did he get my back bloodied, I've thought for a long time that he knew something about my vardo getting burnt. Maybe I can buy you back from him. If it's the same Brandy-Joe I used to know he'll be glad to get rid of you, at any price."

As the people in the camp began to stir, dogs were already searching for food. Lighted lamps appeared at the windows of living wagons, and on poles outside bender tents. The kindling of cooking fires gave off palls of smoke before bursting into flames. The wood was slow to ignite in the light misty rain that softened the ground.

**

At about seven o'clock, Brandy-Joe drank a mug of tea made by Jem. Using the remainder of the hot water, the boy soaped and then shaved away all the hair on his father's head - a safety precaution necessary for anyone using fire in their act. Whiskers quickly singe.

Joe collected his props together and, carrying a large tin of oil, he walked across the field to the empty show tent. He preferred practising in the open air, but because it was still drizzling, he began preparing his complicated equipment in the tent. Once inside, he carefully closed the tent flap. A draught could have fatal consequences.

Joe laid out his torches on a table in a specific order. He placed a bowl of flammable mixture, into which he dipped the torches, on the ground near the table. A special liquid, which he had mixed earlier, stood in a bottle on the table ready for use. During his act, he would blow out a mouthful of the liquid and light it. Flames would shoot across the stage, which would amaze and scare any audience. The tin under the table, which contained the remainder of the oil, was uncapped, ready to refill the bottle.

Brandy-Joe's greased torso and shaven head gleamed in the light of a smoking oil lamp which hung on a nail overhead on the king pole. A sudden draught made the lamp flicker. He saw the figure of a man silhouetted in the doorway.

"What the 'ell are you doing in here? I don't have folk watching when I practice me act." Brandy-Joe squinted at the man who took no notice of his threatening yells and began walking towards him.

"Tawno? Tawno Ardry?"

"You have yourself a new act, Joe. A fire-eater? Finished with burning vardos?" Tawno came closer, pointing a finger at Brandy-Joe. "Now you've taken me woman. She ain't much, I know, but she's mine."

When he recognised who it was, Brandy-Joe clenched his ham-like fists, ready to pummel to death the loathsome toad that had killed his lovely Curlanda.

"I've been waiting for you, beng. Knew you'd come back one day. The whole world will know what you did to my Curlanda. Made her mong to die, did you? Well. We'll see how long it takes to make you mong."

As Brandy-Joe spoke, Tawno continued walking towards the colossal man. With a rush, they locked together and began punching and biting. Both men seemed to be determined to fight dirtier than the other.

Holding her broken arm and whimpering with pain, Synfye followed Tawno into the tent. She could see they were resolved to kill each other, and she tried to get close enough to part them and try to talk some sense into them. Without realising what she had done, her foot kicked over the tin containing the remainder of the oil that had been placed under the table. It spread in a thick mess, saturating the sawdust and straw under their feet. The table toppled over as Synfye tried to separate the men, and the oily mixture intermingled with the flammable contents of the bowl and the unlit torches. They splashed around, feet slipping and sliding, mixing the dreadful concoction on the ground.

Lifting the kicking Tawno with one hand, Brandy-Joe began to beat his back and head against Big Bill, the main structural wooden post. The lighted lamp hanging on the nail above them swung wildly. It fell with a tinkle of breaking glass. Like a living thing, the flames ran across the oil and consumed Synfye's skirt and the men's trousers. Fight forgotten, each person tried to beat out the flames on their clothing, but in seconds they were rolling on the floor and screaming in agony.

"Fire! Fire in the big show tent!"

Others took up Hugo's desperate cry. Everyone in the vicinity raced to the tent. When the tent flap was lifted, black, oily smoke pothered out to meet them. Those nearest began coughing and retching as the smoke billowed into their faces.

"Look out! It's coming down! The canvas is on fire! Get back! Get back!"

They watched in horror as the huge tent collapsed in a heap of burning oiled canvas, ropes and poles. It was impossible to reach those inside without endangering themselves. Swiftly, a human chain was started to move buckets of water from the nearby river to try to douse the flames, but it had little effect.

Leaping from their horses, Culvato and Seth ran towards the burning heap.

"How did this happen? Did anyone see?"

Everyone was milling around, finding buckets and using blankets to beat out the flames. Those near enough to hear Culvato shook their head, their faces pale with shock.

A voice called from the crowd.

"I saw a man. Don't know who he was, a stranger. He was followed inside the tent by Brandy-Joe's wife."

"Synfye? Oh no! Not Synfye." Ursula clung tightly to Lilly, who started weeping. Seth, hearing what was said, stared blankly at those who were still trying to put out the fire.

Eventually, all that was left of the tent was a smouldering mass. The men continued throwing water in a steady flow until they were able to remove the three bodies from under the charred covering.

"Do you know who the other person was, Mr Ardry?" someone asked.

"No one, no matter who should die in such a terrible way as this," he said, shaking his head.

"One was a woman," a man said, pulling a smoking piece of canvas across the grass.

"Someone said they thought they heard a woman screaming," someone else called.

"Mrs Lincolin," Culvato announced, in a flat voice. "She

224

was with Brandy-Joe. Find out if anyone else is missing from the camp," he said, glancing around at the helpers.

Standing alone with an empty bucket in his hand, Jem stood watching the men stripping away the canvas. It was Heather and Belle who gently drew the stricken young man from the scene, and took him to Culvato's vardo. It took a good amount of whisky before some colour returned to Jem's cheeks.

When Culvato entered the vardo, Jem half rose with a questioning look.

"Sit down, lad. Have another drink, and tell me what your dadrus did this morning."

When his glass was refilled, Jem swallowed the contents in one gulp. He wiped his mouth with his fingers, before speaking,

"Nothing. We had a mug of tea as usual, and I… I shaved him. After that I left him and went to clean out Lucky's stall. Before I left, I saw Dadrus collecting his stuff together, ready for practice. He said he'd use the big tent because of the wind and rain."

"Did you see him talking to anyone?"

"No. He might have called 'Good morning' to old Mr Ardry. I saw that he was carrying a couple of rabbits when I was going across the field."

"Mrs Lincolin. Did you see her?"

Jem shook his head, and then suddenly rose to his feet.

"The chavvi. She'll be all alone." As Jem spoke, the door opened and Ursula entered, carrying baby Isopel.

"There's enough womenfolk here to look after the chavvi until you see whether you'll be staying with us or joining your father's people."

"Don't forget she's Seth's half sister too, Rom." Seeing the dismay on the men's faces, Ursula guessed rightly that they had forgotten Seth.

"He came home with me. We arrived back early, just as fire belched out the top of the tent. I saw him running towards the fire, and then we joined everyone else trying to get inside."

"I'll go and find him," Ursula said, thrusting Isopel into Heather's arms.

"Wait. I'll come with you." Ramming his hat on, Culvato followed his wife and Jem out of the vardo. The stench of smoke and the smell of burning hung over the camp. Ursula covered her mouth with the corner of her shawl between bouts of coughing.

Some women had brought clean white sheets from their vardo and had covered the three bodies, which had been moved well away from the remnants of the tent.

They found Seth on his knees beside his mother. Holding his hat, Culvato placed a hand on the young man's shoulder.

"Come to my vardo, lad. Have a glass of something to help with the shock."

Glancing up, Seth saw that Jem was staring at an uncovered brown hand.

"Best you give it to him; seems he needs it more than me."

Although the words held a spiteful ring, Seth allowed Culvato to lead him to the caravan. Jem followed, walking beside Ursula.

***

Later that day, children were playing in the woods near the camp and found a dog guarding Tawno's pack. Because the dog had barked and growled ferociously, they left it and ran to fetch Culvato.

A noose was thrown over the dog's neck and the remainder of the rope tied to a tree: that rendered the animal harmless, although it jumped and strained to free itself. The pack was examined. They found worn clothing and a rope bridle. Then, a pair of leather boots with a knife tucked inside. The knife had a hand-carved bone handle. As he picked it up, Culvato recognised Tawno's handiwork, and felt his stomach churn. The initials T.A, cut deeply into the base, confirmed his fears.

"You know who it belongs to, Sherrekano?" one of the tent men asked.

Without looking up, Culvato nodded.

"My brother, Tawno," he said, getting to his feet. Ignoring everyone who spoke to him, he hurried to his vardo.

As soon as she saw her husband's shocked expression, Ursula immediately shooed everyone out of the vardo.

"The man was Tawno," he said, when they were alone.

For a brief moment Ursula froze. Culvato's eyes brimmed, and she rushed to put her arms around him, and rocked him as though he was a child. It was quite a while before Culvato's sobs turned into hiccups, and then a long shuddering moan escaped his lips.

"Why didn't he come to see me first? He should have done. I would have told him. Broke it to him. I would never have let her marry again unless I thought that he was dead."

"Hush. Hush now. What's done is done. He must have wanted to see her. If she told him that she was now married to Brandy-Joe, they'd probably both went to the tent to find him. It's not your fault."

"Where do you think he's been all these years?"

"Someone may be able to tell us one day, my dear."

"How on earth could such a thing happen?"

"We'll never know that, Rom. You know how quick-tempered Tawno could be. Maybe they argued, or maybe Brandy-Joe was careless."

Culvato rubbed his cheeks with the back of his hand and gave a heavy sigh.

"Not like Brandy-Joe to make a mistake, he was always so careful setting up his act," he said.

The stench of burning still hung in the air when Culvato felt he had enough control of himself to leave his vardo. He went to find Seth. It wasn't easy to tell Seth that his father was the stranger who had died with Synfye. Taking the young man into the woods, they shared their grief in private.

It was Seth who heard a horse whinny. They discovered five horses, all tethered near the place where Tawno had left his pack. The horses had not been noticed earlier because they were out of sight behind bushes.

"Why? Why didn't he bring them into the camp and then come and find me? I never forgot him. I know that he didn't treat my dai very kindly, but I still loved my dadrus." Once again, Seth's shoulders began heaving with suppressed sobs.

"I think it was his way of saying sorry. Perhaps he hoped that one of these days he could turn up as a rich man and take you and your dai away to live together."

All the horses were sound. Running a hand over one of them, Culvato nodded.

"You want to keep this grey, and you'll get a good price for the rest. Tawno always had a good eye for horse flesh."

Seth turned his head away to hide his tears whilst gently stroking the soft nose of the horse.

Leaving the young man to grieve, Culvato returned to his vardo. He had to begin making the funeral arrangements. Men from the fairground were sent on horseback to where he knew friends and families would be camped. News of the fairground disaster quickly spread around the country. When they heard about the tragedy, everyone connected with both the Lincoln and the Ardry family promptly packed their possessions and travelled to attend the funeral.

Ursula and the triplets were constantly busy for the next

few days, cooking and feeding each group of travellers as they arrived. Beer and spirits flowed as each person drank to the departed.

The funeral was attended by so many that the parish church in the small village of Selston was not big enough to accommodate them all. The service was dignified and sombre, as befitted the occasion. Culvato had already suggested to Jem and Seth that it would be better if the deceased were to be buried in separate graves, side-by-side. Seth nodded and after a short discussion with the chief of the Lincoln family, Jem agreed too.

The bell rang in a slow and regular manner as Synfye, Tawno and Brandy-Joe were laid to rest. Thanking the minister for the service, Culvato and his family returned home.

He had made an arrangement for Synfye's vardo to be placed in a field, well away from the fairground. A solemn crowd walked to the field and stood together in small family groups. Jem and Seth stood either side of the caravan, each with a lighted torch. Culvato lifted his hand. As he lowered it, the two young men touched the wood and canvas structure with the torches, and watched as it burst into flames. When the vardo was well alight, they threw the torches inside the open door and turned away. They hurried away in different directions. The only thing left to be decided was which of her half brothers would be responsible for the baby, Isopel.

Chapter 19

Hugo sat on an old wooden box, polishing leather tack. He'd been keeping a watch on the vardo for more than an hour in the hope of catching Rose alone inside. With the tack polished, supple and ready for use, Hugo hung it on a hook at the back of the vardo. He found a brush and began to groom Nipper until the coat of the little brown and white dog shone from his attention. When his mother left the vardo along with Lilly and Heather, he stood on the top step gave a sigh. "At last," he muttered. "Oh! Didn't know anyone was in here."

Looking up from playing with baby Isopel, Rose gave him a smile. It was rare indeed for the couple to be alone. Closing the door and seating himself beside the stove, Hugo watched Rose holding Isopel's hands. The baby beamed and babbled baby talk as she enjoyed the sensation of standing on Rose's lap. Because he was so close, Rose caught a whiff of the leather polish Hugo had been using. Her heart thumped and her cheeks glowed with pleasure.

To cover her confusion, she said: "She'll be walking in a few more weeks. Look how strong she is."

As though to prove Rose wrong, Isopel promptly sat down on her bare, dimpled bottom and began to suck her fingers.

"Wish she was ours," Hugo muttered, between clenched teeth.

At first, Rose thought she hadn't heard properly. Her smile, which had brightened her face at his unexpected entrance, disappeared. Her cheeks paled, and then she blushed crimson. She gave the scowling young man an incredulous look.

"That's wicked, Hugo. You must never... We'll both be in terrible trouble if, if..."

"You feel the same. I know you feel the same as me." His eyes were wide, and both his hands were clenched as he stood over her.

Rose shook her head so wildly that a ribbon fell out of her hair.

"No! Hugo! We can't ever. Don't ever think..."

"I'll never take a wife, if I can't have you..."

"Get out! Go on! You're wicked talking to me like this. The Bible says it's wicked. You'll be damned in hell and me with you."

Tears welled up and ran down the frightened girl's cheeks before plopping onto the baby's head.

Hugo leaned forward.

"You do love me. I know you do. I've seen how you've looked at me when you thought I wasn't watching," he said quietly.

"Yes. Oh, yes. But it's wrong to have such feelings. It says in the Bible that brother and sister must not... When I go to church I always ask God to forgive me for thinking such things."

"Love like I feel can't be wrong. I know it can't. Say you love me, just once more, Rose."

"Yes. Yes, I love you dearly."

The whispered words, low as they were, brought a satisfied gleam to Hugo's eyes.

"I'll go away now I know that. Be better than seeing you every day and knowing I can't touch you."

"No! Oh no, Hugo. Please, my dear one, I couldn't bear it if you went away."

"Wish there was someone I could talk to. Perhaps dadrus?"

"No, Hugo! Dadrus would kill us and then he'd make me marry Seth."

"Seth? Who's said anything about you marrying that weasel?" he cried.

"I once heard Dai talking to Beebee Synfye. It was a long time before she died. They thought it would be a good match."

"Never! You'll never be his woman. I'd kill him first."

"Oh, don't say that. Oh, Hugo what a mess. I'm sure other brothers and sisters must have felt like us. I wonder what they did about it. Oh, I can't bear it."

With a sobbing moan, Rose lifted the baby and buried her face in the infant's soft curls. Hugo echoed her cry, and with a bound he was out of the vardo and running into the nearby woods as though pursued by tigers.

By the time Heather and Lilly returned to the vardo to change into their spangled costumes, Rose had brought her feelings under control and was able to act as normal. If her sisters noticed her reddened eyes and pale cheeks they made no comment.

"I've persuaded Dadrus to let Ben take Lionel's place, and he'll now work with us on the horses. Lionel's wanted to work with Belle for ages. Now they can do that juggling act they've been practising together."

Lilly's voice was light, and her face glowed at the prospect of having Ben catch her in his arms. He was in his mid twenties, very muscular and handsome, his hair in long, loose curls which he tied at the nape of his neck with a ribbon.

They found it difficult, but whenever Lilly and Ben had

the opportunity to meet in secret, they planned their future together. Lilly, just like her sisters, told her love that it was futile. But the couple talked of how they would have a proper Gypsy wedding; it was an impossible dream. Culvato would never be persuaded to let one of his girls marry a Gaujo. Yet neither Lilly nor Ben wanted to feel ashamed of their love and run away, to just live together without the blessing of Ursula and Culvato. They did have the means to leave, since Ben had enough money saved to own a small fair, and the knowledge to run it as a successful business.

Heather sniffed and tossed her head. "He's a Gaujo, and not one of the family."

"So is William Astwood. That doesn't stop you from making eyes at him, and I've seen you talking to him on your own, more than once."

Lilly felt sorry she had spoken so sharply when she saw a bleak look settle on Heather's face.

It was true, but William always kept his distance. He always called her Miss Heather or Miss Ardry, and spoke only of his work.

"No use you mooning after such a one as him. Neither Romani law nor the Gorjios folk would let you live together. If he was a lord or an earl, that would be a different matter. He could take you to the palace in London, and then you would meet the King and Queen. Everyone would want to know you then. No one would have to know that you were born a Gypsy if you didn't tell them."

Heather knew Rose was speaking the truth, but it didn't make it easier to bear. Taking the baby from her sister, Heather nodded towards the door.

"Dai said that she wants you to help her with the cooking, Rose. She's trying to get everything ready for the party tonight. Says she wants everything to be ready for after the Gaujo people have gone home." She glanced at Lilly who was on her knees and reaching into a cupboard used by Ursula for storing lace.

"I've managed to get Dadrus's waistcoat finished without him seeing it. I hope it fits him." Holding up an emerald green silk waistcoat trimmed with gold braid, Lilly bit her lip anxiously. She had copied the pattern from one of Culvato's old waistcoats, but she thought that lately he seemed to have put on some extra weight.

"If you keep bringing it out he'll see it and then his birthday surprise will be ruined," Rose said tartly, as she opened the door.

Lilly and Heather both blinked in surprise when the vardo door banged closed.

"I do wish Rose would say what's making her so unhappy," Lilly said, wrapping the waistcoat in a white cloth, and putting it back in the cupboard.

"She will tell us when she's ready," said Heather, kicking off her shoes. "Perhaps it's because she wants to ride by herself in the ring and do that new trick she's learnt," she added, pulling a fresh spangled tunic on over her head.

With a pensive expression, Lilly shook her head.

"It's more than that. If I didn't know better, I'd say our Rose was in love and can't tell anyone about it, but I can't think who that might be," she said.

***

At last, the customers were drifting away from the show ground. Men covered the smaller rides with oiled canvas sheeting. Candles and lamps in the show booths and tents, and around the children's rides, were snuffed out. The animals had been fed and securely locked up, and the chickens were in their coops, safe from the murderous attention of foxes. Women were bent over open fires, cooking the evening meal; the mixed aroma of food and wood smoke drifted across the field as the moon shed its light on the tired but contented travellers.

Because Ursula had invited a great number of Culvato's family and most of the fair folk to supper, she had made an effort to make the meal special. One of her cooking pots was large enough for two hares, plus vegetables flavoured with herbs. She had already baked batches of Gypsy bread, made with freshly milled flour, butter, milk and cream of tartar. An assortment of fruit pies baked in a Dutch oven stood cooling in rows on a table next to several pots of cream.

Honey balls were always a favourite with Culvato's family. Rose was blending honey with stewed apples and eggs and dropping spoonfuls of the mixture into hot butter when Seth walked up to her. Tossing her hair back from her face, Rose had no idea how desirable she looked. Her face was pink and glowing from the heat of the fire, and her eyes were sparkling.

"Dai told me to make these. She was saying how she used to make them when we were children. We all gobbled them up so fast that there were never enough left for Dadrus," she said.

Rose watched under her eyelashes as Seth walked away without answering and seated himself next to Lionel and Hugo. *Grumpy pig,* she thought. He had a small waist and broad shoulders like her brothers, and he wore the traditional Gypsy bandanna and gold earring. Since the death of his mother and father he was a lonely figure; when he wasn't working, he roamed around in the woods snaring small animals. It surprised everyone but the triplets that the young man had taken a dislike to his half sister, Isopel, and refused to have anything to do with the baby. Jem, in comparison, always made a fuss of the chavvi and encouraged her to smile.

Almost everyone had finished eating when the first rattle of a tambourine was heard. It began jingling in tempo to the haunting sounds of panpipes and a squeezebox. Dancing began. Skirts flared and handkerchiefs waved gaily as the women whirled and paced intricate patterns on the grass in time to the rhythmic music. With laughing glances they invited the men to join them. One by one, the women found partners who danced facing them and clapped with hands held high in the air. Seth joined Rose and danced close enough for their swaying bodies to touch. Springing to his feet, Hugo stood scowling at the couple.

"Sit down, Hugo. They're only enjoying the dance." Lionel pulled at his brother's sleeve, and then pushed his tankard of ale into Hugo's hand. "Watch me with Heather and our Lilly," he laughed.

With a high leap, Lionel landed in front of the two girls, who whirled around faster when they saw who their partner was. As the music finished, the three of them doubled up laughing, coughing and out of breath.

Culvato still held Ursula around the waist as they finished dancing. Pulling her closer and nibbled her ear. "Come with me, woman," he murmured.

She wound both arms around his neck, pressed against him and looked deep into his eyes.

"Where shall we go, Birthday Rom?" she asked in a sultry voice.

Still a little dizzy from whirling round, Ursula staggered on the uneven ground as they walked away. Culvato tightened his grip, and held her even closer as he led her away from the campfire and into the darkness. The music was muted in the soft night air; it faded and they only heard each other's heartbeats and murmured endearments as they made love.

The triplets were laughing with Lionel when Seth caught

hold of Rose by the arm. He drew her apart from the others and was about to lead her into the darkness. Suddenly, he found himself sitting on the ground, looking up into the angry face of Hugo.

"Take your hands off my sister!" Hugo held his clenched fists out towards Seth as he spoke.

"We were dancing. What's got into you?" Seth jumped to his feet, ready to fight, and, as Hugo lifted his fists, Seth hunched his shoulders ready to defend himself.

"You weren't dancing just now."

"She's willing. She wouldn't have danced with me like that if she wasn't," Seth said, scowling at Hugo.

"Where had your dadrus come from on the day Brandy-Joe died?" Hugo growled. "Why was he in the tent?"

Hugo's words were cut short as Seth rushed forward, and the two young men began fighting in earnest. Years of distrust and dislike helped to fuel their anger. Blows to body and face soon brought red swellings and blood. Hugo lashed out with a searing fury at the young man who danced so close to his Rose.

The fight was finished when a short branch hit Hugo at the back of the head.

With fists still raised, Seth looked at Jem Lincolin in astonishment.

"No need for that! I could have beat him," he said sulkily, rubbing his grazed knuckles.

"You don't scrap with your cousin. Family don't fight - they stick together," Jem said, eying Seth with distaste. "Might have knocked some sense into your thick skull."

The triplets were bending over Hugo; Rose cupped his beloved face in her hands and looked up at Jem.

"You might have killed him, hitting his head like that," she spat out. Three pairs of accusing blue eyes stared like flints at the handsome young man, who stared back defiantly.

"Good thing the sprog has a thick head of hair." Standing square in front of Jem, Piramus looked him straight in the eye as he spoke.

With a muttered curse, Jem threw the branch onto the fire and turned away. Everyone watched in silence as he disappeared into the darkness. With a groan, Hugo sat up and put a hand to his head. The girls helped him to his feet and supported him as he leaned against the side of their vardo.

"Shame you had to say that to Seth. He doesn't know what happened to his dai and dadrus any more than we do." Lionel rubbed the back of his hand over his mouth as he spoke, and looked with some trepidation towards two shadowy figures that were laughing and walking towards them.

"What's this then?" Culvato called. "Lost your way up the steps?"

His smile disappeared when he saw the dour expressions and noticed Hugo's battered face.

"A bit of trouble between the boys, Culvato. Jem hit Hugo over the head when he began fighting with Seth."

As he finished speaking, Piramus lit his clay pipe, and with eyes half closed from the smoke, he watched the young folk keenly. There was something here he didn't quite understand. He felt that there was something more than an ongoing dislike between the cousins.

"It's nothing, Dadrus. I thought Seth was dancing too close to my sister, and I said the first thing that came to mind."

They were standing under a lamp, and Culvato saw that Hugo was close to tears.

Giving him a hard look, Culvato turned to face Piramus, who shook his head.

"The boy needs a whipping. Teach him how to hold his tongue and not to lash out with his fists for no good reason," said Culvato, who was beginning to undo the buckle of his belt, when Piramus caught hold of his arm.

"No! No, Culvato. Don't thrash the chal. One is as bad as the other. They've always scrapped over foolish trifles. It wasn't nothing important."

With a quick glance at Culvato, Seth turned on his heel and walked away.

The two men and Ursula followed the triplets and Hugo into the vardo. Hugo looked at his father with a mixture of bravado and fear. If Seth left the fair because of the fight, they would be a sideshow short, and he would be held responsible for the drop in the takings.

"Relax, boy, but say no more about tonight's happening," Culvato said, wagging a finger at Hugo.

Swallowing hard, relief on his face, Hugo glanced at Rose who returned a supportive smile. She was crimson with guilt. *If only I had discouraged Seth from dancing with me none of this would have happened,* she thought. With her eyes on Hugo's pale face, she vowed to be much more careful in the future. Anyway, it was time to retire to bed, for they had to be ready to begin the journey to Scarborough in the morning.

Chapter 20

Salt-laden wind and sand whipped up by the horses blew in the faces of the Gypsies. The long fair hair of Heather and Rose streamed out behind them; they were clearly enjoying themselves as they galloped along the foam-flecked beach of Scarborough.

As usual, Heather led the party. Hugo rode near her, followed by Lionel, Rose and William Astwood. When he realised that Lilly would be occupied sewing costumes for most of the day, Ben had decided to join the riders at the last moment and he brought up the rear. Further back along the beach, a new camel ridden by Jem, plodded along. Jem balanced precariously in the custom-made saddle.

It was Heather who first caught glimpses of the rider high on the cliff. She shouted, and pointed upwards to the right, alerting the others to the rider who galloped the horse as though keeping pace with the party below.

A terrible echoing scream rang out from Heather, and the harsh cry of gulls wheeling round the wave-and wind-torn rock face faded to nothingness. The riders on the beach immediately drew rein. At least one horse reared up with front hooves pawing the air. The Gypsies stared with horror as the horse fell down the cliff. It broke through stunted trees and bushes, causing a shower of stones and earth to fall as it bounced from one protrusion to another. The horse finally landed in a heap on the boulder-strewn sand. At the same time, the rider was in freefall until the body came to a halt, spread across a ledge. As far as the Gypsies could see, the rider made no movement.

Heather, shedding her temporary paralysis and shaking back her hair, glanced to where the fallen horse lay motionless among the rocks. She could see blood seeping into the sand.

"Come on. We can't do anything to help the rider from down here. We'll have to climb to the top." She pointed to a narrow path a little further along the beach. It twisted upwards until it disappeared among the thin trees and scrub. Her comrades quickly dismounted. They saw that Hugo was removing the rope halter from his horse and undoing the knots.

"Best have a length of rope. It's not very long, but it might be useful," he said, draping the coil of rope over his shoulder and setting off for the path.

Lionel hurried to where Jem had halted his camel on the firm sand near the water's edge. Jem had seen the horse fall, but had not noticed the rider until Lionel pointed to where a piece of fabric flapped in the breeze.

"You get our horses back to the camp, Jem, and tell Dadrus what's happened. We'll try to rescue the person lying up there." Lionel jerked his head towards the others who were already beginning to climb the steep path.

"The rider doesn't seem to have fallen too far down, but I'm sure we'll need some help. Tell Dadrus to bring plenty of ropes, and bring some lifting tackle," called Lionel, as he began running to join the others.

The climb to the top of the cliff was difficult and treacherous, with loose stones and scrub with shallow roots, which pulled away at the slightest tug.

"Oh, look - look over there, it's a girl," Rose cried, pointing at the figure, almost hidden by bushes. They were able to see, but were not near enough reach the fluttering skirt of the rider.

"Do you think I could climb over to her from here? There seem to be plenty of handholds," Heather said.

"Best try from the top. Always easier to get down than up and across," William said. He stood so close by Heather's side that he could smell the perfume of her hair.

"Whichever way we choose it's going to be difficult," Rose said, pointing to where more small scrubs and clumps of wild grass hung as though peering over the cliff at the vista below.

Taking the circus horses with him, Jem rode the camel as fast as possible to the fairground a mile or so away. Culvato owned so many attractions that the tents, fair rides, show booths and stalls - selling everything from toffee apples and hot peas to toys and novelties - covered almost an acre.

When the group of young people reached the place on the cliff top where the rider had fallen, they found that boulders had been torn away, and a small tree lay partly uprooted. They glanced at each other with some concern. Only the lightest weight could be supported by the stunted bushes - and only then if the person climbing down the cliff face was extremely careful.

"I can just see her. She isn't very far down. I don't think she has moved. Do you think she could be dead?" Lionel said.

Moving to Lionel's side, William dropped to his knees and together they peered over the edge of the cliff. The rest grouped themselves behind them.

"Hello! Young lady! You down there, can you hear me?" William called.

"The damn sea birds are too noisy. She can't hear us," Rose said, biting her thumb anxiously.

"The wind carries your voice away. Hold me steady and I'll try to reach her," Heather said, grasping Hugo's hand.

"Wait for me, I'm coming down with you," Rose said.

"No!" Hugo shouted in alarm. "Those bushes won't support both of you. Let Heather try, she's lighter."

As she lowered herself slowly over the edge, Heather's eyes met William's and she saw his look of horror.

Only he saw her lips form the words, "Don't worry. I'll be careful, my love."

"Go careful, Heather! Remember to have a good handhold before putting any weight on your feet." Lionel shouted, as she moved further down.

"I have plenty to hold on to. I should be able to reach her. But whether we can get her up again is another matter," she said, frowning with concentration.

Heather inched down the cliff face with the same careful agility as she moved in her balancing acts. Her cheek brushed the stones, handholds and footholds were tested for safety before she used their support. Inch by inch, she descended.

The ledges on the cliff face were full of loose shale at the point where the rider had fallen, and as Heather brushed against them, stones bounced to the beach below.

Glancing up, she took a sharp breath and pressed her cheek closer to the rock face as earth slid towards her from the roots of the fallen tree.

"Make sure the tree doesn't come down, it's right above us!" Heather yelled.

"Come back, it's too dangerous!" Rose shouted.

"I'm near to her now!" Heather called back.

Looking up again, she saw that the men were holding the fallen tree, and Hugo was tying it with his rope halter to a nearby bush.

Hugging the cliff face and trying not to dislodge the loose

rocks, Heather moved slowly further down. She was startled when she disturbed a sea bird, and cried out with alarm.

"Heather! What is it? Can you reach her yet?' Lionel called as he peered cautiously over the edge.

Those above didn't hear her reply, "No. Not yet," for her words were blown away by the wind.

Desperately casting around for help, Hugo noticed a roof and chimneys showing over the top of distant trees. He clutched hold of Ben's arm. "I can see a house over there," he shouted, pointing. "Go and fetch help, Ben. Tell them a young lady has fallen down the cliff, and we are in dire need of assistance. Hurry now."

"I've nearly reached her," Heather called. "She's alive. She's still on the ledge."

"That's one good thing. Now we have to find a way to get them both back up," Hugo muttered, giving a desperate glance towards the house. There was no sight of Ben.

When a few feet away from the girl, Heather tried to attract her attention by shouting, but there was no response. With the questionable support of a slender tree and a couple of bushes, she inched her way closer, and called to the girl again.

"Are you badly hurt, miss? Can you sit up?"

The only answer she heard was a terrified whimper. The girl had lost her hat and whip. Heather saw the girl's loose blonde hair and the long scarlet skirts of her riding habit blowing in the wind, threatening to pluck her from her perilous perch.

"Don't move. Whatever you do, don't move a muscle." The warning was unnecessary, for the young girl lay with eyes closed, stiff with terror. Eventually, Heather stood on the ledge alongside the girl and gave a sigh of relief.

"I'm going to keep talking, and I want you to answer me. It will make you feel less frightened. What do they call you?" she said, crouching down.

244

"My… M-my name is Beatrice," the girl whispered. As she glanced up, Heather gasped in astonishment. Cornflower blue eyes, delicately arched eyebrows and almost white-blonde hair; it was as though she was looking at one of her sisters.

"Are you hurt? Is anything broken?" Heather asked taking hold of one of girl's gloved hands and stroking it.

Beatrice nodded.

"My head hurts, and I've hurt my wrist," she said tearfully, holding out her other arm.

Heather saw a bruise beginning to swell near the girl's temple, and her sleeve was torn showing a long graze.

"Can you move your arm?"

Sniffing back her tears, the girl nodded.

"What about your legs?"

Lifting her skirts, Beatrice cautiously moved first one leg and then the other. As she did so she disturbed some shale which disappeared off the ledge in a rattle and a cloud of dust. Suddenly noticing the beach and crashing waves far below, she gave another terrified whimper and clutched hold of Heather.

"Nothing is broken, thank goodness, but we must try to get you back home, and let a doctor see you," Heather said. "The first thing we'll do is tie the skirts of your habit in a knot, so the wind can't get under it. I don't want you blown away. Help me to take off your petticoats. It's no use wearing them, for you'll never be able to climb off the ledge with all those skirts round your legs."

It took several attempts and a great deal of careful manoeuvring by both girls before the ties of the petticoats were unfastened and the lace-trimmed linen removed. Heather then knotted the voluminous riding skirt.

Throughout, Beatrice clung to Heather, with fingertips white with pressure.

"Th-They c-call me B-Bea," said Beatrice in a shaking voice

once Heather was finished.

"Place your fingers in that crack, Bea. Don't put any pressure on your swollen wrist." Heather waited until Bea found the courage to reach out and place both hands on the rock. "That's right. Now ease yourself up, and put a foot on the roots of that bush," Heather urged.

With eyes tightly closed, Bea shook her head and gave a sob.

"I can't," she wailed.

"Yes you can. I'm here, and I'll tell you what to do. Give me your good hand." Heather gripped Bea's hand. The girl's fingernails dug into the back of Heather's hand, deep enough to draw blood.

Hugo and the others, watching from above, constantly yelled encouragement to the girls, at the same time, keeping an anxious lookout for Ben's return.

With Heather's coaxing, kind but firm words, Beatrice found the courage to climb a few inches upwards. Her progress came to a sudden halt when the narrow projection she was standing on crumbled under her weight. With a cry of terror, she slid back onto the ledge, pulling Heather down beside her. The girls looked at each other in despair. Heather felt a pricking behind her eyes, but with a determined effort she hid her fear and gave Beatrice a smile. She was rewarded with a weak smile in return.

***

With a face white with shock and anxiety, Ben ran towards a house with lawns and gardens that almost reached the cliffs. As he ran, he kept his eyes peeled, and listened for the barking of loose guard dogs. He wore old clothes and could easily be thought of as a vagrant, and a pack of ferocious guard dogs could be set on him.

The house, owned by George Soult and his family, was situated in isolation on the cliff top. The Georgian house was tall and wide, with many windows overlooking the sea.

After sixteen years of marriage, George Soult was as much in love with Charlotte as he had been when they first met. Before their marriage, she had told him she had borne triplets out of wedlock and, haltingly, she had related some of the details to him. Knowing her late brother, and fully aware of his weakness for gambling and the kind of people he had mixed with, George had filled in the remainder of the story for himself. The revelations had not led him to reject her and he, upon learning everything that Charlotte could remember, had sympathised with her deep longing to meet her babies again.

There was a comfortable suite of rooms on the first floor, for the exclusive use of Mrs Bigsby and Nurse Grant.

A parlour maid, straightening Mrs Bigsby's drawing room curtains, became intrigued at the sight of a stranger waving his arms and shouting as he ran across the lawns towards the house. After watching Ben for a moment or so, she decided to go to find the butler and draw his attention to the stranger. He looked over her shoulder to where she was pointing.

"Good God, woman, something must be very wrong!" he shouted, as he hurried to his master's study. He didn't bother to give his usual discreet knock, but instead burst into the room.

"Sir, I fear we have some trouble. A man is running from the direction of the cliff. He looks distraught."

Leaping to their feet, George and his son, Richard hurried to the window and saw Ben running up the steps to the front door. The thunderous banging reverberated through the house and brought servants running into the entrance hall, agog to find out what was happening. The butler opened the door to see Ben, crimson and sweating, pointing in the direction of the sea.

"Sir... Sir... An accident. You must help. A young lady. She has fallen over the cliff. We need help and ropes," Ben panted.

For a moment, Richard stood with his mouth open. The blood drained from George's face as he heard the words 'young lady.' His heart began pounding.

"Is it Beatrice, Miss Soult, who's fallen?"

"A lady in red fell almost half way down the cliff, sir. She's on a ledge, and someone is trying to reach her. Men with ropes are needed to make them both safe."

Taking hold of the butler's arm, George pushed him out of the door.

"Quick, man, run to the stables! Tell Marsden what has happened. He'll know what we need for this kind of situation. I'm going over there."

Richard was already sprinting across the lawns. George followed, with Ben and some others keeping pace with them.

When they arrived at the cliff edge, George saw at a glance what the situation was. He looked with helpless frustration to see if anyone from the house was coming with ropes.

"Is she alive? Hurt? Can she climb?" George asked the questions in rapid succession. When Richard's foot hit a rock near the cliff edge and he stumbled, George closed his eyes in anguish.

"Watch what you're doing, fellow," Lionel said, glaring at Richard. "A falling stone could knock both of them off the ledge and onto the beach,"

Hugo was lying on his stomach peering over the cliff. He glanced over his shoulder.

"She's trying to get the lady to climb back up."

"Who is down there with her?"

248

"My sister Heather, sir. We are acrobats and used to heights. But with this cold wind, they must both be tiring."

A shout of "She's coming," from below brought a "Thank God," from the men above. When they heard Heather call once more, to say that the young lady had slipped back onto the ledge again, they groaned. Relieved sighs came from the travellers at the arrival of a carriage and a wagon drawn by a heavy shire horse. They stood back when they saw people unwinding ropes and hammering strong posts into the ground, obviously familiar with rescue procedures,

Hugo found a coil of rope thrust into his hands, and he tied it to the harness of the shire horse in a special knot before running forward and throwing the rope as far out as he could over the cliff.

Hearing Hugo shout; "Below there!" Heather caught hold of the rope, and reached out for Beatrice.

"That's it, lady. Help has come. Hold onto me, now."

Once the rope was holding Beatrice securely, Heather relaxed. Another rope uncoiled, and then another. Heather made a safety loop and attached it to the rope which already held Beatrice. She smiled, and Beatrice managed to smile weakly in return. With the co-operation of the girl, the climb to the top would be a little easier for Heather.

"Let go of me. You won't fall now. Remember what I said about using both feet against the rock. As we push ourselves out from the cliff, the men above will pull us up." Heather tried to keep her voice steady, but their situation, together with the weight of the girl and the constant gusts of chilling wind, had severely taxed her strength.

A sudden shower of shale and rocks caused the girls to close their eyes hastily and huddle against the side of the cliff.

"Are you all right, Bea?" Richard asked. The girls saw with amazement that Richard hung on a level with them. He was suspended on a rope and reaching out for Beatrice.

"What do you think you are doing, you fool? You could have had us both killed if those rocks had swept us from this ledge, Richard!" Beatrice yelled in fright.

"No chance of that happening, Bea. The rope would have held," the young man said in a self-assured manner.

"No use it holding if our brains had been dashed against the rock and spilled onto the beach," Heather said in a frosty voice.

Without much care for Heather's safety, Richard took hold of Beatrice around her waist, and yelled for the men above to pull on the ropes.

As Beatrice and her brother began their ascent, another rope, which hung near the ledge, swung away from Heather. It hung tantalisingly close to her outstretched fingers. Gritting her teeth, she moved to the right to get a higher foothold. Suddenly the rock crumbled under her weight and she fell in a skin-scraping slide. Desperately, she lunged for the rope.

From his position on the cliff top, Lionel saw what was happening.

"Hang on. Hang on," he screamed. He yelled for another rope to be thrown to Heather.

Hugo gave a loud groan of despair and closed his eyes. He dared not peer over the edge. His eyes flew open, however, when he heard a voice.

"Come on, slow coach. I'll race you home."

In spite of her sore hands and legs, Heather had managed to catch hold of the rope and climb it. Her face was level with Hugo's feet. His hands went out to help her climb the rest of the way to safety. He was trembling as much as she was.

A cheer went up as they reached firm ground. Rushing forward, George swept Beatrice into his arms and held her tightly. He looked at Rose, who was hugging her sister, and his eyes widened with amazement. Even accounting for the sisters' age and weary expressions, the likeness of the girls to Beatrice was uncanny. But his attention swiftly returned to his daughter when she swooned. With her hair hanging over his arm in a platinum curtain, George carried her to the waiting carriage, and handed her into the care of her nurse and two parlour maids.

The sisters had finished hugging each other, and were just about to hug their brothers, and William and Ben who were coiling the ropes. The young men grinned sheepishly at each other, and hastily moved to stand closer to the carriage.

As her nurse and maidservants wrapped Beatrice in blankets, George turned to shake the young men by the hand.

"I don't know what to say. Beatrice is my dear daughter, and all I can say to you is, thank you."

His eyes met those of Heather and Rose as he spoke. Suddenly, he remembered the night of the ball all those years ago, and Charlotte's clear blue eyes when he had asked her for a dance. In that moment, George had no doubt that these were Charlotte's illegitimate daughters.

"I am certain that my wife will wish to thank you herself. Mrs Soult and I will be pleased to receive you in our home tomorrow at eleven, if that suits you?"

Hugo stepped forward and gave a bow.

"We would be honoured to meet Mrs Soult, sir. I also know that my parents will be very pleased to meet you."

"Of course! My invitation extends to your family. I look forward to meeting them, sir."

"Sir, the horse - the young lady's horse. I'm afraid it's lying on the beach, dead," Hugo said.

"I'll have it attended to immediately, thank you." With a heartfelt sense of relief that his daughter hadn't met the same fate as the horse, George climbed into the carriage. As he returned home, he wondered how to tell Charlotte about the rescue. He also pondered on how to tell her of his conjecture about the two Gypsy girls. George recalled talk of triplets. Could these young women really be two of Charlotte's lost babies?

Richard had also noticed the resemblance. He had no chance to ask questions, however, for servants were nearby and both his father and his mother gave Beatrice all their attention when they arrived home. He vaguely remembered someone once saying that Nurse Grant had taken care of his mother when she was a girl. *I shall speak to nurse when I have the opportunity to be alone with her,* he thought.

Chapter 21

The young travellers sat well back from the edge of the cliff as they rested on the grass. They were almost too exhausted to discuss the dangerous rescue of Beatrice and were aware of how the wind was blowing chilly moisture from the sea, making everyone shiver.

They watched in silence as George Soult's carriage and the farm wagon were driven along the winding path leading to the house. Eventually, the vehicles disappeared from view among the trees.

William Astwood had managed to sit close enough to Heather to speak to her.

"You were very brave, Miss Ardry," he murmured.

Heather blushed.

"Everyone else was just as brave as me. We all did it together. Dadrus has always said that we must work as a team." Heather spoke with her head bent. Knowing she should not be so close to William, she kept her voice low and glanced sideways at the others, but they were busy with their own thoughts, they hadn't heard the couple or noticed where Heather was sitting.

"I feel very strongly that you should not have put yourself at such risk, but I'm very proud of your success," he said.

William turned and stared out to sea when he noticed Hugo glance in their direction. It was the first time in ages the couple had been able to speak. The last occasion was when they had been in the large show tent. Heather had been collecting some riding equipment after a performance when William had happened to walk in. They were alone in the huge sawdust-scented arena. Unable to keep silent any longer, he had drawn Heather to a seat and, kneeling beside her, had told her how his father and brother had died in an accident and that he was now Lord William Astwood. Seeing his distress, and the grief and the loneliness in his eyes, Heather had wept with him and held his hand tightly. It had seemed no time at all before the couple had reluctantly had to part.

Seated so close to his love, William caught the scent of sea breezes in her hair. He watched as her eyelashes fluttered like dark crescents as she looked down so as to hide her guilty love from her family. The soft down on her cheeks reminded him of the peaches grown by the gardeners at the Astwood Estate. How he wished he could take her in his arms and kiss the grazes he saw on her hands and arms.

It was Ben who first heard the shouting, the pounding of hooves and the sharp crack of a whip.

"It's Mr Ardry!" Ben cried, jumping to his feet. Running forward, he waved both arms to attract attention.

They saw Culvato driving one of his flat wagons at top speed towards them, and Ursula clung with white fingers to the wagon's seat as the vehicle bounced over rocks, small gorse bushes and rough grass. Disregarding the very real danger of rabbit burrows in the sandy soil, Lilly galloped her horse beside the wagon.

"What happened? Are you all safe? Was it an accident?" The questions were called out as soon as the wagon came within earshot.

254

"It's all right, Dadrus. We're all safe," Hugo shouted as he ran forward to catch hold of the bridle of the nearest sweating horse.

Rose and Heather climbed aboard the wagon; Ursula tightly hugged and kissed them both. When she saw the state of Heather's clothes, and her bare legs, she lifted her eyebrows and quickly passed her a blanket. Lilly didn't waste time tethering her horse, but tossed the reins to Ben before jumping in the wagon and hugging both her sisters. The young men nodded, and each of them shook hands with Culvato in a Gypsy greeting.

"What's happened to the rider? Jem told us that somebody fell down the cliff," Ursula asked, looking around for a stranger. "I hope the rider hasn't met the same fate as the horse."

"Her father and some men came to help us, but there was no way of saving her horse. It's dreadful that such a beautiful animal had to die like that," Heather said.

"The girl landed on a ledge. Our Heather stayed with her until people from the big house came with ropes. They were able to lift them both to safety. Then her dadrus took the girl home in their carriage."

Although Hugo revealed only the bare bones of the incident, and spoke in a matter-of-fact tone, Culvato gave him a sharp glance. He wasn't fooled for one moment about what danger the young people had just faced.

"Who was she?"

"The gentleman didn't say what his name was, but the girl's name was Beatrice," Heather said.

"Ben fetched everyone from that big house on the headland, Dadrus." Lionel pointed back with his thumb to where windows shone through the trees, and smoke rose from tall chimneys.

"Dai, he said we were to all call and see him and his wife

tomorrow morning at eleven, but we haven't anything fit to wear." Heather looked at Ursula with an expression of dismay. "We can't go to a Gorjios home wearing these."

Heather's riding clothes were torn beyond repair. So that her skirt wouldn't impede her progress on the cliff face, Heather had ripped it and tied the ends around her waist before beginning her climb. She sat on a coil of rope in the wagon with the horse blanket wrapped around her covering her bare legs.

"You must ride there. Wear the riding habits you use in the show ring. Take off all the trimmings, and give them a good brushing, and you will look very well." Ursula spoke briskly. Her heart was still thumping with shock, and suddenly, she announced, "I shall come with you."

Turning to Culvato, she said: "You must have our best carriage cleaned and ready for tomorrow morning, Rom."

Hearing the authority in his wife's voice, Culvato nodded agreement.

Mounting Lilly's horse, and riding alongside the wagon, William gazed with admiration at Heather. Fortunately, the family were too busy talking about their experience to notice his enamoured expression.

***

At mid-morning the following day, the travellers rode sedately along the drive leading to the Soult's residence. Culvato wore a dark blue tailcoat. His white hat, low of crown and wide of brim, was set at a jaunty angle. His cherished diamond horseshoe pin twinkled in his black silk cravat and a heavy gold watch and chain spanned his yellow waistcoat. He rode in his green and gold painted carriage with Ursula. She wore a black silk gown with tight sleeves, and sat primly by his side, holding a red silk parasol high over her bonnet. As they drew closer to the house, Ursula felt not only a great sense of unease, but an intense tingling on the backs of her hands.

The young people rode their own horses, with well-polished but plain leather tack. The triplets looked beautiful. They wore their hair swept back high into an elegant chignon. They had chosen riding habits of different colours, with matching top hats and veils that partly covered their faces. A froth of white lace at their throats completed the bewitching picture. Heather wore lavender velvet and an amethyst necklet; it had been given to her some years ago, when she had helped Ursula to nurse Synfye after the birth of Isopel. It was Heather's most cherished possession. Lilly, in cream and brown, looked charming. Rose had chosen a deep pink. A young man, wearing a coat to complement the colour of her outfit, escorted each girl. Rose matched by Hugo, Lilly and Lionel, and Heather and William. Ben rode behind, dressed in a sober russet brown.

When the party arrived at the front entrance, a small army of grooms ran forward to hold the horses and lead them to the stable block. An unsmiling lackey helped Ursula to alight, and he bowed to Culvato. A row of footmen and maids, curious to see who had rescued their young mistress, waited in the entrance hall to receive gloves and cloaks. The butler bowed, and acknowledged Culvato's greeting with a nod.

"The master and mistress are expecting you, sir. They await you in the family drawing room. Please follow me." The butler led the way through the entrance hall where sunlight streamed through the jewel-coloured windows to pattern the wall tiles along the carpeted corridor.

Heather let her gaze rove over the dark wood panelling and crystal chandeliers. Rose noticed a large portrait of a horse and a lady rider who somehow looked familiar. Lilly's eyes were huge as she took in the richness of the furnishings, and threw a glance over her shoulder at Ben.

Beatrice Soult sat quietly on a chair by one of the windows, watching for the arrival of her new friends. Her brother Richard stood beside her.

"Mr Ardry and party, sir," announced the butler, opening the door. George stepped forward, and approached Culvato with a warm smile and his hand held out.

Charlotte sat on a sofa; her back was straight and her skirts were arranged becomingly. She used her fan in nervous strokes in an attempt to cool her flushed cheeks. It had taken a great deal of soul searching the previous evening before George could bring himself to tell his wife whom he thought their visitors might be. He had become alarmed when Charlotte turned deathly pale, but she had assured him that it was only the shock of his announcement and that she would be quite herself after a good night's sleep.

"So pleased you were able to come with your family, sir. Please may I present my wife, my son Richard, and my daughter Beatrice, whom some of you have already met."

Beatrice looked very young in her sprig muslin gown and green velvet sash. As her name was mentioned, she moved quickly forward to wrap her arms around Heather's waist. With a smile, Heather realised the girl was surviving her shock well, and although the bruise on her temple had deepened in colour, the swelling had partly subsided. A bandage, starting from just below her puff sleeve, covered the long scratch on Beatrice's arm and finished at her wrist.

Heather recognised Richard immediately. He was the young man who had been so discourteous to her on the cliff face; later, when they stood on the cliff top, he had taken hold of her hands, and had given her fervent thanks for saving his sister. Heather returned his smile.

The travelling men bowed, and Charlotte murmured

a greeting. Ursula was proud of her sons' courtesy to the company. Mrs Lovell had spent many hours teaching them the correct way to bow for different occasions and, when the girls were small, she had been the one to show them how to execute a graceful curtsy.

"This is my wife, Mrs Ardry. These are my two sons, Hugo and Lionel, my three daughters, Rose, Lilly and Heather, and two of our friends."

With a gasp, Charlotte turned pale, and her eyes fastened on the amethyst necklace worn by Heather. Years ago, she had seen a Gypsy fortune-teller wearing a piece of jewellery such as this.

Beatrice's clear voice carried bell-like though the room and she tried to draw Heather forward.

"This is the lady who climbed down and stayed with me on the cliff, Mamma."

Taking a deep breath, Charlotte used her fan and smiled at Beatrice and Heather, but her eyes never left the amethyst necklace which was so similar to the one once owned by her mother.

With a rueful glance at the other visitors, George drew Beatrice away from Heather, and told her, softly, to curtsy to Mr and Mrs Ardry and to each of the other visitors.

When Ursula looked at Charlotte, her heart sank. She had been correct to worry about her premonition yesterday. Her assumption that there might be trouble brewing in the house on the cliff top was right. The lady seated in front of her was an older version of her daughters, and the lines on her face showed Ursula that Charlotte had lived through a period of worry and despair.

As everyone sat discussing the events of the previous day, Ursula noticed Charlotte's eyes constantly scanning the faces of the triplets and thought that the woman seemed to watch their every expression and movement with a positive yearning.

When the door opened and Mrs Bigsby, escorted by Nurse Grant entered the room, Charlotte took the opportunity to ask Ursula how old the triplets were.

"They are seventeen, Mrs Soult," Ursula murmured. She pretended not to notice Charlotte's gasp, or the way the stricken woman put a handkerchief to her mouth.

Ursula smiled gently at Beatrice when the girl came shyly to stand by her. She shook her head when Beatrice asked if she could ride in the shows with Heather and the others.

"Training must start in babyhood, and you are too old now, Beatrice."

Charlotte snapped her fan closed, and spoke sharply.

"Beatrice. Go and sit over there. Where are your manners, girl?"

Nurse Grant turned pale when she recognised the three girls from the fairground in Nottingham. She hadn't dared tell George or Charlotte her assumption at the time and after all those years, Nurse Grant had forgotten about her visit to the fairground.

Using a walking stick, Mrs Bigsby hobbled across the room and stopped to peer at the faces of the triplets. The previous evening she had overheard some servants gossiping about the drama on the cliff top, and they had discussed the likeness of the Gypsy girls to Beatrice. The old woman had drawn her own conclusions about who the two girls were, and she wondered if the third baby had survived. Everyone fell silent when the she suddenly broke into peals of wild laughter and pointed to each of the sisters in turn.

"They are just the image of their mother at that age! The past is never hidden for long; it always comes back to haunt a body." She turned and looked at Culvato, who was standing with his mouth open. "Did Mr Bigsby, my son give you something with the babes, Gypsy? I want more proof than a pretty face."

Culvato stepped forward, and glanced at Charlotte and George before facing the old woman. Although he was shocked by the unexpected encounter, he was not at all intimidated.

"Yes, ma'am."

"What was it?"

"A ring and a lantern clock, Mrs Bigsby."

"Ha! I knew I was right." The old woman spun around to face Charlotte. "As soon as you saw them walk into the room you knew as well, didn't you daughter? Of course you did. I can see it in your silly face. Jonas should have drowned them at birth, not given them to the Gypsies."

"I can show you the proof, Mrs Bigsby," said Culvato pulling back his shoulders. "I was given money as well as the clock and ring on the night of their birth. I kept the money as a dowry for the girls. If you wish, I can bring everything to the house tomorrow."

"Clock? He has my clock! Thief! Murderer! Give back what is mine!" The screeching shouts echoed around the room as Mrs Bigsby, her walking stick thrown to one side, rushed towards Culvato with both hands stretched out, ready to clutch his throat.

Nurse Grant and a parlour maid threw themselves at the distraught woman, and pinned her arms to her sides - but they were unable to stop her accusations.

"Nurse Grant! Take your mistress to her room and give her a dose of physic. She's not well enough for company." George said.

With his face as pale as everyone else's; George thundered out his instructions to the nurse, who threw a frightened glance at Charlotte before ushering Mrs Bigsby towards the door.

"Come back to your room, Mrs Bigsby. I think you should

have a nice warm glass of milk, and one of those little pills the doctor left for you." Talking gently to the old lady, Nurse Grant and the maid coaxed her with soft words out of the drawing room, but the company heard the demented woman screaming more abuse at the nurse as she was taken along the corridor.

George wiped his sweating face with a handkerchief. He hadn't expected his mother-in-law to venture out of her bedchamber so early in the day. Ursula sat as though turned to stone, whilst Charlotte wept silently into her handkerchief. With the scrap of lace against her trembling lips, she shook her head.

"My... My mamma is not well," she faltered.

The triplets were ashen and trembling. They glanced at each other in bewilderment, and then towards the young men, who had moved and were standing together near a window. Was it true? Was the crazy old woman their grandmother? Why had they never been told that Ursula and Culvato were not their real parents? Looking at Charlotte and Beatrice, they could see the family resemblance for themselves.

Running a finger around his suddenly tightened collar, Culvato saw a mixture of shock, incredulity and disbelief on the faces of those he loved best in the world.

Ursula leaned forward and looked into Charlotte's eyes.

"We love your girls dearly, and have raised them as though they were our own," she said quietly. "They've had years of acrobatic training, and are quite capable of earning their own living."

"Yes. Yes. They have performed in front of the Queen, the Duchess of Kent, and Mrs Fry, the Quaker. The Duke of Newcastle once gave each of them a gold piece," said Culvato, with a proud smile.

"P-performed?" Charlotte murmured weakly, in a

262

subconscious imitation of her mother. She dabbed at her eyes, and then used her fan with such vigour, that others in the room thought the slender ivory sticks would break.

"From childhood they have been constantly chaperoned, Mrs Soult. If I am not able to be with them, then our good friend, Mrs Lovell supervises and tutors them and her own daughter," Ursula said.

George cleared his throat.

"Have you given any thought as to their future, Mr Ardry? Have they prospects? What I mean is; we could possibly offer them more? Present them to the polite world as my daughters," he said, glancing sideways at his wife. George was finding the room very warm.

Culvato moved to stand beside Ursula's chair, and placed a hand on her shoulder. "Suitable husbands will be found, but not until the girls wish to marry. I will not have them pushed into a union that they have no stomach for. That, in my opinion, is the road to a lifetime of misery."

Ursula gave a dignified nod of agreement.

The triplets sat primly with hands on their laps, flushed with embarrassment. They eyed George with dislike. They had never before been discussed as though they were not present, and they didn't care for it.

As Culvato was speaking, William, Ben and Hugo moved and stood close to the triplets. Giving a polite cough, William stepped forward, and gave a slight bow towards Culvato and Ursula.

"In view of what has been said today, this may or may not be the best time to ask you, Mr Ardry, but I wish that you would allow Miss Heather to become my fiancée. We have loved each other for a very long time, and we wish to be married."

Blushing scarlet, Heather gave a guilty glance at Ursula and

Culvato, before staring at the floor.

When Ben moved to William's side, Heather heard a gasp from Lilly. She took hold of her sister's hand to give them both some courage.

"I want to rommer Lilly, sir. Now I know she is not born a Romani, I see no reason why we can't be man and wife, Mr Ardry." Ben said.

With his eyes bulging and his mouth hanging open in astonishment, Culvato turned to Ursula.

"Did you know of this, Romni?"

Putting her fingers over her mouth, Ursula shook her head.

Culvato spun round to face the sisters, and glared at Rose. She stared back defiantly.

"Have you been scheming and plotting to run off behind my back as well?"

Rose shot a desperate look towards Hugo. "No, Dadrus."

Charlotte gave a slightly hysterical laugh.

"This has been a day of surprises, hasn't it? You do know that if you girls marry these men that you will be Gypsies for the remainder of your lives. Stay here and I will transform you into the young ladies you should be, and I promise to introduce you to polite society as my relations from the country. Then, when I think you are ready, I will bring you to the attention of well-bred men of substance. You then will each have a settled future to look forward to." Charlotte gave a brilliant smile, as though she had solved the triplets' and everyone else's problems.

William turned to face Charlotte and legged a courtly bow as though she were royalty. She was quite unaware of the irony in his gesture.

"May I be permitted to introduce myself, ma'am. I am Lord William Astwood, and I have an estate near to Nottingham Town. I first fell in love with Miss Heather Ardry when she was only fourteen. Against my father's wishes, I joined Mr Ardry's troupe of tent men and travelled round England in their company."

"L-Lord Astwood?" Charlotte stuttered. With her cheeks flushed, she began using her fan again.

Knowing the shock Charlotte had sustained, William spoke very gently. "My father and my brother Henry both died some time ago in an accident. So you see Mrs Soult, your daughter - with Mr Ardry's permission, of course - is marrying a man of substance."

For a moment, the room was silent. Proffering her hand to George, Ursula rose to her feet.

"We must take our leave of you, sir. We have a matinee this afternoon, and we must make preparations," she said.

Culvato gave her a sharp glance; there was no performance until the evening.

With a relieved sigh, George bowed over Ursula's hand.

No one spoke on the way back to the fairground. Ursula sat with her shoulders stiff, while Culvato stared unseeingly, a dour expression on his face, at the passing landscape. He fiddled with the buckle of his belt. When they arrived home, the young people exchanged anxious glances. Jumping to the ground, Culvato pointed a finger at William and Ben.

"You two. In the vardo."

Heather's eyes were like stars. As she was not born a Romani, surely there would be no barrier against her marrying William. She caught his eye, and smiled so brilliantly that his heart gave a leap.

Rose looked at Hugo and saw him swallow hard. They couldn't ever remember Culvato being so angry. With a frown, she shook her head. To tell Culvato about their secret love would be the height of folly whilst he was in such a mood.

"Dai?" Heather caught hold of Ursula's arm. "What do

you think Dadrus will say?"

"I don't know. Such a lot of secrets told about in one day have thoroughly upset everyone. We'll just have to wait and see."

"Are you very cross with us, Dai?" Lilly asked, putting her arm around Ursula's waist and kissing her cheek.

"Deary me, what a question. No one can say who they will fall in love with." Ursula looked over Lilly's head, and saw Rose staring at her, her eyes full of tears. Then she saw Hugo walk up to Rose and put his arm around her shoulder. He whispered something that brought a look of radiant joy to her face. In that moment, Ursula knew their secret. She wondered how she could have been so blind and have unwittingly caused the couple to have had so many years of heartache because of her silence.

"The events of this day will alter all our lives, my dears," said Ursula, wondering how she was going to tell Culvato about the latest development in their family.

Chapter 22

Lord William Astwood sat by the campfire, biting at a torn fingernail and making wild plans in his head. Ben sat beside him. He had been whittling a piece of wood for the past three quarters of an hour and there was only a piece of wood the size of a tent peg left. Both young men were unhappy about the earlier tongue-lashing they had received from Culvato Ardry. Although they had put forward a good case for them to marry Heather and Lilly, Culvato didn't listen properly; he was too angry. So they waited, dejected and with drooping shoulders, to hear what Culvato had to say to his family. Whatever conclusion he came to, all their lives would change.

Piramus was seated nearby, wishing there was some way he could help the young people. He had been hovering near the vardo, hoping to hear about the meeting at the Soult's residence. Seeing the way the carriage had been driven into the camp, and hearing the way that Culvato had ordered the young men inside the vardo, the old man had quickly sidled behind the vehicle, well out of sight. He realised from the worried faces that something was dreadfully amiss. *At least no one has been injured*, he thought.

The heat from the fire was comforting to the old man, but

he bent over with a grimace, and tried to rub away the pain of rheumatics in his thin legs while keeping an eye on Culvato's door. When he saw the vardo rocking on its springs, the old man grabbed a walking stick and rose to his feet without noticing the pain. William and Ben also sprang up. They took a tentative few steps forward and glanced at each other as they heard raised voices coming from the closed door.

"I don't care. We love each other. I shall take her away," William muttered.

"There's other fairs for me to work in, or I'll buy some kind of business," agreed Ben, nodding in firm resolution. It was no idle threat for Ben was prudent with his wages. He had gradually amassed and safely invested a large amount of money, and he owned several prestigious properties in Nottingham Town.

***

Inside the vardo, Culvato had undone his brass-studded leather belt and held it wrapped around his fist. Hurt and angry by what he thought of as degenerate and provocative behaviour by Heather and Lilly, he threatened to thrash both the girls, such was his temper. He felt almost as angry towards Ursula. In his opinion, she was as much to blame for the situation; she had not kept a close enough watch on the girls' activities.

Ursula sat tense and still, her face pale and her mouth tight as a result of her husband's unjust accusations. Her dark eyes flashed towards the upset young women as they tried to make their viewpoint known to their parents.

The family had never quarrelled so violently and bitterly and they were all tearful and extremely distressed.

Heather stood, her back to the bed, with both hands on her hips and her chin jutting out. She faced Culvato bravely, trying

268

to ignore the strap in his hand.

"I shall marry William Astwood, Dadrus. I love him and he loves me."

"I say, no, girl! That's final." Culvato's voice was just as loud as hers.

With a whimper, Heather slid down, and ended up crouched on the floor with her back leaning against the bed. Turning her head away, she covered her face with both hands. A lifetime of obedience to her parents stifled her rebellion.

Seeing Lilly open her mouth, Culvato turned to her with a pointing finger.

"Don't you start! None of you are old enough to think of getting married yet, anyway. You all have a duty to your Dai and me for the years we've spent on bringing you up. Wasn't easy to take on three babies together with our own, and with nothing but a barrow to put you all in. And there's another thing to think on. What about your work? Will you be throwing everything away? All those years of training, all that hard work, done for nothing? Them two out there, they won't want folk knowing you've worked in a fairground. They'll want you to become like those young ladies of fashion. At least, Lord bloody Astwood will."

Hugo sat near the door, Rose pressing close to his side. He kept his hands pushed deep in his pockets, hoping that it hid his trembling. His family thought that the strained expression he habitually wore was quite usual. It was no use - he couldn't keep quiet any longer. Leaning forward, he cleared his throat, and looked at both his parents.

"We haven't been able to say anything before. We only spoke about it ourselves the other week." Swallowing hard, Hugo glanced at Rose, who was chewing her knuckle. Her big eyes stared back at him, terrified.

Ursula closed her eyes. There was no time to prepare

269

Culvato for his next shock. She was unable to keep sharpness from her voice, although she guessed what he was about to say.

"What are you saying, Hugo?"

"W-We want to get m-married, Dai." Hugo's usual healthy complexion had faded, and he stumbled over the words. All Ursula could see was the back of her son's scarlet bandanna, for he sat with his head hanging, staring at the well-scrubbed floor.

"Who? What are you saying, Hugo? What girl do you want to marry?"

Culvato was puzzled by the way the conversation had changed. He stared at his eldest son, and looked at Ursula for some kind of explanation. She shook her head with dismay.

Somehow Hugo found the courage to look his father in the eye.

"We thought that we were wicked and dammed to think of such a thing. But now, after today..."

With her hand covering her mouth, Ursula looked squarely at her eldest son.

"Hugo. Look at me, son. Who is it you want to marry?" Culvato said.

Putting her hand on Hugo's arm, Rose stood beside him, and faced Ursula and Culvato.

"Hugo wants to marry me, Dadrus."

A gasp came from five throats. For a moment nobody moved. Then Rose cowered back, and Hugo put out an arm to protect her as Culvato lunged forward with the belt hanging from his raised fist.

"Has everyone gone mad? She's your sister, chavvi. Is there a curse come on this family?" He cast a bewildered look at Ursula.

"No." Hugo stood in front of Rose with his arms held

out to protect her from his father's belt. "She's not my sister. Neither is our Heather, nor Lilly. Don't you both know what's happened? We've kept silent for a long time. We thought we were unnatural, freaks. Now we know we have different parents. Well, now we can love each other in a clean and true way, like what you both do."

Father and son were so close that their curls touched. Taking a grip of Hugo's coat lapels, Culvato propelled him towards the door, and when he reached Rose, he pushed them both outside.

"Get out! Get out of here. Go and do some work." After slamming the door, he turned with a shocked face towards Heather and Lilly who needed no telling to sidle past him and leave the vardo. Sitting quietly, watching and listening, Lionel thought he hadn't been noticed until Culvato spun round to look at him, and snarl. "You don't want to marry, as well, do you?"

"No, Dadrus!" Lionel knew this was not a good moment to tell his parents he wanted to marry Belle, and in any case he would need to approach her parents first.

"Then get out. I want to talk to your dai in private."

When the door closed behind Lionel, Culvato gave a sob, and dropped to the seat next to Ursula. Gently holding him, she drew his head down to rest on her shoulder.

"Should we have told them earlier? Perhaps it would have been best to have said something when they were too small to understand," he said, with a break in his voice.

"We have always done what we thought was right, for all our chavvies. But now, they are all grown into young people, even Ben. If we aren't very careful how we treat them, we'll lose the girls and Hugo. He's very like you, my Rom. He'll do what he thinks is best to care for his own."

"The tent man, that William Astwood; what do you think

of him?"

"It's what Heather thinks of him that matters. I haven't heard anyone saying they dislike him. I don't think he drinks very much - at least I've never heard of him being put to bed drunk," said Ursula, slowly.

"He's a good worker. Never known him get into a fight, and he goes to church regular," Culvato said.

The couple were silent, with Ursula stroking Culvato's hand as it lay on her lap. After a while, he looked up,

"When we were leaving the house, Mr Soult gave me permission to raise the fair on one of his fields. It's a prime site, near the town, and right against the sea." He gave a sharp laugh. "But it won't be no use keeping the fair now. Not if the all the girls marry and leave us."

"Who said anything about leaving? Hugo and Rose didn't. Ben will stay with Lilly. I'm not so sure about Heather and William, though."

"Heather's my star turn."

"If you keep Rose and Lilly - and don't forget Belle Lovell, her parents always draw a good crowd - the fair will continue to be a success. You will still have plenty of acts - and don't forget the show booths, they always bring in a steady income."

"Mmm. Lionel works well with Belle." Culvato turned sharply to look at Ursula. "You don't think…"

"Maybe. They've always got on well together. But that young lady was told Seth had sold his last lot of horses for a good profit. She's always been one to look after herself. And I think that Jem Lincolin once took her fancy."

"They're all such chavvies. It seems no time at all since they wouldn't wear breeches, or wash their faces."

They sat in silence, remembering happy days. Ursula glanced at her husband, her eyes twinkling.

"I was only fifteen when you persuaded me to run away

with you. It was Synfye who should have been your bride. Everyone thought you soft because you didn't thrash Tawno. Remember how we talked for weeks on end, long before we dared to face my father?"

"I didn't want to fight my brother. He was bigger than me, and anyway he needed all his strength with just getting married to Synfye."

Giving a giggle at the memory of the brothers eying each other before shaking hands, Ursula thought it best not to say that she knew Synfye had warned Tawno beforehand not to fight.

Ursula felt a deep sense of relief when Culvato's frown disappeared, and his usual good-natured smile reappeared. With a sigh, he rose to his feet, stretched his back and yawned. Ursula stood and looked at him with a roguish expression.

"Go and fetch them all in. Say they can marry with your blessing, Rom."

Reaching out, he gently drew her close.

"No. Let them wait. How long ago is it since we were left completely alone in our home?"

With a smile, Ursula shook her head. She allowed herself to be led closer to the bed, and began undressing her Gypsy love as though she was a young bride. His waistcoat and shirt were folded and put on a chair. She knelt as she unfastened his trousers. Her tongue fluttered over his belly. He moaned with pleasure as she moved further down.

***

When Ben and William returned to the fire, they sat down next to Piramus, and told him about the dangerous rescue of Beatrice Soult from the cliff face and of Heather's bravery. The old man tut-tutted, and shook his head as he heard about

273

the sad manner in which the horse met its end. But Culvato had already discussed the rescue with him and Piramus was more interested to hear about the meeting of the triplets with Charlotte and George Soult; he nodded wisely when his probing questions were answered. The young men then confided that they hoped to marry Heather and Lilly. The wrinkles in his sunken cheeks and the laughter lines around his dark eyes deepened, and he grinned broadly.

"Likely the chief will have something to say about that. Apple of his eye, them girls are. Wants them to marry Romani. Can't say I blame him. He wants to keep them close."

"Now that she knows who her mother is, she might get him to change his mind, for Heather is a born lady," William said with hope lighting his face.

Without answering, Piramus lifted an eyebrow and grinned even wider, showing his toothless gums. *Even fine ladies get caught with unwelcome chavvies*, he thought.

The door of the vardo opened and Rose and Hugo jumped to the ground, both young men rushed forward. Seeing how distressed the couple were, they halted and, confused, they stood side-by-side. Then, Heather and Lilly left the vardo and ran towards them. Throwing their arms around their loved ones, the girls began to sob. William and Ben glanced at each other in dismay over the heads of the girls, before leading them away across the field so that they could speak in private. Rose and Hugo, their arms entwined, stood beside the campfire, and looked at Piramus without speaking.

"Bad, was it?"

Hugo nodded.

"He don't want to lose his girls. Can't yet see that they've now grown into women, and that you are now a man, full grown," Piramus said.

"We've found out that we aren't brother and sister, Uncle

Piramus. We'll be able to marry."

Rose still had traces of tears on her cheeks, and a teardrop trembled on her eyelashes, but she smiled radiantly at Hugo as he spoke.

Years ago, when he had met them in the small town of Eastwood, the old man had rightly guessed that the girls were not the offspring of Culvato and Ursula. Now, at last, the truth was out. With his doubts confirmed, Piramus felt a deep pity for the troubled couple. He shook his head.

"Culvato don't often change his mind. Maybe your mother will be able to make him see sense."

Seeing Heather, his brother and Uncle Piramus talking beside the fire, Lionel walked slowly across the grass to join them.

"They wanted the best for you, brother. They love us."

"Ha!"

With a wide gesture, Lionel waved his hand to take in the showground and stock. "It's true. He built all this for you and me." With a scowl, Lionel glanced at Piramus. "If Hugo and the girls leave the fair, he'll have nothing left but the freaks and liberty horses. It'll kill him."

"And us, chavvi. Your dadrus will have us until the girls return, and they will, mark my words. No one who's been a traveller from birth will settle for long in a permanent home," said Piramus, with a knowing nod.

Once the girl's tears were dry, and tentative plans had been made, the three couples met inside the big show tent. It was dim, deserted, and smelt strongly of animals. The red plush seats had litter scattered underneath, and the sand in the arena had not been swept since the last performance and was covered in footprints. The triplets sat at the edge of the arena, their loves beside them.

"We leave tonight." Glancing towards her sisters, Lilly bit

her trembling bottom lip whilst clutching Ben's hand tightly. The thought of leaving her sisters and everything familiar was terrifying. Lilly had even wondered, very briefly, if she loved Ben enough to make a fresh start, away from her family and the fairground.

"Oh no! Wait a day or two. See if Dadrus changes his mind." Rose felt Hugo's arm steal around her waist as she spoke. Still shy at showing their feelings publicly, the couple blushed.

Holding Heather's hand, William spoke up quietly.

"You could all come and live at my home. That is, until you find out where it is you want to live. Plenty of space for vardos and bender tents, you know."

"Your home? Do you mean at Astwood House?" Hugo's puzzled expression brought a smile to William's face.

"I heard a long time ago that my father and brother had died. Sometimes, I leave the fair and return home to attend to my estates. Luckily, I have a good steward and manager to look after things for me when I'm travelling." There was a silence as everyone considered William's offer.

Hugo's face lit up at the prospects of a home near to Mr Watson's wood yard. He had already decided to have a vardo built in Eastwood town.

"I always wondered where you disappeared to for weeks on end, but I didn't like to ask," he said.

Everyone felt cowed and on edge, and they sprang to their feet when Culvato's voice boomed across the tent.

"Why are you not getting those liberty horses ready for tonight's show? You girls need to get your costumes trimmed up again, and the carriage is still out there in the field, with mud on the wheels."

With a gasp, the young people turned to see Culvato standing at the entrance of the tent, with Ursula by his side.

Piramus peeped over her shoulder. He was grinning like a tortoise with pink gums.

Hand in hand, William and Heather stepped forward.

"We have all decided that we are no longer going to do our acts, Mr Ardry." William's mouth was thin with temper. He glanced towards the other two couples, they nodded and murmured their agreement.

"No work, no weddings!" Culvato said, sharply.

For a long moment the only sounds in the tent came from three tethered horses. The incredulous expressions on the faces of the young people brought chuckles and wide smiles from the group standing at the entrance. There was no need for Culvato to explain his statement. With a rush, and loud squeals, the two groups met. Culvato and Ursula were hugged and covered with kisses from the triplets. Ben and William thanked Culvato by shaking his hand. It was Ursula who pulled her son close, and kissed his cheek. Clinging to his mother, Hugo tried to hide his emotion.

"Thank you, Dai," he whispered. He knew his father would never have agreed to the weddings without his mother's calming influence and commonsense. Hugo and Rose would have needed to leave, and would have had to find another fair to work in.

Lilly looked at Ben with tears in her eyes. There was no need to leave her family; they could marry and stay with Culvato's fair.

"Let us go and put away the carriage," William said, pulling Heather towards the tent opening.

The End

Glossary

Atrashed: Frightened
Balanser: Sovereign-Guinea
Beshle: Stanley-gypsy tribe
Barvali: Rich
Beebee: Aunt.
Beng: Devil.
Bister: Forget.
Cant: Language.
Chop: Bargain.
Chai: Daughter, Girl or Young Woman.
Girls rather than boys go out hawking with their mothers and to watch fortune telling.
Chavvi: Son -Boy
Chave: Child
Chal: Youth
Chavvies: Children.
Chani: Frog.
Chore: Steal
Choramengro: Chorer: Thief.
Coffle: Long train of vehicles
Chik: Dirt. Earth.
Chop: A bargain.
Corbed: Finished.
Dablo: An Exclamation
Dai: Mother.
Didikai: Rough Traveller.
Diddecoi: Tinker from Ireland
Dinnelo: Fool Imbecile
Dordi: An exclamation
Dukkering: Going door to door.
Drom: Road.
Dukkerer: palm reader. Use a tent in the summer and the vardo in the winter.
Gonner: Bag. Sack.
Gorjified: Living in a settled home.
Grai: Horse
Gaujo: None gypsy man.
Gorjios: None Gypsy's.
Hobben: Food.

Kannengro: Hare.
Kalo: Black
Kaka:Uncle.
Lovva: Money.
Lil Book: Letter
Lubne: Harlot
Patteran: (1) The name of a leaf or a tree. (2) The handful of grass or straw, Gypsies strew on the roads as they travel, to give information to any of their companions who may be following.
Petalengro: Blacksmith.
Pral: Brother.
Matchka: Cat
Mendi: Us. We
Mendis: Ours
Monging: Begging.
Mochadi: Can mean in different ways - dirty, immoral, unhygienic, polluted.
Mokto: Box.
Moila: Donkey, Ass.
Morg: Hare
Minaw: My own – My darling.
Mullo: Ghost.
Mullered: Killed.
Musgros: Police.
Mullered: Dead.
Mutterimengri: Tea.
Nasher: Be Hanged.
Pikie: Tinker married to a Romani

Ratt: Blood
Ratfelo: Bloody
Rauni: Lady
Romni: Wife.
Rom: Husband - Master.
Rommer: Marry.
Rommered: Married.
Romani: True-blooded gypsy
Rinkeny: Pretty – Beautiful
Rye: Gentleman
Taters-in-the-mould: Cold

Roolie: Wagon.
Rokkeramengros: Lawyers.
Riffli, Mongy: Poxy
Sonakai: Gold. Golden Jewellery.
Shushi: Rabbit.
Tikni: Little, Child.
Tiknies: More than one child.
Tradderly: Carefully.
Vardo: Caravan.
Vesh: Wood or forest.
Victuals: Food.
Wafodu: Bad - Wicked
Waffedipen: Evil.

Almond-rocks: Socks
Chevy-chace: Face
Skating-rink: Drink